Praise for *The Jade Peony*

" [An] absorbing novel...[Wayson Choy] is a consummate story-teller with such a keen ear for dialogue that he imbues each of his distinctive characters with an authentic voice."

—*Rocky Mountain News*

"Like all of literature, *The Jade Peony* is a book of layers...[from] Choy's careful word choices, {to} the weaving together of English with snatches of Chinese dialects, [to] the flavor."

—*The Honolulu Advertiser*

"Eloquent, confident...complex...Childhood lessons are quietly, powerfully drawn here, with Choy's evocation of harsh immigrant reality [that is] nothing short of masterful."

—*Kirkus Reviews*

"Choy has rewritten a history that is both painful and eloquent."

—Emily Baillargeon, *Seattle Weekly*

"*The Jade Peony* offers a true and touching insight into a largely unrecorded wartime world. It's human and moving without being sentimental, and the child's-eye viewpoint is very well-handled....A genuine contribution to history as well as to fiction."

—Margaret Drabble

"A lyrical tale...intelligent and sensitively told, with dialogue that crackles with wit and familiarity. I didn't want it to end."

—Denise Chong, author of *The Concubine's Children*

WAYSON CHOY

PICADOR USA

THE JADE PEONY. Copyright © 1995 by Wayson Choy. All rights reserved. Printed in the United States of America. No part of this book may be used or reproduced in any manner whatsoever without written permission except in the case of brief quotations embodied in critical articles or reviews. For information address Picador USA, 175 Fifth Avenue, New York, N.Y. 10010.

Picador® USA is a registered trademark and is used by St. Martin's Press under license from Pan Books Limited.

For information on Picador USA Reading Group Guides, as well as ordering, please contact the Trade Marketing department at St. Martin's Press.
Phone: 1-800-221-7945 extension 488
Fax: 212-677-7456
E-mail: trademarketing@stmartins.com

The publisher gratefully acknowledges the assistance of the Canada Council and of the British Columbia Ministry of Tourism, Small Business, and Culture.

Lines from the poem "Translations" from *Expanding the Doubtful Points* (Bamboo Ridge Press) copyright © 1987 by Wing Tek Lum and reprinted with the author's kind permission.

Library of Congress Cataloging-in-Publication Data
Choy, Wayson.
    The jade peony : a novel / Wayson Choy.
        p. cm.
    ISBN 0-312-18692-4
    1. Chinese—British Columbia—Vancouver Island—History—Fiction.
I. Title.
PR9199 3.C4967J33   1997
813'.54—dc21   97-801
                                                                  CIP

First published in British Columbia, Canada, by Douglas & McIntyre

First Picador USA Paperback Edition: May 1998

D 10 9 8 7 6 5 4 3 2 1

THE
JADE
PEONY

A NOVEL

NEW YORK

To my aunts,
Freda and Mary,
and in memory of
Toy and Lilly Choy.

Contents

Author's Note

Four volumes contained the key information that helped to ground my early memories of Vancouver's Chinatown, for which I extend grateful acknowledgement: Paul Yee's *Saltwater City*; Ken Adachi's *The Enemy That Never Was*; the collected oral histories found in *Opening Doors, Vancouver's East End* by Daphne Marlatt and Carole Itter; and Kay J. Anderson's *Vancouver's Chinatown*.

This book is a work of fiction. Therefore, any references to actual historical events and locales, and any references or resemblances to persons, mythic, living or dead, are used for the purposes of fiction and are entirely coincidental. I am also responsible for any rendering of Chinese phrases and complex kinship terms into English equivalents, and for the adoption of the different sets of rules for the spelling of Chinese words.

I thank the *UBC Chronicle*, the *Toronto Star*, and the *Malahat Review*, in which portions of this book, in slightly different versions, first appeared.

Tòhng Yàhn Gāai was what
we once called
where we lived: "China-People-
Street." Later, we mimicked
Demon talk
and wrote down only
Wàh Fauh—"China-Town."
The difference
is obvious: the people
disappeared.

—Wing Tek Lum, "Translations"

PART ONE

JOOK-LIANG, ONLY SISTER

ONE

THE old man first visited our house when I was five, in 1933. At that time, I had only two brothers to worry about. Kiam and Jung were then ten and seven years old. Sekky was not yet born, though he was on his way. Grandmother, or Poh-Poh, was going regularly to our family Tong Association Temple on Pender Street to pray for a boy.

Decades later, our neighbour Mrs. Lim said that I kept insisting on another girl to balance things, but Stepmother told me that these things were in the hands of the gods.

Stepmother was a young woman when she came to Canada, barely twenty and a dozen years younger than Father. She came with no education, with a village dialect as poor as she was. Girls were often left to fend for themselves in the streets, so she was lucky to have any family interested in her fate. Though my face was round like Father's, I had her eyes and delicate mouth, her high forehead but not her high cheekbones.

This slim woman, with her fine features and genteel posture, was a seven-year-old girl in war-torn China when bandits killed most of her family. Found hiding between two trunks of clothes, she was taken to a Mission House, then taken away again, reclaimed by the village clan, and eventually sold into Father's

Canton merchant family. For years they fed her, taught her house duties, and finally put her on a steamship to Canada. She was brought over to help take care of Poh-Poh and to keep Father appropriate wifely company; but soon the young woman became more a wife than a concubine to Father, more a stepdaughter than a house servant to Grandmother. And a few years later, I, Jook-Liang, was born to them. Now, in our rented house, she was big with another child.

Poh-Poh, being one of the few elder women left in Vancouver, took pleasure in her status and became the arbitrator of the old ways. Poh-Poh insisted we simplify our kinship terms in Canada, so my mother became "Stepmother." That is what the two boys always called her, for Kiam was the First Son of Father's First Wife who had died mysteriously in China; and Jung, the Second Son, had been adopted into our family. What the sons called my mother, my mother became. The name "Stepmother" kept things simple, orderly, as Poh-Poh had determined. Father did not protest. Nor did the slim, pretty woman that was my mother seem to protest, though she must have cast a glance at the Old One and decided to bide her time. That was the order of things in China.

"What will be, will be," all the *lao wah-kiu*, the Chinatown old-timers, used to say to each other. "In Gold Mountain, simple is best."

There were, besides, false immigration stories to hide, secrets to be kept.

Stepmother was sitting on a kitchen chair and helping me to dress my Raggedy Ann; I touched her protruding tummy, I wanted the new baby all to myself. The two boys were waving toy swords around, swinging them in turn at three cutout hardboard nodding heads set up on the kitchen table. *Whack!* The game was to send the flat heads flying into the air to fall on a roll-out floor map of China. *Whack!* The game was Hong-Kong made and called ENEMIES OF FREE CHINA.

One enemy head swooped up and clacked onto the linoleum floor, missing its target by three feet. Jung started to swear when

Father looked up from his brush-writing in the other room. He could see everything we were doing in the kitchen. Poh-Poh sat on the other side of the table, enjoying Kiam and Jung's new game. Bags of groceries sat on the kitchen counter ready for supper preparations.

"I need a girl-baby to be my slave," I insisted, remembering Poh-Poh's stories of the time she herself once had a girl-helper in the dank, steamy kitchen of the cruel, rich Chin family in Old China. The Chins were refugees from Manchuria after the Japanese seized the territory. Not knowing any better, Poh-Poh treated the younger girl, her kitchen assistant, as unkindly as she herself had been treated; the women of the rich Chin family who "owned" Poh-Poh were used to wielding the whip and bamboo rods as freely on their fourteen servants as on the oxen and pigs.

"Too much bad memory," Poh-Poh said, and then, midway in its telling, would suddenly end a story of those old days. She would make a self-pitying face and complain how her arteries felt cramped with pain, how everything frustrated her, "*Ahyaii, ho gitsum!* How heart-cramp!" Though she was years younger than Poh-Poh, Mrs. Lim would shake her head in agreement, both of them clutching their left sides in common sympathy. It was a gesture I'd noticed in the Chinese Operas that Poh-Poh took me and my brothers to see in Canton Alley.

Whack! Another head rolled onto the floor. Kiam swung his toy sword like an ancient warrior-king from the Chinese Opera. Jung preferred to use his sword like a bayonet first, and then, *Whack!*

"Maybe Wong Bak—Old Wong—keep you company later, Liang-Liang," Poh-Poh said, happily stepping over one of the enemies of Free China to get some chopsticks from the table drawer. She was proud of her warrior grandsons. "Kill more," she commanded.

Poh-Poh spoke her *Sze-yup*, Four County village dialect, to me and Jung, but not always to Kiam, the First Son. With him, she spoke Cantonese and a little Mandarin, which he was studying in the Mission Church basement. Whenever Stepmother was around, Poh-Poh used another but similar village dialect, in a more clipped fashion, as many adults do when they think you might be the village fool, too worthless or too young, or not from their district. The Old One had a wealth of dialects which thirty-five years of survival in China had taught her, and each dialect hinted at mixed shades of status and power, or the lack of both. Like many Chinatown old-timers, the *lao wah-kiu*, Poh-Poh could eloquently praise someone in one dialect and ruthlessly insult them in another.

"An old mouth can drop honey or drop shit," Mrs. Lim once commented, defeated by the acrobatics of Grandmother's twist-punning tongue. The Old One roared with laughter and spat into the kitchen sink.

Whack!

Another head fell.

Stepmother rubbed her forehead, as if it were driving her mad.

"Wong Bak come for supper tonight," Poh-Poh said, signalling Stepmother to start preparing the supper. The kitchen light caught something gleaming on the back of her old head; Poh-Poh had put on her jade hair ornament for Wong Bak's visit tonight. He was an Old China friend of Grandmother's; they were both now in their seventies.

Wong Bak had been sent from the British Columbia Interior by a group of small-town Chinese in a place called Yale. He was too old to live a solitary existence any longer. Someone in our Tong Association gave Father's name as a possible Vancouver contact, because Old Wong might know Poh-Poh, who had once lived in the same ancestral district village.

Most Chinatown people were from the dense villages of southern Kwangtung province, a territory racked by cycles of famine and drought. When the call for railroad workers came from labour contract brokers in Canada in the 1880s, every man who was able and capable left his farm and village to be indentured for danger-ous work in the mountain ranges of the Rockies. There had also been rumours of gold in the rivers that poured down those mountain cliffs, gold that could make a man and his family wealthy overnight.

"Go to Gold Mountain," they told one another, promising to send wages home, to return rich or die. Thousands came in the decades before 1923, when on July 1st the Dominion of Canada passed the Chinese Exclusion Act and shut down all ordinary bachelor-man traffic between Canada and China, shut off any women from arriving, and divided families. Poverty-stricken bachelor-men were left alone in Gold Mountain, with only a few dollars left to send back to China every month, and never enough dollars to buy passage home. Dozens went mad; many killed themselves. The Chinatown Chinese call July 1st, the day celebrating the birth of Canada, the Day of Shame.

Some, like Old Wong, during all their hard time in British Columbia, still hoped to return to China if they could somehow win the numbers lottery or raise enough money from gambling. But now there was the growing war with the Japanese, more civil strife between the Communists and the Nationalists, and even more bitter starvation. Hearing all this, Poh-Poh gripped her left side, just below her heart, and said she only wanted her bones shipped back.

Father always editorialized in one of the news sheets of those Depression years how much the Chinese in Vancouver must help the Chinese. Because, he wrote, "No one else will."

In the city dump on False Creek Flats, living in makeshift huts, thirty-two Old China bachelor-men tried to shelter themselves; dozens more were dying of neglect in the overcrowded rooms of Pender Street. There were no Depression jobs for such men. They had been deserted by the railroad companies and betrayed by the many labour contractors who had gone back to China, wealthy and forgetful. There was a local Vancouver by-law against begging for food, a federal law against stealing food, but no law in any court against starving to death for lack of food. The few churches that served the Chinatown area were running out of funds. Soup kitchens could no longer safely manage the numbers lining up for nourishment, fighting each other. China men were shoved aside, threatened, forgotten.

During the early mornings, in the 1920s and '30s, nuns came out regularly from St. Paul's Mission to help clean and take the bodies away. In the crowded rooming houses of Chinatown, until morning came, living men slept in cots and on floors beside dead men.

Could we help out with Wong Bak? Perhaps a meal now and then, a few visits with the family ...? asked the officer from the Tong Association. It turned out that Poh-Poh indeed knew Wong Bak when they were in China, more than thirty years ago.

"Old-timers know all the old-timers," Third Uncle Lew said, taking inventory on his warehouse stock with an abacus. "Why not? The same bunch came over from the same damn districts," he laughed. "We all pea-pod China men!"

And now, tonight, Wong Bak was coming for dinner.

I looked up past Stepmother's swelling stomach, at the kitchen counter beside the sink with the pots and pans. Father had splurged on groceries: a bare long-necked chicken's head, freshly killed, hung out of the bag he had carried home. Poh-Poh also unwrapped a fresh fish, its eyes still shiny. Once it was cooked, Kiam and Jung would fight over who would get to suck on the hard-as-marble calcified fish eyes. I wanted the chicken feet. I wondered which part Wong Bak would want.

Father was worried about our meeting him for the first time. Wong Bak, I sensed from Father's overpreparation and nervousness, was indeed not an ordinary human being. He was an elder, so every respect must be paid to him, and *especially* as he knew the Old One herself. Grandmother must not lose face; we must not fail in our hospitality. Excellent behaviour on the part of my two brothers and me would signal our family respect and honour for the old ways.

Father looked at his watch and put down his writing brush.

"Let us talk a moment," he said to my brothers, and they left their game and stood before him. He told Kiam and Jung that Wong Bak might appear "very strange," especially to me, as I was so young, and a girl, and therefore might be more easily frightened.

"Frightened?" Stepmother said.

My ears perked up.

Father answered that the boys, being boys, would not be as easily scared about you-know-what. He spoke in code to Stepmother but whispered details to Kiam first, then Jung, whose eyes widened. After the whispering, Father delivered to the three of us a stern lecture about respect and we must use the formal term *Sin-saang*, Venerable Sir, as if Wong Bak were a "teacher" to be highly respected, as much as the Old Buddha or the Empress of China.

Respect meant you dared not laugh at someone because they were "different"; you did not ask stupid questions or stare rudely. You pretended everything was normal. That was respect. Father tried to simplify things for my five-year-old brain. Respect was what I gave my Raggedy Ann doll. I knew respect.

"I don't want you boys to stare at Wong Sin-saang's face," Father warned, which I thought was odd. Old people's faces were all the same to me, wrinkled and craggy. "Wong Sin-saang's had a very tough life."

"We know how to behave," First Brother Kiam insisted, waving the toy sword over the buck-toothed "WARLORD" nodding on the edge of the kitchen table. Jung poked his sword, bayonet-fashion, and two other heads nodded away, waiting for decapitation.

Third Uncle Lew had given Kiam the ENEMIES OF FREE CHINA game for his tenth birthday. Third Uncle had imported some samples from Hong Kong with the idea of selling them in Chinatown. Kiam read the game instructions written in English: "USE SWORD TO SMACK HEAD. COUNT POINTS. MOVE VICTORIOUS CHINESE AHEAD SAME NUMBER."

The Warlord was one of three Enemy-of-China "heads." The other two were a Communist and a Japanese soldier named Tojo.

All three had ugly yellow faces, squashed noses and impossible buck teeth. It was a propaganda toy to encourage overseas Chinese fund-raising for Free China.

Watching Kiam and Jung jump up and down was far better than having them force me to play dumb games like Tarzan and Jane and Cheetah. Kiam had seen the picture *Tarzan* three times. Kiam got to be Tarzan; Jung, Cheetah; and I got to be Jane doing nothing. I embraced my Raggedy Ann and watched another swing of Jung's sword *Whack!* take off Tojo's head. Father said that Tojo, a Japanese, was in command of the plot to enslave China for the Japanese.

Whack!

The third head went flying.

"Don't forget," Father repeated, thinking of the worst, "no staring at Wong Sin-saang's face. No laughing."

"Tell Liang-Liang," said Jung, waving the wooden sword at me. "She'll stare at Wong Sin-saang's face and behave like a brat."

"Jook-Liang will be too shy," Stepmother said. "I promise she'll do nothing but run away. At five, I would."

"Jook-Liang almost six," Grandmother interjected. "She look. I look."

Stepmother turned away. Jung swung. *Whack!*

"Liang-Liang'll say something to Wong Sin-saang," Kiam said. "She'll say something about Wong Sin-saang's face."

"You will, won't you, Liang-Liang?" Jung said, following First Brother's cue to be superior at my expense.

I looked up at them through the flowered wall and tiny windows of my Eaton's Toyland doll house. I put Tarzan's Jane, whose doll legs would not bend, in the front room. At Sunday School, I had learned how all visitors, like the Lord Jesus, for example, and even Tarzan and his pet chimpanzee, Cheetah, should always politely knock first, before you invited them into the front room of your house. At Kingdom Church Kindergarten, I also learned to say the words "fart face," and that upset Miss Bigley.

"Fart face," I said.

Jung opened his mouth to reply. Kiam looked darkly at me.

"If you have eyes, stare," Poh-Poh said to me. "Eyes for looking.'

Just as Jung was putting away the game box and taking my Raggedy Ann from me, and Stepmother and Kiam were setting the oak table, someone banged on our front door. A rumbling *Boom... Boom...* tumbled all the way from dark hallway to kitchen. Grandmother and I were waiting for the rice pot to finish cooking.

"Thunder," Poh-Poh commented, sniffing the air. The autumn damp would tighten her joints. She was midway through telling me a story about the Monkey King, who was being sent on another adventure by the Buddha. This time, the Monkey King took on the disguise of a lost boatman, and with his companion, Pig, they rode the back of a giant sea turtle to escape the fire-spouting River Dragon. "No one crosses my border," Poh- Poh said, in the deep voice of the River Dragon.

Boom... Boom...

"It's the front door," I said, comfortable against Poh-Poh's quilted jacket, listening.

"Thunder," Poh-Poh insisted, "ghost thunder."

There were in Grandmother's stories, always, wild storms and parting clouds, thunder, and after much labour, mountains that split apart, giving birth to demons who were out to kill you or to spirits who ached to test your courage. Until the last moment, you could never know for sure whether you were dealing with a demon or a spirit.

"Liang, stay in the kitchen," Stepmother said, wiping her hands on her apron. I heard Father struggling with the swollen front door, pulling, until the door surrendered and slammed open. "Step in, step in ..."

I jumped off Poh-Poh's knee. Everything in our musky hallway was suddenly lit by the outside street lamp. I could make out a hunched-up shadow standing on the porch, much shorter than Father. I thought of the burnished light that lingers after thunder; a mountain, after much labour, yawning wide.

"It's Wong Sin-saang," Father nervously called back to us, as if the shifting darkness might otherwise have no name.

Is it a demon or spirit? I thought, and nervously darted back to join Stepmother standing quietly at the end of the parlour. Jung and Kiam raced to crowd around Father; he waved them away. I grabbed Stepmother's apron.

In the bluish light cast by the street lamp, a dark figure with an enormous hump shook off its cloak. My eyes opened wide. The large hump continued shaking, struggling, quaking. Something dark lifted into the air. The mysterious mass turned into a sagging knapsack with tangled straps. Father hoisted the knapsack above the visitor's head and took away a black cloak. The obscure figure gave one more shudder, as if to resettle its bones; now I could see, against the pale light, someone old and angular, someone bent over, his haggard weight bearing down on two sticks.

"This way to the parlour," Father said, turning to put the cloak and knapsack away in the hall closet.

The stooped stranger, leaning on his walking sticks, confidently push-pulled, push-pulled himself into our parlour. My eyes widened. Everyone was anxious to see his face, but so sloped was the visitor, yanking his walking sticks about, that at first only the top of a balding grey crown greeted us. Finally, he stopped, half-standing in the parlour, a runty frame rising just under First Brother Kiam's chin; the narrow torso, fitted with a grown man's broad shoulders, thrust against an oversized patched shirt. Powerful legs angled out from his suspendered work pants. He looked like a half-flopped puppet with its head way down, but there were no strings moving him about. Suddenly, the old man snorted, cleared his throat, but did not spit. The force of his breathing told you he was ready for anything to happen next. Now it was your turn to breathe or to speak. Or to clear your throat. Your turn.

No one moved except Jung. He tried secretly bending his knees to peek at the very face we had been warned not to stare at; Kiam quickly elbowed Jung up again. Did the old man notice? No one said a word. The old man began to breathe more heavily, sawing, as if to inhale strength back into his lungs. Still no one could see the face. We examined the rest of him. Sleeves were rolled up over frayed longjohn cuffs; dark pants, freshly pressed. Gnarled thick fingers curled tightly onto bamboo canes. Scuffed boots pointed in skewed directions. Except for a cane on each side of him, his crooked legs looked no worse than some of the one-cane bachelor-men I'd seen sitting on the steps of Chinatown, hacking, always hacking, with grey-goateed heads bowed to their knees.

"*Sihk faahn mai-ahh?* Have you had your rice yet?" Father asked using a more formal phrase than Stepmother's village *Haeck chan mai-ah!* greeting—Eat dinner, yet!

To answer, the visitor straightened himself as far as he could, which was not far, and shook his head sideways: the overhead light bluntly hit Wong Sin-saang's face. A broad furrowed brow came into view. Wrinkles deepened. Jung gasped; the back of Kiam's neck stiffened. Father's warnings echoed in our minds: *Remember not to stare.* How could we help it? We all stared. Even Stepmother stared. I stared until I felt my eyes bulge out. The old man's face was like no other human one we had seen before: a wide-eyed, wet-nosed creature stared back at us.

A thrill went through me: this face, narrow at the top and wide at the bottom; this face, like those carved wooden masks sold during the Year of the Monkey; this wizened face looked directly back at me, perhaps like Cheetah, but more royal. I heard ghost thunder. A mountain opened, and here, right in our parlour, staring back at me, stood *Monkey,* the Monkey King of Poh-Poh's stories, disguised as an old man bent over two canes. But I, Jook-Liang, was not fooled. It could not be anyone but mischievous *him.* The air intensified; the world seemed more real than it had ever been for me. Poh-Poh was right: she heard ghost thunder when I heard only the door. A spell was cast in our parlour. Kiam pushed against it, trying to be sensible; First Brother asked the Monkey King, "Have you eaten, venerable sir?" Kiam used the formal dialect, just as Father had instructed him.

Monkey grimaced, showing large tobacco-stained teeth.

"No, not yet, thank you, so good of you to ask," he said, with Monkey smoothness, in a Toisan dialect, meaning that we, the family, needn't be so formal. Kiam tried discreetly to clear his throat, gulped, and stepped back, leaving Jung to stand alone. Now Monkey King, exactly as if he were holding court, looked steadily at Jung.

Jung said nothing. There was a long silence; it was Jung's turn as the Second Son to give his own greeting. Jung kept staring, open-mouthed. I thought of a sword flying through the air— *Whack!*—Jung's head, tumbling. I laughed, a short unstoppable titter. Stepmother's hand quickly covered my mouth.

"Wong Sin-saang," I heard Stepmother say, "you must be hungry."

Pulling a red handkerchief from his shirt pocket, Wong Sin-saang blew his nose noisily. Perhaps to signal his companion, Pig, waiting outside for instructions. I looked past the lace curtains, saw only the one-eyed street lamp.

"Who's there?" Poh-Poh shouted from the kitchen, all this time waiting for one of us to call her politely to come and meet the visitor, so she wouldn't seem too rude or too anxious. We'd forgotten. She banged on a bowl and banged on a plate and stayed in the kitchen, waiting.

The Monkey King seemed to hear nothing; he had turned his sable eyes on me. I let go of Stepmother's apron and slowly walked towards him. Stepmother reached out to grab me; I slipped past her. I pushed Jung and Kiam aside. Father began to fidget in the hall.

Across the room, Wong Sin-saang seemed not much bigger than me. His grey head drooped, as if it needed to bend lower. I stepped towards him. Stopped.

"This must be Jook-Liang," Monkey finally said, and his voice trembled, "the pr-pretty one."

I ran the last few steps and reached out to him, at once burying my head against his bone-thin body: *Here was the Monkey King!* After all, I heard his voice tremble—*the pr-pretty one*—a signal to any child not to be afraid of him. Not to doubt him. His disguise as an old man and his two canes were not meant to fool me, especially the canes. I knew what these really were: the two walking sticks, which he could instantly rejoin to become the powerful bamboo pole Monkey used to propel himself across canyons and streams; the same pole he employed to battle monsters, mock demons, shake at courage-testing spirits. I laughed and felt Monkey awkwardly embrace me; very awkwardly of course, so as not to betray his disguise as an Old One with two canes.

His gesture broke the ice; everything was familiar again.

I heard Stepmother and Father welcoming Wong Sin-saang in a jumble of ritual phrases: "Stay, stay for dinner!" "No, please don't stand on ceremony." "How good of you to visit." Even Jung finally spoke, though he did not remember every word. "Have you your rice?" No one felt it necessary to notice how Monkey blew his nose again—and again—or how quickly he wiped his eyes. A signal to Pig, hiding under our porch.

The aroma of twice-cooked chicken filled the air; we could hear Grandmother preparing the food for the table; she stepped into the parlour and boldly stared at Monkey. *Eyes for looking.*

"*Aiiiiyah!* Wong Kimlein!" Poh-Poh exclaimed, calling him by his birth-name in a voice loud enough to break up the hubbub. "It's truly you! They say you come back from Yale. Not die there. Die here, in Salt Water City, in Vancouver."

"Die here, maybe," Monkey said, looking up. "How goes your old years? Are you well?"

"Die soon," Poh-Poh said. "You and me too old for these days."

Stepmother took my hand and led the way to the dining room.

"You hear from Old China?" Poh-Poh took Monkey's arm, as if she would lean on his walking stick, too.

"We must talk, Wong Kimlein, just you and me," Poh-Poh commanded. "Come, come, sit for dinner."

I rushed to take the seat beside Monkey, and Poh-Poh pulled back a chair for him and sat down to be on his other side. She suddenly spoke to him in a different dialect, more pitched and strange than I had ever heard. *Monkey talk.* Poh-Poh waved Father into the kitchen to bring the food. Monkey chattered back to Grandmother, matching her odd, lurching vowels. Stepmother and Kiam and Jung brought in bowls of rice and steaming dishes of pork and vegetables and fish and bitter melon soup.

"Let's all sit and eat," Father said, bringing in the twice-cooked chicken.

All through dinner, I sat next to Wong Sin-saang, looking up at Monkey devouring his rice. He was careful not to miss a single grain so he would not have a pock-marked bride, and kept monkey-talking in that strange way with Poh-Poh. Jung could see what I was thinking. Being seven, he could still think like a kid, but not completely. When Jung brought over my own bowl of bitter melon soup, he whispered to me, "He's just a man, stupid."

I admit I was still not entirely sure and I kept arguing with myself: if Wong Sin-saang knew Poh-Poh—who said *she* felt older than even Miss Bigley's Bible friends, like Moses—how could Monkey be just a man? An ordinary man?

I drank all my soup, but hardly ate any rice. I was too excited, though Poh-Poh was drawing away most of the Monkey King's attention. She grew more animated, grew flushed with excitement to hear a voice matching the servant dialects of Old China. She listened with glee to the resonant *slurrrph* the old man sounded at the edge of his soup spoon, a sound not encouraged at our table. (Father had taught us to sip our soup slowly, noiselessly, in the Western way.) Poh-Poh hardly ate anything, barely touched the green vegetables Father dropped into her bowl. She had turned her attention completely to the old man, speaking Old China secrets. Poh-Poh nodded, sometimes laughed, but both of them—more often than not—sighed with longtime sadness. Grandmother's eyes grew wide with remembering; the more she talked, the more she had to say. Monkey kept eating, nodding; between bites, he spoke a moment or two, then let Poh-Poh chatter on. He was hungry.

I thought of all the stories Poh-Poh had told me since I was two: Monkey King, in all kinds of disguises, adventuring through the world of ordinary people: "He could look like an old woman with a hooked nose and crooked fingers, or turn as lovely as Kwan Yin standing in a white silk gown; sometimes it suited him to be a country farmer with dirt on his brows... but all the time he was as hungry as a bear from his travels. You could trick the Monkey King with food, especially if you offered him ripe peaches." Poh-Poh smacked her lips. "Lunch and dinner were perilous times for Monkey."

My eyes were in pain from so much staring. I could not help myself: *here* beside me, the Monkey King sat, playing at being an old man as ancient as Poh-Poh, yet wielding chopsticks with youthful ease. I imagined juicy peach slices, delicately held by those same chopsticks, skinned slice after skinned slice, smoothly disappearing into his mouth. Wong Sin-saang ate every piece of stir-fried celery, bean cake, carrot, bok choi, eggplant, pork, fish and twice-cooked chicken offered to him, and ate, and ate, into his third brimming bowl of rice. *Hungry as a bear.* When the Monkey King ate, not a drop of sauce fell, not one grain of rice was lost. Father nudged Jung to stop staring at the old man.

I fidgeted with joy. Looking up at Wong Sin-saang, watching him carry his third bowl of rice to his mouth with such a sigh of pleasure, I sensed no one knew what else I knew: here, too, right beside me in his patched-up shirt, with his soft eyes, like liquid— sat the marvellous Cheetah of the matinee movies; Cheetah, Tarzan's friend. Poh-Poh had educated me about this. After Jung took Grandmother and me to the Lux to see my first Tarzan movie, Poh-Poh announced that Cheetah was another one of the Monkey King's disguises. It was a way for the Monkey King to be with his monkey tribe and still keep in touch with Buddha's commands, for Monkey could not do without human company, black or white or yellow. After all, people were closest to Buddha, Poh-Poh told me.

First Brother Kiam always argued that Poh-Poh's stories were just *stories*, nothing more, like the stories about the blonde Jesus Miss Bigley told us. At home, after Sunday School, Kiam always demanded to know: "How can anyone walk on water? How can so few baskets of bread and fish feed hundreds?" And Santa Claus never once visited our house. Doubt grew in me. Jung's insidious whisper was doing its job: *He's just a man, stupid.* The more I looked at Wong Sin-saang's animated face, his cheeks flushed with food, the more I felt I needed to know for sure. Slowly, a single question began to disturb my child's mind: *He's wearing a mask... I thought... like one of those Halloween demons...* I wanted all at once to make sure he was not tricking me, not wearing a monkey mask, like those demons who came banging on our door and sent me crying with fright back into the kitchen. At once, I stood up on my chair. I dropped my chopsticks, turned, and grabbed Wong Sin-saang's large ear, tugging his Cheetah face towards me. Father banged his hand on the table.

"You Tarzan monkey," I said to Wong Sin-saang. "You Cheetah..."

Stepmother gasped.

Poh-Poh reached across to stop me. "Let go!"

Wong Sin-saang started laughing.

"Let her pull, Old One," Monkey said, "let her pull away. Jook-Liang has your *lao foo* spirit." He looked into my eyes and announced, "Liang is tiger-willed."

I looked into his eyes. His dark eyes focussed and refocussed. They were real, reflecting life. I touched his deeply wrinkled forehead, studied both sides of his head to look for a telltale string. Nothing but straggly hair. Even the pen-brush tufts that stuck out from his ears were honest. I felt proud of myself, unable to hold back the news: *"Gene-goh Mau-lauh Bak!"* I said to the soft eyes. "A *for-real* Monkey Man!"

Stepmother swallowed deeply. Jung giggled. Wong Sin-saang pushed himself a foot away from my chair. Father tried to say something, but Monkey shook his head. Everyone sat with chopsticks poised. Silent.

The old man bent his head lower. We were eye-to-eye. He knew I knew his real name. My lips soundlessly mouthed the words: *Monkey Man. Mau-lauh Bak. Monkey Man.* He denied nothing. But he said, "Will you call me Wong *Suk*?"

I tried out the name: "Wong *Suk*."

Suk meant someone about Father's age, or much younger. *Suk* was more informal than *Sin-saang*. *Suk*, I thought, and knew he was younger than Father even if he was very old on the outside.

"I like *Suk* very, very much," he said. "Oh, much better than Wong *Bak—Old* Wong. Make me feel younger. Call me Wong Suk. Okay? Maybe everyone call me that. Okay?"

I nodded. He was giving us his secret magic name as a blessing.

Then I said the next thing Father insisted no one was supposed to say out loud.

"Wong Suk," I said, loudly, in Chinese, "you all twisted up, *crooked.*"

Wong Suk swallowed; he reached out and held me gently at arms' length, though it seemed to me, his long fingers, his wide palms, were too awkward to hold an almost-six-year-old with such unearthly gentleness. Wong Suk's eyes grew strange. He spoke to me in the family dialect:

"M-pai Mau-lauh Bak?" Wong Suk's voice was a half-whisper. "You not *scared* of Monkey Man?" I shook my head, took a closer look at Wong Suk, touched his for-real wide nose, delicately tugged at the curving tufts of salt-and-pepper hair that formed his bushy eyebrows. I recognized his hair tonic; it smelled of the stuff Father always used. I leaned closer. Crooked arms enfolded me. *M-pai... m-pai...?* I heard Wong Suk chant. *Not afraid... you not afraid... m-pai...?*

It seemed he could not stop his chanting nor his heart's rapid beat, nor could he let go his hold on me. I only knew to hold him tighter, lean into him like a cat, a tiger, catching the herbal scent of his body. The air felt hot.

"This child not afraid of me," I heard him say to everyone. "She not afraid."

"Don't be foolish," I heard Poh-Poh saying, in the dialect I understood, and I could feel her tugging away at my arm. "Don't be foolish."

He's mine, I wanted to shout. *He's mine!* Something old sprang from me, something struggled to defy even Poh-Poh. I pulled my head away from Wong Suk and looked back at her. Something like an ancient sword swooped— *Whack!*—striking her against the wall, though outwardly nothing happened to Grandmother, or to Wong Suk, or to me.

Wong Suk let me go. I slumped back into my chair and picked up my chopsticks. Poh-Poh turned back to the table. Everyone went back to steadily eating supper, went on breathing the heated air. After Wong Suk settled back and slurped his soup, loudly, he and Poh-Poh spoke no more in their secret language to one another, though their lips smiled and moved with the memory of something deep and savoury.

TWO

"JOOK-LIANG, if you want a place in this world," Grandmother's voice had that exasperating let-me-remind-you tone, "do not be born a girl-child."

"This is Canada," I wanted to snap back, "not Old China."

Sitting on the kitchen stool, I bit my tongue. For years, I had been nagged to remember to wash diapers and generally clean up after my baby brother, who was now three years old and sickly. I was tired of his always leaking at both ends.

I liked to think I was almost nine, and much, much older than Sek-Lung. I recalled how Sekky had received twice the number of jade and gold bracelets that I had got as a baby, and how everyone at the baby banquet toasted his arrival and how only the women noticed me in my new dress, and then only for a few minutes to compare Poh-Poh's and Stepmother's embroidery.

Poh-Poh and I were alone that cloudy morning, except for Sekky. She was down on one knee between me and the oversized crib, doing me a favour, getting ready to tie ribbons on my tap-shoes. His thumb in his mouth, he looked like a pale China doll sleeping in its wicker crib.

Baby Brother was sick again. Always sick. Always getting all the attention; always snoring because of his congested lungs, though he had no fever. Everyone was afraid his illness might be TB. Afraid Sekky might die. Then, our two-storey wooden house would by law be cursed by the Vancouver Health Inspection Board: a cardboard sign would be posted on our front door, a sign boldly visible from the street: CONDEMNED. Everyone would pass by our house, pointing at our family as if we were lepers, like the Chau Lims or the Negro Johnstons down the street.

But the official white doctor from St. Paul's Hospital—so far—could not find TB. "Perhaps it's just a stubborn cold," he said to my father. "A flu." It was good that no one else in the family had any signs of illness.

For weeks, Poh-Poh's Chinese herbalist had instructed her to slip mysterious pink pellets, like tiny BB's, into the warm, honey-sweetened chicken broth she patiently spooned into Sekky's mouth. We were lucky: Sekky had no fever, and he kept greedily swallowing the soup.

Grandmother glanced at the crib, and her white hair brushed against my creamy taffeta skirt. I took a deep breath. The persistent damp, woodsy smell of our old house reminded me of the oncoming fall.

"A girl-child is *mo yung*—useless," Poh-Poh grunted, shifting down her other knee to give me, as always, reluctantly, my measure of attention.

I was getting ready for my performance time with old Wong Suk, and wishing, with the will of my almost-nine years, that old people would move faster. I ignored Poh-Poh's remark about being a girl-child. After all, she was a girl, too, even if she was, as my father respectfully called her, the Old One.

At last, with both knees down, and a great sigh, Poh-Poh began engineering the ribbon laces of my tap-shoes, twisting and turning each end until the satin strips danced between her bony fingers.

My friend old Wong Suk had last week gone tottering on his two bamboo canes through Woodward's store aisles to buy me three lengths of crimson satin ribbon.

"From Liang's bandit-prince," he had said, snatching out of a small paper bag a fistful of red ribbons and, like Robin Hood, scattering the dishevelled strands across our round oak table, "a gift for my bandit-princess!"

There was one length for my hair and two longer ones for my tap shoes.

"How much you spend on that?" Poh-Poh asked, lifting them up to feel their quality.

"Fifteen cents," Wong Suk proudly announced. It was the Depression. Fifteen cents was equal to an hour of bachelor-man labour.

"A waste of good money," Poh-Poh pronounced in her contemptuous *Sze-yup* village dialect. She always chose her tone and style of words according to her judgement and mood. "All useless!"

Old Wong Suk gave me his semi-toothless smile and was pleased. Wong Suk liked to irritate Grandmother, and when he succeeded, he always winked at me. The satin ribbons slipped gracefully from Poh-Poh's hand, falling back onto the dark table. Poh-Poh felt flattered that her worthless granddaughter merited such bounty. Wong Suk had promised me the ribbons many weeks ago, and my bandit-prince would never fail me; just as our hero bandit, Robin Hood, would never fail Marian, his fair maiden. Wong Suk always called me his *chak neuih gung-jyu*, his bandit-princess.

I shifted restlessly on the stool, impatient for Wong Suk's arrival.

"Raise your legs." Poh-Poh needed to see better. Whenever she was alone with me, the Old One snapped at what she saw as my lack of humility.

"Feet so stinky. Not pretty girl feet. Cow feet."

I stretched my thin child's legs into the rectangle of grey light coming from the window overlooking the wicker crib. It was a rain-threatening Vancouver morning, but there was enough light for Poh-Poh's nimble fingers. She knew how to tie knots blindfolded. Besides, I dared not suggest turning on the naked light-bulb hanging over us: *Waste of money!*

I had pestered Poh-Poh for days to help me tie Wong Suk's gift into show-off bows for my tap-shoes.

"But you do everything so prettily," I said to her ancient head, for it was true. "And Wong Suk spent so much good money on these ribbons..."

Finally, after days of nagging and begging, she was indulging my foolishness, but barely: *Aiiiiyaah! How one China girl be Shir-lee Tem-po-lah?*

Grandmother delicately pulled, and commenced twisting and tucking the drawn-out ribbon strands. We decided to make three small blooms for each of my shoes.

"Point your toes down," she commanded, holding a single dangling strand in each of her hands, "and push your stinky feet away from me."

I did, pushing down at my steel toe-taps.

Before my eyes, curls of red slowly shifted—lifted—then unfurled into two bouquets of three flowers each. I looked in amazement.

Teach me, my heart said, but I held back the words.

It was a ribbon-tying trick only Poh-Poh knew, taught to her long ago in Old China when she had served as a "house-daughter" to a refugee Shanghai family. The First Concubine threatened to break her fingers if she did not learn fast enough how to knot pom-pom flowers and how to hand-weave sun-dried, skin-cutting grass stalks into flat "eternal love" patterns so seamless that each design revealed neither a beginning nor an end. Poh-Poh told me how her fingers bled while, as a girl not yet ten, she frantically practised tying rough kelp filaments together, tying them endlessly until she perfected each design. Finally, she could tie even the thinnest silk strands in the most subtle patterns. The rich loved their pleasures in miniature, she told me, like

American gold coins, diamonds and carved emeralds.

"Make smaller," Poh-Poh said, imitating the pitched voice of the First Concubine. "Always that pig-lady say, 'Make smaller!'"

Poh-Poh refused to teach me any of her knots. Once she did try, when I was six, but I seemed too clumsy, too awkward, not fearful enough of failure. My six-year-old fingers slipped; I clutched at Grandmother's body, glimpsed her hand raised above me, ready to slap. Then she froze, her hand in mid-strike, held back; tears welled up in her eyes. "No, no, *no!*" Furious, she shook me off. "No more teach!"

At seven, children in Old China laboured in fields, rode bone-crushing oxen, crawled with oiled bodies into narrow coal seams and emerged bent-backed forever. At seven, Grandmother was told how lucky she was to be a house servant and not one of the field servants. Then, the First Concubine's fists fell on her lucky body; some days, her thin child's back was whipped with a knotted belt and beaten with a switch. Cowed, shaking, Grandmother was dragged by her long hair and flung back into her narrow bedding by the kitchen door. "Learn or die," First Concubine screamed, her long fingernails clawing at the air.

Now I was almost nine, swallowing, knowing nothing.

And there was no other way to learn. No one could ever follow her quick-moving fingers. She would later teach Baby Brother some juggling, tell him paperfolding stories, even show him how to make simple toys, like paper cranes, toss rings—or windchimes when he grew old enough. But all her womanly skills she would keep away from me, keep to herself until she died: "Job too good for *mo yung* girl!"

Poh-Poh knelt back to look at her handiwork: each of my tap-shoes was crowned with a perfectly delicate, perfectly brilliant bouquet of red pom-poms. Not even the silk-tasseled shoes of the First Concubine could have been lovelier. Old Wong Suk would be delighted.

Shaking my stiff ringlets (still smelling faintly of Stepmother's curling iron), I felt like a grown-up girl. I knew to keep quiet, stay properly humble: that is, not play out Poh-poh's usual games, except to say thank you and hug her jacket-padded body and wait for her to push me away. But the word "useless," *mo yung,* jumped out at me:

"I'm not *mo yung,* Poh-Poh," I protested, "even though I *am* a girl!"

"*Aiiiiyahhh*—a *girl!*" Grandmother shook her head. "Too late then!" She slapped my shoes. "Finish! *Mo yung* girl!" I looked down again to focus on the small petals of those rare, exquisite flowers. My spirits lifted.

"So beautiful," I said spontaneously, with a hug, which she elbowed away.

"*Mo yung* girl!" she said, as if I would never learn a thing, however much I wanted to be taught. "Too much spoil!"

I hopped off the kitchen stool, smoothed my cut taffeta dress against my spindly legs. The patent surface of my tap-shoes glimmered back at me; the shoes no longer looked second-hand, not at all as if they came from a throwaway church bazaar sale, which they had. I lifted each heel, heard two satisfying *tap taps.* I felt light as air, in control again.

"Looks nice," I said slowly, in English, catching a glimpse of myself in the hall mirror. The grey morning light softened everything into half-shadows. Poh-Poh refused to look at me. I took my favourite pose, the one Shirley Temple does with her tiny hands tucked under her chin; you know, bright eyed—*My goodness!*—just before all the grownups praise her for a song well sung, a dance well danced. I could hardly wait for Wong Suk. Why was he so late this morning? I looked down at the flowers glowing on my feet.

"Too fussy," Poh-Poh said, her back to me. "Useless!"

My chin lifted, that stubborn voice of mine charged ahead: "Father says after the war is over, things will change for everybody, even girls."

"War over?" Grandmother chuckled, shifting her dialect. "Always war in China. First, bandit wars in South China,

Communist—*Gung Chang*—wars everywhere, and all those sun-cursed Japanese dogs yapping into North China..."

I thought of the newsreels, smoke and bombs: Europe and Germany were at war. Britain was at war. The Chinese were for-ever at war with the Japanese invaders. War everywhere but here in Chinatown.

"There's no war in Canada," I said. "This is Canada."

Poh-Poh sighed deeply, gave me a condescending look.

"*You* not Canada, Liang," she said, majestically, "*you* China. Always war in China."

I hated the Old One: Grandmother never let me get on with my movie-star daydreams. And now the late morning sky seemed more threatening: if it rained, how could I dance on the porch for my bandit-prince? Surely Wong Suk would be here any minute now, with his semi-toothless smile and wrinkled kind eyes, antic-ipating my best performance.

The ribbons burned in the half-darkness, and my feet would not keep still. Undaunted, I pushed myself back onto the stool, clenched my fists. Waited. I shuffled. Sekky began to smell of pee; he turned on his side. I grew restless. The wicker crib creaked. Poh-Poh sat down on her rocker. Always waiting.

I waited, just as Poh-Poh once had waited until the First Concubine summoned her to come to her *mahjong* tea table. While learning how to wait, to serve, to obey, Poh-Poh said she thought of her poor mother, the mud-walled room she last shared with her, but mostly her mother's smile, her mother's hope that things would turn out lucky. I saw myself on our dilapidated porch, tapdancing and whirling about, and I thought of Wong Suk's delight. I began to sing, not one of Grandmother's riverboat songs, sung to amuse the First Concubine and her gambling cronies, but my tapdance song, "Mama's little baby loves short 'nin', short'nin' ..."

"*You* China," Grandmother said.

I sang louder.

"*Mo yung* girl!"

I could barely keep still. A week of tapdance practice lay coiled in my dreamer's body: "... *short'nin'* ... *short'nin'* ..."

The wooden porch facing the street was the stage for all my performances. There, in good spring or summer weather, wearing Stepmother's old dresses, her junk costume jewellery protruding from my tied-back hair, hung about with silk scarves, I mimicked the Chinese Opera heroines: the warrior-woman, the deserted wife, the helpless princess. And, lately, in my movie costumes, I tapped steps as deftly as Shirley herself. I hung up old bedsheets for skies, draped ropes for rivers, piled up orange-crates for mountains, just like the Canton Alley operas, with their fine silk and dazzling sequins and plain wood props.

I took care to set a perfect make-believe world before Wong Suk, my old guardian, my adopted uncle; *Wong Suk*, my one and only true friend since I was five. Others said he was ugly, old, with squashed lips that gave him a hapless monkey-face. True, Wong Suk was doubled-up and cruelly crippled, but to me, Wong Suk ambling along on his pair of thick bamboo canes seemed only different, unusual. I, his Shirley Temple princess, always saw only a bandit-prince in disguise.

Wong Suk and I spent Saturday mornings and afternoons together. Often, after I'd sat by his side around our oak dining table, listening to his story-telling (as violent as Poh-Poh's, but more ghost-driven and fantastical), he would indulge me by watching one of my miniature performances. As I took my bows, I drank in the way Wong Suk applauded, banged his two bamboo canes, and laughed and ooohhhhed and ahhhhhed at my efforts.

Delighting in each other's company, the two of us would walk as fast as we could down Pender Street to get a snack of Chinese pastry, served with a bowl of "daily soup," or pace ourselves so that we would arrive in time to catch the movie house matinee at the Lux or Odeon around the corner on Hastings Street.

"Jook-Liang," Wong Suk said to me one perfect day, "you are my little girl, my family."

I was happy. I knew our adopted relationship was a true one: Wong Suk would otherwise have been only one of the many discarded bachelor-men of Chinatown—and I, barely tolerated by Poh-Poh, would merely be a useless girl-child.

"Go to Odeon or Lux?" Wong Suk would ask me.

If we hadn't seen the movie, and Father gave us some extra coins, I always chose the Odeon. It had a gold ceiling with painted angels, and between movies there were magicians, singers, a chorus of dancing girls and dog acts. Sometimes there were acrobats and jugglers; then Poh-Poh might come with us, that is, if Stepmother or one of my brothers could stay home with Sekky. My favourite movies starred Shirley Temple; Wong Suk liked Tom Mix, any old picture with Tarzan (to tell the truth, he identified with the smart and smart-alecky Cheetah), and we both liked Laurel and Hardy. But we absolutely gloried in the Sherwood Forest world of Robin Hood. "So much like the heroes of Old China," Wong Suk told me. My two older brothers, Jung and Kiam, used to go with us to see the gangster and Charlie Chan movies, which I hated, so much talking and no action until the end—but soon these two, especially Kiam, had their own friends, the onrushing war to worry about, and jobs to go to. These days I had Wong Suk nearly all to myself.

Today, if only the sun would peek out, if only it would not rain, I was going to delight Wong Suk with my best performance. I could see that Poh-Poh wanted Wong Suk to be pleased with me, if only because my performance would reflect on her. Wong Suk was only a few years younger than her seventy-seven years; he was her equal; he was a man whose approval meant something. And Wong Suk had bought her granddaughter ribbons for her dreams. A princess! Poh-Poh understood the appeal and danger of dreams. She broke into a chain of half-dialects.

"Too much playing," she said, shaking her head and rocking herself impatiently. "Too much fancy! Learn nothing!"

Then she used a kind of half-English pidgin and half-Chinese which usually sent Wong Suk rollicking, for he knew more English than Poh-Poh. But he was not here.

This useless only-granddaughter wants to be Shirlee Tem-po-lah; the useless Second Grandson wants to be cow-boy-lah. The First Grandson wants to be Charlie Chan. All stupid foolish!

"In China, Jook-Liang, you no play-act anything." She looked up at her obviously spoiled granddaughter. "In China, they tie up your feet like this—" With her hands, she made tight, bent-back fists. "—No can dan-see!"

"Well," I said, with my best sense of dignity, mustering up the Toisanese words, "I'm only play-acting for Wong Suk." This was a lie: I also play-acted for myself, imagining a world where I belonged, dressed perfectly, behaved beyond reproach, and was loved, always loved, and was not, no, not at all, *mo yung*.

I pulled at my chin and sucked in my thick cheeks to lengthen my "look," just as Stepmother said the actress Anna May Wong always did. If Poh-Poh was going to launch into the story of "the old days, the old ways," I wanted to escape.

It was tiresome to hear again how she hadn't been deemed worthy enough to have her feet bound: back in China, the village match-maker had destined Grandmother to be sold to a well-off family, to be their house servant.

"*Too ugly,*" the midwife had pronounced at Grandmother's birth. And her father, an old farmer wishing for a son, spat at his wife and left them forever.

Grandmother had come into the world a month too early, a cursed girl-child with a misshapen birth skull, pads of skin over her face, and a fold of hair around her neck.

"At ten she will be even uglier—monster ugly!" The midwife rinsed her bloodied hands in the wooden birth pan, and spat out onto the dirt floor the bad water and evil smell caught in her throat. "Get rid of this useless girl-child."

I got off the stool and took a pose before the half-length mirror in the hall entrance. The stiff white taffeta dress I'd begged Stepmother to buy me from the Strathcona School Rummage Sale looked really pretty. Elegant, even. I knew the breeze on the porch would catch the folds and lift them like a dream. And then, as I turned and spun, lifting my arms...

Grandmother kept shaking her head.

"Maybe it rain soon," she said, darkly. She was always saying something discouraging. I know now she was only warning me to be patient, not to tempt the gods. Poh-Poh always said the unlucky thing to bring back the luck: for example, if you worried about her health, she would say, "Maybe die soon."

"It's only cloudy," I said. "Cloudy isn't rain."

She refused to acknowledge me. Her rocker kept its steady motion.

Poh-Poh's mother had said, looking at the wretched baby, twice-cursed for being born ugly and a girl-child, "Maybe die soon."

For weeks after Grandmother's too-early birth, Father told me, Poh-Poh's stubborn village mother fed her with a rubber syringe given to her by the Heavenly Gate Mission lady. She filled the bulb-shaped syringe with her own breast milk, sometimes mixed with three drops of ox blood saved for her by the village butcher. The mission lady brought blankets, mysterious potions, biscuits. The hard biscuits were slowly chewed into a warm pulpy spittle by Poh-Poh's mother, and dabbed into the baby's hungry mouth. Father told me that slowly the flabs of skin lifted up from Poh-Poh's face, the skull grew to be normal; her coarse, black hair rose up richly to cover her head. The hideous, twice-cursed baby survived, grew up, married, had one son—my father.

In fact, Poh-poh had become quite pretty, with high cheekbones that made her seem ageless for her first sixty years. Now she was seventy-seven. And I was almost nine, getting ready to tap-dance for Wong Suk: *One shuffle, kick-back, kick-side, two shuffle, step-toe, step-back... kick, kick, kick....*

The Old One grew bored with my self-absorption. She had more important things to do. Carefully, she bent over to look at Sekky, now struggling to wake up. She gently rocked the crib and began cooing at him. My baby brother was her chief concern; I was a distraction, a nuisance. She was always happy to see me go off with Wong Suk.

"Rain, rain, go away," I sang under my breath, "come again some other day…"

Poh-Poh hated English tunes that sounded like bad-luck chants. When would her *mo yung* granddaughter learn not to tempt the gods? She reached down to pick up Sekky; he was waking up slowly, arms unfolding beneath him, in that stupid way all babies do, even Canadian-born ones. Poh-Poh liked to whisper blessings in his ear, always whispering softly, so that Sekky could never really repeat them; softly, so that the gods could not hear; she liked to sing to him, pat his hands and back, to enchant him with stories and songs.

"Well, when is *Mau-lauh Bak* coming?"

"Don't call him that," I protested. My bandit-prince was not anyone's Monkey Man. "Call him Wong Suk."

"Why not?" Grandmother said, in a half-whisper, now that baby Sekky was stirring from his nap. "*Mau-lauh Bak* ugly like me—he Ugly One. We know world. No one spoil us."

She got worked up and her dialects fell into a kind of controlled disorder. "No one care for us. Not like you—spoiled Jook-Liang—always play. Wong Suk and me too ugly—*ahhyaiii… Git-sum! Git-sum!* Heart-cramp! Heart-cramp!"

In the old pictures of Poh-Poh, even the fading sepia ones with their cracked edges taken by the mission lady, the photos where she clings to her mother's black pants, no one would never think her ugly. But when the village midwife had pronounced fresh-born Poh-Poh hideous, the judgement stayed. Why not? A beautiful girl-child from a poor family is even more useless than an ugly one from a rich family, unless you can sell either one for a jade bracelet or hard foreign currency. Then you can feed your worthy sons, give them educations, arrange marriages, make them proud men. But a girl-child? If no one else appreciated me, Wong Suk knew my worth: he would never desert me. I was his family. He told me so.

I shifted my weight, did a simple turn, and watched the cream-coloured skirt lift and ripple above the dancing rosettes on my patent shoes. Above the tap-tap-tap, the soft taffeta rustle embraced the silence. *I'm not ugly*, I thought to myself, *I'm not useless*. Oh, if only it would not rain, I thought, and whirled.

Above the house, the clouds broke up.

Suddenly, the light from the window brightened and poured over the crib; the sitting room and hallway became brilliant, full of sun.

My heart almost burst with expectation. I looked again into the hall mirror, seeking Shirley Temple with her dimpled smile and perfect white-skin features. Bluntly reflected back at me was a broad sallow moon with slit dark eyes, topped by a helmet of black hair. I looked down. Jutting out from a too-large taffeta dress were two spindly legs matched by a pair of bony arms. Something cold clutched at my stomach, made me swallow.

Sekky started to wail. Grandmother lifted him up into the light, whispering.

[handwritten, right margin:] cross-racial identification

[handwritten:] → = liberation. Interesting

I looked down: masses of red clustered at my feet. I thought of old Wong Suk leaning on his two canes. And I danced.

[handwritten annotations below:]
WHAT IS HAPPENING HERE?
— she is frustrated
— solace + strength from Wong Suk
HOW DOES HE LIBERATE HER?
— Gma doesn't support her.
— Wong Suk lets her call him by informal, be a child, call her pretty, lets her touch + feel + encourages her dreams + fantasies.

THREE

Waiting for Old Wong Suk to come and see me dance, I stood on our porch—back straight, eyes forward—and did a practice *toe-tap, shuffle-kick, turn.* It was my tap version of the Castle Walk. Last week, Wong Suk had asked me, in his best English, "Liang, next time show me Shirley Temple. Show me so I never to forget you, okay?"

When I got the dress and tap-shoes at the last Strathcona School Fall Rummage Sale, Miss McKinney threw in an oversized book, *Professional Tap-Steps in Twenty Easy Lessons.* The book cover featured Fred Astaire side-stepping with Ginger Rogers. The book came with fold-out pages stamped with shoe prints I could follow with my own feet. Like *glide*-one, *glide*-two. Otherwise, for the actual tap-steps, I imitated the movie shows that occupied my head and smiled and curtsied, just like Shirley did.

The white taffeta dress was actually a creamy white, a colour that made my skin look more canary than I liked. There was a faded raspberry stain near the collar.

"If you don't look for it," Father said, "you won't notice it."

The taffeta dress was going to be a surprise for Wong Suk, only I wished the dress had colourful polka dots, too, but it didn't. Wong Suk loved polka dots.

Maybe the plain white dress was a sign; the raspberry stain, a sign. Poh-Poh told me there were always signs, if only one was paying attention, like the time she dreamed of me falling off the porch when I was a baby. I didn't fall off. But I was learning to walk and I did trip and bump my head on the bannister. Even today, you can spot a tiny nick just above my left eyebrow. Poh-Poh likes to hold my head a certain way and point out to people how she foretold the scar.

Maybe I should have known it was a warning—a sign, I mean—when after Poh-Poh tied all those ribboned pom-poms on my tap-shoes, she didn't ask me to help her rinse out the stinky pail of diapers. "Keep your dress clean," was all that she said, throwing the rinsed diapers into the galvanized tub herself.

Everything seemed right that Saturday except Wong Suk was late. He usually appeared by eleven o'clock, latest. The spring sun overhead reminded me it was nearing twelve o'clock: the mill whistle by the B.C. docks would blow soon. The air felt wet and warm, spring and summer, though it was mid-spring. Small clouds scudded cross the mountain tops.

Wong Suk and I were, as usual, going to have a lunch of leftovers, then walk two blocks down Pender, cross Main, down to Hastings near Carrall, to the Lux movie house. Hastings Street, outside of Chinatown, was where people always stared at the two of us—stared at this bent-down agile old man with the funny face leaning on his two canes, at this almost nine-year-old girl with her moon face—but we didn't care.

"Look," a teenage boy once said, loud enough for everyone walking by to hear, "Beauty and the Beast."

His two pals giggled. Wong Suk didn't quite understand, but I knew the English words and I knew the story from one of my school readers. I had loved Wong Suk since I was five, loved his wrinkled monkey face, so it didn't matter what people said.

The Lux was showing a Festival of Cartoons plus two main features. Wong Suk and I stayed late to catch the newsreel. China was at war, fighting the Japanese invaders. Wong Suk liked to start the clapping whenever Chiang Kai-shek appeared on the screen. Then we would all hiss the enemy if they showed up, especially if General Tojo marched into view, or if we saw the western-dressed Japanese going in and out of the White House, chattering away with the Americans. If enough Chinatown people were there, the hissing was as loud as the clapping. Grown-up white people clapped every time they saw President Roosevelt, Chinatown people booed every time they saw the Japanese, and children cheered every time Mighty Mouse showed up. I always looked forward to the Petunia Pig cartoons and *only the Shadow knows* mystery serial.

The old porch creaked. I did another tap-step. Turned once. Turned twice. My Shirley Temple ringlets smelled of Stepmother's curling iron; my hair felt floppy against my neck. No one was home except Poh-Poh, Sekky and me. My older brothers were working at Third Uncle Lew's warehouse. Stepmother was busy in Chinatown on some errand with Father. That was, I now realize, another sign. Of course, I thought they were busy selling raffle tickets to raise funds for China's battle against Japan.

"Stay out of Poh-Poh's way," Stepmother had said to me, as she stepped out of the house that morning. "Sek-Lung's been coughing all night again. He needs extra sleep today."

I did keep very quiet and let Sekky sleep away most of the morning. Gladly. In fact, I hardly bothered Grandmother at all, except to ask her to knot and tie the ribbons on my shoes. (Sicky Sekky still took most of Poh-Poh's attention, though.) I myself tied the strand of red ribbon holding back my curls. I didn't want the curls to melt away on my brow in the wet-warm morning air, especially with Stepmother away, unable to help me "freshen up" like the big girls did.

I pressed my head against one of the fluted porch pillars, leaned my clean dress against its length and listened to the birds chattering in the Douglas fir across the street. I started to day-dream about my friendship with Shirley Temple. It was a fact we were both nearly nine years old. If we'd had a chance to meet, it was a fact she would have been my best friend. Besides Wong Suk, I mean. Of course, just as I got into sharing a double banana split with Shirley (and she was just about to tell me how pretty I looked), Poh-Poh's sharp voice intruded.

"Dress all dirty now."

Grandmother pulled me away from the pillar and with her other hand presented a large white plate before my eyes: braised chicken feet and cut-up sausage meat bumped up against a chunk of coarse bread. The bread was spread with honey and thick lard. *Cw*

"Sit down."

"I'm not hungry," I protested. Poh-Poh spread out a clean diaper, pushed me down. I sat. She firmly tucked a tea towel under my neck and put another tea towel on my lap. Finally, she pressed the plate on my lap.

"Eat."

I picked up the hard bread and took a tiny bite. Poh-Poh stood over me, watching. I chewed and made a big swallowing noise. I sensed her waiting for my next question. She had a grandmother's instinct for being important.

"Where is Wong Suk?" I asked.

"Very late today," she said, with full authority, hinting at some mystery. "Paper day for Wong Suk."

"Paper day?"

The old woman looked at me. I had to take another bite.

"Paper, paper, *paper*." she said. I was to know that each repetition explained the previous one. She gently rapped my head.

It worked: last Saturday came back into my head.

Last Saturday morning, Wong Suk had taken off his black cloak, leaned his two canes against the wall. He and Father had sat around the oak table, pulling out neatly tied bundles of paper from a heavy brown cardboard case. I could see half-folded documents stamped CP RAILROAD, B.C. WORK PERMIT, letters from China, old bills, certificates with Chinese words in black ink, signed with red chop marks ... all important papers.

"You kept so much," Father commented. "Good. Good."

"Never know what government do," Wong Suk said. "One day they say Old Wong *okay-okay*. Next day, Wong *stinky Chink*."

I picked up a paper with official-looking stamps.

"What's this one?"

"Tell her," Wong Suk urged Father. The two men looked at each other. Father hesitated. Wong Suk nodded, as if encouraging him.

"This certificate says that Wong Suk arrived in Canada when he was twenty—*what?* Not clear here," Father said.

Wong Suk seemed disappointed. His face was still saying *tell her*. Another sign. *Tell her*. Father turned away, seemed too busy to obey Wong Suk's plea. Father looked at the year of birth on the certificate and figured out that Wong Suk was *maybe* seventy-five. On another document, *maybe* seventy. In Chinatown, the saying went: *Walk young for young job; walk old for old job*. Father held up another document—a sheet that looked like the first one but gave a different birth year.

"Maybe this paper say five years younger," Wong Suk sighed, his *tell her* face surrendering to Father's fidgeting with the papers.

"Or five years *more*," Father said, respectfully. The two men looked at each other, and Wong Suk gently smiled with pleasure.

Adding years, I knew, made one Honourable. The more life-years relatives and friends added to your paper-years, the more Honourable one became.

I understood all that.

For example, I had always wanted to be older—be fifteen paper-years at least—like Florence Marsden and be stuck-up and wear lipstick and rouge and pencil my eyebrows and get treated to sodas by the boys from the pool hall. Of course, Flo Marsden couldn't pluck her eyebrows yet. *That* would be really grown-up.

But in all the talk about paper-years, I was baffled about how old the old man really was.

"How old *is* Wong Suk?"

"About the same age as Grandmother," Father answered.

It was no answer at all. I had witnessed Poh-Poh giving different numbers to different people.

"Poh-Poh, how—?"

"*Ancient,*" Poh-Poh answered. Then she tried to be helpful, looked up at the ceiling to count the years flying away. "Paper-years number... maybe eighty... maybe more."

I started thinking of my own age, my paper-years, and grew puzzled.

"*Ga-ji nin*—paper-years," Father said, looking at me, "always different from Chinese years."

The thought excited me. I started to count my fingers: nine *plus* five... *equals*... fourteen!"

"Am I fourteen?" I asked, imagining fresh apple-red gloss on my lips.

"You *juk-sing* years," Poh-Poh laughed. "You Canada years."

"You to be nine years soon," Wong Suk said, trying to be kind. "Lucky nine."

Father cleared his throat and all the grownups quickly turned their attention back to the papers on the table. Poh-Poh picked up a washed old bedsheet and began to scissor it into diaper-size squares.

No grownups ever gave you a plain answer, unless they were saying no. I watched Father sort out the packages and decided to look more carefully at the documents. Being in Upper Grade Four at Strathcona, and being one of Miss McKenzie's Very Best Readers, I could figure out most of the English words. But of course I was unable to pay attention and read the signs. As Poh-Poh always warned me: *Look closely... listen carefully.* I stupidly thought, *There's nothing left to tell.*

Wong Suk's papers, like Poh-Poh's, which were stored in a covered shelf in the top lid of a metal trunk, were neatly tied with twine and smelled of moth balls. Father carefully untied each package and folded out only important-looking papers. There were bundled letters with Old China postage stamps, but these he left alone. Father then read off or translated the titles of certain official papers. Wong Suk liked to hear his own history, just like Grandmother; neither of them could read, but both liked to hear what the words on the papers could say.

There were papers dated in the year 18-*something* that said Wong Suk was to pay back, through his labour, the steerage fare from Canton, his bonding tax, plus give back so many years of his wages for shelter, food, and the privilege of being allowed to pay interest on his debts. These contracts had been made years before I was born, signed with Wong Suk's carved chop stamped in red, stamped and sealed way before Father and Stepmother and my oldest brother arrived in Canada. The papers documented long-term debts, now paid in full.

Wong Suk looked at Father, then at me, then back to Father. *Tell her.*

"We must only use the papers that have exactly the same birth month and year," Father said, softly, like a conspirator.

Wong Suk nodded.

Father selected some papers.

"This one, and maybe this—yes—this one for the Benevolent Society. The Head Tax Certificate for the government—that's all they need... Some of the rest we can trade or—"

Wong Suk half-whispered, as if it were a delicate matter to mention, "Maybe negotiate with the... the *Tong*—?"

Father looked agreeable. Poh-Poh cleared her throat.

No one would say anything more: a child with a Big Mouth stood beside the oak table. Big Eyes. Big Ears. Big Careless Mouth. A Mouth that went to English school and spoke English words. Too many English words. Poh-Poh looked at me cautiously.

I knew that every brick in Chinatown's three- and five-storey clan buildings lay like the Great Wall against anyone knowing everything. The *lao wah-kiu*—the old-timers who came overseas from Old China—hid their actual life histories within those fortress walls. Only paper histories remained, histories blended with talk-story. Father said to me, "Jook-Liang, don't you need some spring air?"

I did. The smell of those documents, packed so long ago and undisturbed between packets of moth balls, prickled my nose. I took my tap-dance book with me and walked out to the front porch and looked up and down the sun-washed street.

I wondered if all the clapboard houses along the street harboured as many whispers as our house did. Those damp shacks decaying on their wooden scaffolding, whose doors you reached only by negotiating rickety ramps—all the one- and two-storey houses parallel along Pender and Keefer, Georgia and Union—did each of those broken, scarred doors lock in their share of whisperings? Some nights I would hear in my dreams our neighbours' whisperings rising towards the ceiling, Jewish voices, Polish and Italian voices, all jostling for survival, each as desperate as Chinese voices.

I could see the North Shore mountains from our porch and imagined Wong Suk and Father still murmuring behind me, their words lifting against the ceiling. I laid open the *Easy Lessons* book and did a *shuffle-tap-kick*. My best step, my favourite one, was the *full turn, double-tap curtsy*. It involved a furious spinning motion, my starched crinoline noisily swirling above my tip-tap tapping feet—drumbeats, I suppose—to beat out all the whispering.

After Wong Suk finished his business with Father, he came and sat down on the porch steps beside me. He pulled out the Head Tax Certificate, unfolded it carefully, and pointed at the two-inch square photo pasted on the bottom right-hand corner. I looked down and inspected a shoulders-up shot of Wong Suk as a young man. He was wearing a plain shirt.

"Liang," Wong Suk said, "what you see?"

There was a man in a white shirt. There was no sign of the black woollen cloak he wore in most weathers, the same kind of woollen cloak gentlemen in England wore. I was disappointed. For some reason, I had expected the cape to show up on his shoulders even in the old photograph, something that was simply always a part of him, like his two arms and two crooked legs.

But that was foolish, just because I had always known Wong

Suk with his grand cape. I had heard the story of the cape, heard him tell it many times. Heard him talk-story about it when Poh-Poh mended it for him, or when Stepmother patiently restitched the lining and patched up the secret pocket for the tenth time.

Wong Suk had inherited the cloak when I was five years old, from a man named Johnson who lived in Victoria. Roy Johnson had once been Wong Suk's Number Two Boss Man "in olden CPR day," as Wong Suk referred to the years after 1885 when he helped build one of the last sections of the Canadian Pacific Railroad.

Johnson was over six feet tall, a *dai huhng-moh gui*—a giant red-haired demon—who, on his deathbed decades later, remembered Wong Suk as a friend. Johnson asked Chinese old-timers in Victoria if a man whose birth-name was Wong Kimlein, famous for his monkey face, was still alive.

"No one else could have such a face," he said, and with the fingers of each hand pulled at the corners of his mouth to demonstrate.

"Yes, yes," they said, and told Johnson everything. Monkey Man was living in Vancouver in one of the rooming places near the Winter's Hotel in Gastown, a place run by the Chinese Benevolent Society. They said he could write to any B.C. old-timer in care of *The Chinese Times* newspaper. Then Roy Johnson gave instructions to his oldest son to have a message translated into Chinese writing by one of the Chinese elders, and to send this message to Wong Kimlein.

Wong-Suk told me, "Johnson bess-see Boss Man," and with a flourish threw the cloak around himself, remembering why a demon on his deathbed would call him friend. Of course, Wong Suk sat back in our big cane chair and told us the story.

It began, he said, in one of the last rail camps set up to extend the CPR rails to Granville, now called Vancouver. Wong Suk that early winter evening was taking a heavy sack of supplies back to one of the few remaining Chinese work camps in the interior of British

Columbia, and—as he told the story—noticed a sudden shadow, looked up, and saw an eagle flying angrily overhead. It circled majestically and sent down a screeching sound, soared, then swooped down so close that Wong Suk recalled forever the loud snap of its bent beak and the oncoming rush of its broad powerful wings.

Wong Suk ducked his head quickly. As he did so, his eye caught sight of something between the tracks ahead, something humped up against a distant reflecting curve of rail. Wong Suk thought the lump on the track was a wild animal, maybe worth some extra money—its spleen or heart or liver could be sold for medicine. Instead, as Wong Suk hurried along with his heavy sack, feeling lucky, he just as quickly felt his heart turn on him. It was a human shape lying inside the tracks, a giant body slumped low against the steel track. He could make out the head positioned on the rail, waiting to be crushed. The head had red hair. Wong Suk recognized at once that it was Johnson, Number Two Boss Man.

Wong Suk later learned that Johnson had shared his last bottle of whisky with a new drinking partner. The two ended up wandering drunkenly along the tracks. Johnson's new friend became abusive, knocked him down from behind; when he refused to stay down, the friend took out a handy pocketknife and cut him up for his lack of co-operation. Whoever it was took Johnson's pocket change and a gold watch. Whoever it was also took his wool jacket and his new vest, then neatly leaned his head against the steel rail and left him to die.

When Wong Suk dropped his sack and stood over the slug of a body, the giant's orange beard was already beaded with ice, his breath shallow, his nostrils frost-clotted; the left side of his head was swollen purple. His shirt had been cut open; his chest crisscrossed with thin lines of blood scabbing from the cold. Luckily, Roy Johnson had drunk enough to keep his blood from freezing. At this point of the storytelling, Wong Suk always laughed and rubbed his tummy and smacked his lips.

"I think maybe find dead animal—maybe big, *big* deer—

make good food—make good medicine—make stew."

The old man would smack his lips.

"No stew! Just no-good Johnson!"

He barely managed to pull Johnson up, dragged him off the rails and wrapped the huge man in one of the two new Hudson's Bay blankets he had just bought from the supplier. Wong Suk knew enough to keep the half-conscious Johnson walking, back and forth, back and forth, happily slapping Number Two Boss Man, until his blood circulated again and pain snapped him awake. The Boss Man never forgot.

During the last week of his dying, Johnson related his old times as the camp Boss Man to his son: how he had once been beaten and robbed—how freezing to death was like burning in fire—how someone managed to slap him alert, kept him walking, kept him warm against the plunging mountain temperature. And when his eyes cleared enough, how he had seen to his amazement the wizened Monkey Man, the camp cook's Chinaman assistant, staring back at him, slapping him silly, laughing like a crazy coyote. "You lookee good!"

It was Wong.

Johnson wanted to reward Monkey Man, but anything he offered—a wool vest, food, a kerosene lamp—was abruptly refused.

"Wong come to *Gim San*—come for *gim*, for gold—" Wong Suk said, sternly pushing the giant Johnson and his gifts out of his makeshift tent, "—no gimme *gim*, no gimme thanks!"

"Monkey Man only wanted gold," Johnson told his son. "He knew of course none of us had any damn gold, just these railroad chits to trade for food and supplies, and some emergency cash to buy bootleg liquor. I never got to thank that Chinaman properly."

Johnson's son said to him, "I'd like to thank him, too."

Later that month of September, Wong Suk received a large parcel covered with both Chinese and English writing. The English words read, "TO MR. WONG KIMLEIN, c/o CHINESE TIMES, Vancouver, B.C. FROM ROY JOHNSON."

Father read aloud the Chinese letter inside, explaining the origin of the gift in the flowery words of a Chinese elder.

The son wrote he had come home from studying at Oxford to be with his sick father. Now Johnson had died, and the son was going back to England. Here was the son's new cloak, "a blanket," the son wrote, "to replace the one you wrapped around my father."

The note itself was wrapped around a heavy American gold coin. Engraved on one side of the coin was an eagle, its beak as bent as Wong Suk remembered it.

I loved that story

"Eagle good luck," Wong Suk told me, but I thought his cloak was even more lucky. I always leaned against its thick warmth and begged Wong Suk to let me drape it over my shoulders, to let me fly about, become Robin Hood's bandit-princess, turning rapidly around and around in the imaginary forest of our back yard, the cape lifting, like wings, lifting above the earth. And the Monkey King would roar with laughter, clap-clap his two canes in a drumbeat; I was dizzy with pleasure. We would not stop until the neighbours loudly slammed their doors against such invading, clapping, joyful madness. Then we would sit quietly together on the back steps, to catch our breath. Sometimes Second Brother Jung stepped out and sat with us. Wong Suk would tell us one of his stories from the past. Jung liked that. He would listen intently, hugging his knees, his eyes as dreamy as Wong Suk's, his need as deep as my longing for Wong Suk to be sitting close to us, like this, with Jung and me, forever.

But, of course, when Wong Suk and I stood on the porch that day, looking at his Head Tax photo, the young monkey face I stared at had not yet gone into the mountains, nor lifted the camp cook's heavy armour of pots and pans, nor met the giant he called Boss Man Johnson, nor seen a huge eagle diving between the sky and mountain wall: he had just arrived in the Customs House in Victoria. The immigration official had just freshly glued his photo onto the document, impressed a seal on it, and taken fifty dollars cash for the Head Tax that Chinese immigrants had to pay to the Dominion of Canada.

I craned my neck to inspect the old photo. My almost-nine-year-old eyes looked back down at Old Wong Suk, then back at the photo: two faces, almost fifty years apart. Yet each was the same wide-eyed monkey face. The porch creaked. I sensed Wong Suk wanted me to say something, maybe about the young face that stared unchanged back at both of us.

I could see the same square jaw, the large teeth, intact; oiled-slick hair, eyebrows thicker brushes of black. Fewer wrinkles. Definitely fewer wrinkles.

"What you think, Liang?" Wong Suk asked me, holding the photo against a shaft of porch sunlight. He sounded sad.

I moved closer to the old man, craned my neck again. Refocussed against the sunlight. Last week I had decided, for absolute sure, to become Shirley Temple. Little Shirley was his favourite dancing girl, but Wong Suk said he would be just as happy to have the movie star Miss Anna May Wong come visit him any time.

To me, Miss Anna May Wong was an old lady—more than twenty-five years old—yet Wong Suk insisted he would like her to visit Vancouver's Chinatown, just as Shirley Temple had during the city's Golden Jubilee when we waved to her and she waved back. After all, he said, he had in me alone both his Little Shirley *and* bandit-princess. I wasn't old enough to be Miss Anna May Wong; she reminded him of someone he'd known from afar in Old China.

"Not close like you, Liang," Wong Suk explained.

"How close?" I had to know.

"Meet her maybe three times in Old China. I never to forget her. Last time I gave her plum blossoms." Wong Suk looked far away, became quiet.

"What did she do?" I asked, meaning was she a movie star.

"What she do?" Wong Suk looked far away. "She spit." His voice softened. "Throw back at me all the blossoms."

I looked at his face in the photo and the face before me: the sadness was still there.

"You look the same," I told Wong Suk and took a tap position.

"You look same, too," he laughed. He looked up at me and raised his hand high enough to brush my curls. "Still Jook-Liang, but dance bess-see."

Which was a lie; I couldn't tap without tripping, but I liked being lied to. I felt he wanted to say something else. The screen door squeaked open. It was Father.

"Good," Father said. "You two haven't gone."

Father stepped onto the porch and handed Wong Suk a lucky red envelope of money. We only ever spent thirty cents together, including treats; this was *real* money, *folding* money.

"Take Liang to the show and get some extra treats on me," Father said. "Keep the rest."

Wong Suk waved his hand in refusal but Father insisted, pushed away his hand, and stuffed the lucky envelope into the old man's shirt pocket.

Lucky money was awarded on birthdays or maybe when a report card was all A's. I couldn't think why today was special at all, but sometimes one is lucky, I thought—and thought of an eagle against the mountain and the sky, thought of how the blanket Wong Suk had wrapped around Johnson turned, years later, into a cape. Lucky and fun, as when Wong Suk and I, in the back yard, played out Robin Hood of Sherwood Forest, and I was his bandit-princess, the cape royally spread around me.

Later, at Benny's Ice Cream Parlour, when Wong Suk opened up the lucky envelope, a fifty-dollar bill slipped out. I saw the orange-coloured paper and the number *50* before he could put it away. Wong Suk began to stare at the Coca-Cola calendar on the wall; he just gulped and said how much prettier I was than that little girl holding onto the Lassie dog. A few people, probably new to Benny's, stared at us and whispered. Perhaps that was a sign, too, and I did not pay enough attention.

I was eight plus, grown up, slurping up my second cherry soda at Benny's, but I remembered that at age five and six I had confused Wong Suk with the Monkey King or Cheetah. I knew most of Chinatown called him *Mau-lauh Bak—Monkey Man*—usually behind his back. He knew that, too. He looked like an old grouchy monkey and he was my Best Friend.

And I didn't like sharing Wong Suk, either. Even my two closest girlfriends, Jenny Soo Yung and Grace Ventura, knew that they didn't rank any place near my never-ever-going-to-split-up Best Friend.

I always pestered Wong Suk for stories. Whenever Second Brother Jung tagged along with us, Wong Suk's stories took place in rail camps; he told us how he survived climbing up sheer mountain cliffs, how one limb after another got broken; and he told us about fights he had with white demons in lumber mills, late at night, by campfires, when all the men were surrounded by the glowing needle eyes of wild animals. I preferred the stories with demons and ghosts, like those Poh-Poh used to tell me before she got stuck on my baby brother Sekky and had no more time for me.

I liked the stories Wong Suk told of being friends with some Siwash natives on the rocky shores of the B.C. coast. There were Indian ghosts, as incredible as Chinese ghosts; forest ghosts and animal and bird spirits. Wong Suk had even witnessed sacred Indian pow-wows and smoked special tobacco called sweet grass and traded gold nuggets and gold dust for bear paws, antlers, herbs and wood fungus. In his stories, men changed into spirits, animals, birds and demons, had names like Boss Man Johnson, One-eyed Smith, Broken-tooth Cravich, Thunder Tongue and Clever Fox.

In spite of all his stories about the past, Wong Suk really said little about his earlier times in Old China. When I asked, "What was it like when you were a little boy?" he roared with laughter or sighed deeply. "Too long ago," he would say, and leave me guessing. Others speculated, too. Wong Suk was a topic of conversation in Chinatown. Everyone knew everyone's daily business, but not always everyone's past. I did everything to hear conversation *about* Wong Suk, unusual conversation.

Around the *mahjong* tables that Stepmother took me to while Father was many times away at different seasonal jobs during the Depression, some of the Chinatown ladies, clinging to Old China ways, speculated about Wong Suk and his monkey face:

How do you think Monkey Man got that face?

It was all curious talk, though the women would never discuss these matters in front of the men, and certainly not within Wong Suk's hearing. The women's *mahjong* gaming tables were a cozy haven, like a club gathering, a sorority. With their men often away on seasonal work, the women got to swear as hard as any man, said the outrageous without hesitation and with much delight, traded shopping tips and imparted gossip before anything bad festered into reality. Gossip was a way everyone warned everyone else about what was known ("Someone thought they saw you going into Mr. Lim's car..."). Or warned you about what was to be discovered ("They say you should worry about your First Son's fondness for too many late nights at the Good Fortune Club...").

Late into the night, when the *mahjong* ladies thought I and the two younger Lee kids, Mary and Garson, were fast asleep on the large sofa, Stepmother and her friends sat around the *mahjong* table, slapping down the playing cubes, and giggled and wondered aloud about Wong Suk's *penis*. It was a word Second Brother Jung always used when he swore in Chinese at stone-throwing white boys; it was a word that alerted my ears. Half-nodding in my practised fake sleep, I got to hear most everything Stepmother and her friends shared:

"How long his penis, you think?"

"Like my old man's—long enough to have babies—"

"—and too damn short to have fun!"

Everyone laughed. The ivory pieces clacked back and forth.

"Perhaps a hairy ape back in the Old China village frightened his mother."

Cards were discarded. I imagined a hairy ape, gorilla-size, chasing Wong Suk's poor mother.

"Ahhh, perhaps she fell in love with a monkey!"

Someone discarded her last pieces. Someone swore. Then the ivory pieces clacked again.

"How you think monkeys do it?"

"Men and monkeys, do-do, do-do, all the same!"

Do-do what, I puzzled.

The women's voices pitched higher between the smacking of the game pieces, then settled like musical notes. Tea was being poured.

"I hear *Mau-lauh Bak*'s family was eating live monkey brain... you know how they carve that stuff out, with razor-sharp spoons, and—"

"—they forgot to blindfold the creature!"

"Yes, yes, the expectant mother walks by and—"

"—*aaiiiiyahhh*—"

"—the Demon-Monkey threw a curse on the unborn baby, just like that. The poor mother grips her opening, she feels wetness and pain, she gives birth—a monkey boy with a monkey face!"

I was proud of Wong Suk. Not even Rosie Chung's one-eyed, monster-faced uncle, Chung-Guun, drew so much attention. Chung-Guun's face had been divided by a thrown axe after a card-cheating episode in a fish cannery up the B.C. coast near Bella Bella. To cheat at cards and get caught—what did Chung-Guun expect? Luckily for him the axe only sliced his face open. In Chinatown, as in Old China, so many men walked about with scarred faces and limbs. Who did not have a tale to tell?

The long awaited mill whistle blasted into the air. *Noon*, it said. Countless birds flew up from the giant Douglas fir across the street and noisily resettled. The porch step I was sitting on felt hard. The plate of food sat heavy on my lap. Should I wind up the RCA gramophone? Why was Wong Suk more than an hour late?

If I had been allowed to stay to listen to more of their talk last Saturday, Grandmother would not be holding her hint of mystery over my head: "Paper, paper, *paper*"... so what if there was? If only I had stayed longer, I might have found out something. *Tell her*, Wong Suk had urged. And Father could not.

Today he had promised to see me decorated in his gift of red ribbons, the ones Grandmother this very morning tied into pompoms on my tap-shoes. Today I was dancing my new *Short'nin' Bread* tap-steps for him. Then we were going to line up at the Lux, stay twice to see the newsreels. "You'll see the Japanese bombing Shanghai," First Brother Kiam had told us at dinner. "You'll see bodies everywhere. There's a baby crying by the railway tracks, his mother dead beside him." I imagined the bodies scattered all over. But we're safe in Canada, I thought.

Suddenly, I was aware of Grandmother behind me, watching me. I hated being watched as much as I hated waiting. I took a big bite of bread and picked up a piece of sausage and started chewing.

"Swallow first," Poh-Poh said. "Eat slow like lady."

She stepped back into the house. I heard her picking up my sickly baby brother and lifting him up so he could giggle for her. He could never get enough attention. I think she wished I was one of those rich children she had to serve when she was a young girl back in Old China. They daintily chewed their food while she stood by in silence and wiped their heart-shaped lips with silk napkins. It was one of the rare stories I heard being told between Wong Suk and Grandmother of their time in Old China.

Wong Suk and Grandmother remembered how they first met, in one of the kitchens of the rich families: how they would talk in their clan dialect or switch to their secret slave dialect; how they would meet at the marketplace and trade secrets and laugh at their household masters and mistresses. And how they, this monkey-boy and defiant girl, once showed their whip scars to each other, shared healing balms and kind words, and wished their lives would end. Stepmother told me that as children they had been sold to rich merchant families as their house servants.

Grandmother stepped back onto the porch carrying Sekky. He was more weak than strong, which made Poh-Poh spoil him even more. I bet no one carried me around like that when I was three, except to pass me along to someone else. When I was six, Grandmother already had me folding diapers for Sekky, and when I cried, I cried on my own.

"Poh-Poh," I begged, "why is Wong Suk so late today?"

"He come now," she said. "He tell you."

I stood up, looked in the direction she pointed. There came towards me the familiar bamboo canes tap-tap-tapping on the sidewalk. Wong Suk, with the help of his two walking canes, push-pulled himself up the stairs to our house. His dark cloak caught a gust of wind, opened wide and partially blocked my view; then, coming up behind him, I saw Father carrying two suitcases, one larger than the other. Seeing Monkey Man, Sekky burrowed his face into Poh-Poh's shoulders. He was always shy around Wong Suk, afraid of his monkey face and roaring laugh.

The old man reached our porch landing, breathless. Our porch steps were nothing to him. He had climbed the Rockies, decades before I was born, and seen others, like him, climb up the steepest mountain slopes, then come skidding down, legs and arms flying, to escape dynamite blasts, rockfalls.

Wong Suk leaned his two canes against the porch pillar and limbered down beside me. Before I could ask about the two suitcases, everyone and everything—Father, the suitcases, Grandmother and Sekky, the plate of food on my lap—all disappeared into the house, leaving Wong Suk and me abruptly alone. And that was a sign, too. Wong Suk sat on his cloak, which neatly cushioned under him; he moved closer beside me and touched my ringlets and smiled how pretty I looked.

"Poh-Poh tell you?" he asked, in Toisanese.

"Tell me what?"

"About the bones—the bone shipment."

I was puzzled. I wanted to hear him speak Chinglish—the mix of Chinese and English we threw together for our own secret talks. I used Chinglish to tell him all the movie stories we ever saw, about Tarzan and Shirley Temple, about Fred Astaire and Ginger Rogers, about Robin Hood and how he, Wong Suk, my Best Friend, was like the bandit-prince and how I was his bandit-princess. What did *bones* have to do with us? I remembered Father carrying in the two suitcases, one larger than the other. Suitcases meant *hello* or *farewell*. My stomach tightened. The chicken feet may have been too rich; the bread, too coarse. I waited for our Chinglish conversation.

Wong Suk talked instead only in *Sze-yup*. He said, "You listen to me, Jook-Liang, I tell you about the bone shipment."

He took my hand in his. I thought that meant I should stand up. I wanted to spread out his cloak, hang it up as we always did for our stage curtain. I wanted to do my Shirley Temple dance and shake my ringlets. I wanted to sing and watch the pom-poms on my tap-shoes catch his eyes. However, he didn't let my hand go. I didn't move. He did not notice anything I had on, not even the taffeta dress, not even the ribboned shoes; he only looked at my face, intensely, with unfamiliar wetness in his eyes, as if he were trying to memorize forever my half-opened mouth, my wide-apart eyes, my ringlets. This is the Monkey King, I thought, as if I were five years old again, deeply enchanted. I gave him all of my attention, so that even the wind and the birds grew soundless to me, everything went quiet, except for his voice.

"I'm going on the *Empress* steamship this afternoon," I heard him say. "I'm going back to China with the bone shipment."

"But we're going to the Lux today," I said, "to see the cartoons and the news about China. Kiam said they bombed Shanghai."

I pulled away from him.

"And you're late," I said.

"The bone shipment," Wong Suk kept on, "that's all the bones of the dead Chinese, the Chinese who died in Gold Mountain. The bones come from all over B.C. I'm going back with the shipment to Hong Kong first, then to Mainland China, then back to my—"

The old man could see I was not listening to him properly, but he kept talking.

"Two thousand pounds of bones going home to China. Liang-Liang, isn't that wonderful?"

In my mind, I saw a pile of bones, a mountain of dead people's bones: it was horrible. Like all the dead people lying about the railroad in Shanghai.

"Stupid bones!" I said. "You promised me we would go to the movies today. Father gave you big money last week. We could go to movies for years and years."

I got up, had to, and reached through the open parlour window and churned the handle of the second-hand RCA gramophone. I lifted the needle arm and put it down gently. No matter how carefully I put it down, the needle bounced, then threw itself back-forth, back-forth, making a sound like a heartbeat, before it would at last snap-skip into play. A Negro voice sang out. *Mama's little baby loves...* Banjoes and drums jangled in light-hearted unison. I danced.

The sky was blue and the air smelled of fresh wet leaves. I danced away with eight-year-old thoughts of stardom and the miracle of Wong Suk, my best friend, travelling to Hollywood with me. Then, the music over, the needle went back-forth, back-forth, until I shut it off. I sat down again.

"Just likee moo-vee star," Wong Suk said, at last, in Chinglish. I did not respond.

Wong Suk nudged me, "What thinking, Liang?"

Neither of us said any more. Father came out and told Wong Suk his lunch was ready. He should eat something before he sailed; it was a long way to China. The old man leaned on his two canes, hauled himself up, and push-pulled into the house, his cloak swinging. I felt Father touch my shoulder.

"Come in and finish your lunch," he said. "You can sit beside Wong Suk."

I didn't move.

"Kiam and Jung will be home soon. Later, Stepmother will be arriving in a taxi to take Wong Suk and all of us to the docks."

I wished everyone would go away and stay away.

Even Wong Suk.

Even me.

I stepped back from Father, felt sweat on my head. The large tree across the road seemed to bend. It was very hot. Father looked at me, touched my forehead like he would baby Sekky.

"All right," Father said. "You stay here if you want."

I sat down on the porch. Time went by, a minute, an hour. Jung and Kiam walked up the stairs, looked at me, said nothing, and then stepped into the house. My mind seemed to go blank. A horn honked. It was Tom's Taxi. Stepmother waved for me to come down the porch steps. I helped her carry some boxes into our house; they were belongings to be shipped back later to China when Wong Suk sent for them. Then everyone put on jackets because Father said the docks would be windy and chilly.

"I'm too hot," I said, and shrugged off the jacket First Brother Kiam attempted to put over me. No one insisted.

We stepped out of the house and started towards the taxi. Stepmother got in first.

"Come on," she said to me. "Get in."

I did. My white taffeta dress made crinkling noises.

Wong Suk came in beside me, clutching his two canes, while the taxi driver and Father put the suitcases in the trunk of the car. I felt the deep warmth of his cloak and moved away. Kiam climbed into the front; Jung sat giggling on First Brother's lap. Then Father stepped in beside Wong Suk and I was put on Stepmother's lap. As the taxi backed up to make a U-turn, I could see, on the porch landing, Poh-Poh with Sekky squirming in her arms; Grandmother looked at us without a word.

The taxi went smoothly forward, down our street, down streets soon unfamiliar to me. In no time we were driving past the docks, past huge ships bobbing like monsters. Tall cranes lifted up crates and steel pipes hung dangling in the air, clanging against each other. The air tasted salty. Thousands of gulls rose into the sky and dove down into the waters to feed on floating debris.

We all got out of the taxi, stepped onto the pier, and felt it move with the waves breaking beneath on the pilings. Here, I thought, the Sea Dragon lives. My tap-shoes were noiseless against the cry of the gulls and the clamour of the waters slapping against the dock. Stepmother and Father helped Wong Suk out of the taxi. Brothers Kiam and Jung took the pieces of luggage out of the trunk and led the way towards large wooden gates and a sign that said: ALL VISITORS STOP HERE: CUSTOMS.

We were not allowed to go past the customs landing and departure gates. Everyone started to say goodbye. The dock felt unsteady under my feet; everything smelled like iodine and salt and the sky was bright with light. Father gave a man in a uniform some money to carry Wong Suk's luggage past the gates. I could only look about me, robbed of speech, spellbound. I remember Father lifting me up a little to kiss Wong Suk on his cheek; he seemed unable to kiss me back. His cheek, I remember, had the look of wrinkled documents. He looked secretive, like Poh-Poh, saying nothing. I felt his hand rest a moment on my curls, then a crowd of people began to push by us.

"Hurry," Father said, gently lifting the old man's hand from my head.

Wong Suk shook his shoulders so that his cape opened up; he shifted on his two bamboo canes, push-pulled, push-pulled away from us, but against the noise of the docks and the chaotic loading of baggage on huge carts, I could not hear the familiar tapping of his two canes. People stepped aside, made room for him; they openly stared, pointed, shook their heads. Wong Suk never looked at them, and he never looked back. The hump of his back animated his cloak. The sea-salt wind lifted up its mended edges.

Fighting the wind, Wong Suk's cloak began to flow away from him. The cape continued to move, as if in slow motion, to unfurl. *Farewell, chak neuih*, I thought it said, *Farewell, my bandit-princess.* I waved frantically back.

Father lifted me up. Higher and higher.

It was not a dream.

Higher and higher, Father lifted me.

The ship blasted its horn, a short, sharp shriek, like the sound I imagine an eagle might have made. The crowd closed in. There was nothing more to see: Monkey Man had gone into the Customs House with all the other passengers. At the other end of that huge dockside warehouse, Father explained, Wong Suk would make his way up a plank stairway and board the *Empress of Russia.* Against the afternoon light, I strained my eyes to catch a glimpse of Wong Suk. An English woman pointed at me and said to Stepmother, "What a pretty dress."

Father put me down on the ground.

I forgot I still had on my taffeta dress; I forgot to ask Wong Suk how he liked the way the dress danced when I danced. I forgot to cry and shout his name and urge him: *Turn around! Come back! Come back!* We stood with others on our side of the gates, watching. Someone put a thick sweater over me. I think we waited a long while. First Brother said, "Let's go." But Father said, "No, not yet, not until Liang wants to leave."

The *Empress's* whistle gave a loud, long, last cry, sent seabirds soaring into manic flight; the giant engines roared, churned up colliding waves; the dock shook. The ship began to pull away. I think I saw Wong Suk on the distant deck of the ship. Then, as in a dream, I was standing beside Wong Suk, felt his cloak folding around me under the late afternoon sky. We were travelling together, as we had promised each other in so many of my games. I wondered how he felt, unbending his neck against the stinging homeward wind.

What wealth should a bandit-prince give his princess? Wong Suk once had asked me, as I turned and turned and his cloak enfolded me, with its dark, imperial wings. And I answered greedily, too quickly, my childish fingers grasping imaginary gold coins, slipping over pearls large enough to choke a dragon, gripping rubies the colour of fire... *everything*... for I did not, then, in the days of our royal friendship, understand how bones must come to rest where they most belong.

Dear Wong Suk, I never to forget you.

PART TWO

JUNG-SUM, SECOND BROTHER

FOUR

BEFORE I discovered it, the hissing *lao kwei* had been in our outbuilding for seven days. But no one had thought to tell me about it.

When Dai Kew got off his kitchen-galley duty on the *Princess* ship and arrived with the wooden crate at our house, I was asleep. It was 2 A.M. As he always did, Dai Kew brought us tins of tea biscuits, crusty bread rolls, tiny soaps with the letters CPR carved in them, and other sundries or gifts, all generously pulled out from two duffle bags. Dai Kew called this loot "my salary bonus." Then he would rush off to go gambling in a smoky Chinatown bachelor-club, with its all-night kitchen and fast night company. The men of Chinatown, who were lucky to be hired on, worked for weeks or months in the hellhole kitchens of the steamship lines, touring the B.C. coast from Seattle and Vancouver to Alaska.

We might see Dai Kew again in two days, two weeks, or two months—depending on his Chinatown winnings or, more often than not, on his losses. Dai Kew always looked for omens directing his luck. One day, a stevedore, as a joke, put a turtle in Dai Kew's locker, and that very afternoon, in a crapshoot on the docks, Dai Kew won over a hundred dollars and escaped with only a bruised eye. He kept the turtle with him for two years, moving from ship to ship, until one day he was caught feeding it soft-boiled eggs.

And so the turtle, the *lao kwei*, arrived in a crate at our house. Father helped Dai Kew to lift the crate and put it down in a corner of our garage-sized woodshed.

Then it finally became my turn to bring in, for our hungry stove, buckets of sawdust and armloads of wood. All the old men who visited our house considered me weak and spoiled. They were from Old China, after all, remembering the calluses already forming on their own hands at five and six and seven. And here I was, ten years old, with hands like silk.

"No work, no will," some of the bachelor-men warned my father, waving old sinewed hands with missing fingers and bent joints.

I was home between going to English and Chinese schools when Stepmother told me to fill the sawdust buckets. The mid-September evenings were quickly getting colder; the stove crackled with hunger.

"Heat, more heat!" Poh-Poh demanded. "Not heat for me! Too old for heat!" Grandmother smiled attentively at Stepmother, who was expecting her third-born in Canada: "*Fung sup, hai, m'hai-ahh?* Too damp-cold, yes?"

However warm Stepmother felt, she always nodded.

The herbalist had warned Stepmother that her third child might be born weaker than Sek-Lung, with his early years of coughing and lung infection. Since China was at war, there were shortages of women's herbs to warm her blood. Poh-Poh and Mrs. Lim got together a concoction of leaves and roots, and steamed them into a tea for Stepmother. The balance of wind-water in a city like Vancouver, a city of fog and chills, of dampness and endless grey days, could affect the condition of the baby. Stepmother sat for hours in the rocker beneath the parlour shelf that held the Goddess of Mercy and the God of Longevity with his bald, protruding forehead, and I could tell she was worried.

Our clapboard two-storey house, which people called "a

Chinaman special," was shaking with cold. The wide cracks in the walls had been stuffed a generation before with newspapers print-ed in a strange Eastern European language. The woodshed—large enough to hold a truckload of sawdust, piles of broken shipping crates, and a cord of hardwood—was a perfect mate to our cedar-grey, paint-peeling house.

Father handed me the large empty pails to fill with sawdust.

At the woodshed, I rattled the tin pails as I pushed the high, creaking shed door open and made gruff, manlike noises. Loudly banging the buckets was how Stepmother taught me to scare off any Depression hobo who might have taken shelter inside, and disguising my high voice was my added touch.

When I walked into the dark, sweet-smelling shed, the beams of the low afternoon sun outlined an open crate. Inside the crate, something solid and dark... moved... shifted. Suddenly, in the silence, came a loud hissing, scratching noise. My heart nearly stopped.

"WHOooo's there?" I half-shouted, my voice rising in pitch.

The scratching grew louder, more frantic. It was coming from the crate.

The crate was barely two feet high and three feet wide and had black letters reading GLASS FRAGILE on its side. No hobo or desperate enemy could hide in a box this size. I took a deep breath and calmed down. But what could *hissssss* so frantically? Perhaps a squirrel? A raccoon? A cat? I brightened. Bobby Steinberg and I had seen a movie about an old man and a boy who lived in the forest and made friends with all kinds of creatures. Since then, I'd had daydreams of having a wild animal for a pet. My fear turned to impatience. Without thinking, I dropped the two empty buck-ets and ran over to examine the crate.

There, peering up at me, rose the poking, snakelike, angry, fearless, eye-glittering head of a turtle. I gaped. The shell was the size of a large oval serving-plate, and the creature was knocking against its wooden prison and pushing a webbed foot into a deep pan of water. The crate smelled like a stale swamp. But the animal was incredibly, monstrously splendid: dark and greenish-brown, with a slate-black shell above its long, outstretched neck, its sharp jaws opening and shutting between hisses. A *snapper*. Exactly the kind of turtle that I had seen in a picture book at the library. The turtle looked at me unafraid, twisting its fist-sized head to one side, one yellow eye now taking me into its brain as vividly as my own eyes had taken in its majesty. I ran back into the house and told Poh-Poh what I had found.

"That old thing," Grandmother said, trying to put another sweater on top of the two she was already wearing. Stepmother helped her push her arms through the sleeves. "Dai Kew left it here last week."

"But what does it eat?" I asked, excited.

"Table scraps," Stepmother said.

"Is that all?" I said, imagining a more glamorous diet for such a monster.

"It eats that or it dies," Grandmother said. "What you think it eats?"

"It eats everything," Stepmother said. "Dai Kew says on the steamship he trained it to eat anything."

"*Anything?*" I said, imagining an enemy or two.

"Your Dai Kew has had that *lao kwei* with him for two years. Last week he got caught by his kitchen-boss."

"It bites, and it's stinky," Grandmother said, stretching her two palms like the back of the turtle and wetting her lips. "Still, turtle very good fortune. Long life."

"But it's lonely out there."

"Stupid boy," Grandmother said. "Turtle talk to ghosts—all the time, ghost-talk!"

"Maybe, Jung, you'd like to take care of it?" Stepmother said, a little discomforted by her big stomach. *Take care of it?* My mouth fell open: *My* turtle! Seeing my excitement, Stepmother went over to the stove and pointed to the two pails. "Fill these with water and change the turtle's water pan."

I rushed to pick up the buckets and ran to the sink and started half-filling each one with water. *The turtle was going to be mine!*

"Watch out for ghosts!" I heard Grandmother shout as I slammed the back door.

I believed in ghosts, like everyone else in Chinatown, and I knew that sometimes enemies, like hobo runaways from the tent city on False Creek, like Japanese from Japtown and Indians from dark alleyways—like ghosts—could lurk in the woodshed. Fights, muggings, knifings, these were not uncommon. There was treachery in the world. But there were good ghosts and bad ghosts, and you had to be careful not to insult the good ones nor be tempted by the bad ones. And you had to know a ghost when you saw one.

But that day ghosts were not on my mind.

I had to figure out how to clean the turtle crate and change the water. It took nerve, believe me. I stared at the yellow eyes, the hooked mouth grinding away, ghost-talking. The plush, snakelike folds of its neck told me how well fed it was. Slowly, I tipped over the crate, let everything spill out against the sawdust pile: the murky water, decaying food scraps, the plate-sized turtle, *thump!* When the metal water pan fell out, with a crash, the turtle smartly pulled its head into its shell as far as it would go. It was not as fearless as I thought. Dai Kew must love this turtle very much to keep it so well for two years. Good fortune, Grandmother had said, long life.

Now, I thought, he's mine!

Of course, I knew that Dai Kew would one day find a way to get the turtle back on board some other ship, as I would, if the turtle were really my own pet. Until such time, the turtle really *was* mine. All mine. "Hello, Lao Kwei," I said. "Hello, Old Turtle."

I cleaned everything with splashes of water. Finally, with a board, I carefully shoved the turtle into the tipped crate; then I righted the crate and heard the thick turtle *thump* into place; next, with my calculating pilot's eye, I dropped the water pan down and sloshed fresh water into it. I filled the empty wet buckets with sawdust, took one more look at the crate. *The turtle is mine*, I exulted, and shut the shed door like a vault. *I have a pet like the old man and the boy in the woods!*

Every day, between English and Chinese schools, I ran home and looked in on the turtle, who looked back at me with glistening eyes. Every three or four days, I flushed the crate with fresh water, cleaned and filled up the pan, and tossed in fresh table scraps. It was wonderful. The turtle seemed to know how much I appreciated his presence. In spite of myself, I was sure his ancestry belonged to the Great Turtle in Old China, the one who held the Dragon, the Phoenix and the whole world on its back. I told Bobby Steinberg about Lao Kwei, but he only looked into the crate and said, "So?"

By the second week, I had lured a few more boys from my English school to come and admire my turtle. I also got to show Bobby Steinberg and Peter Brodlin how I could hold up carrot tops and cause the turtle slowly to stretch out its neck and snap its jaws. Even Bobby Steinberg thought that was neat.

By the third week, I had gone to the library at Main and Hastings and looked up the scientific name of my turtle, followed its ancient lineage all the way back to the time of sea-swimming dinosaurs. Between my chores and my helping sometimes at the warehouse, I would take the turtle out into our backyard and let it move a few feet here—a few feet there—and pull it back by the rope-harness that First Brother Kiam had made for me. I could slip the harness back and forth onto Lao Kwei and pick him up, swinging, to carry him out of the crate and out into the daylight.

By now, Lao Kwei politely pulled in his head and strong limbs, and rarely snapped at me: he knew he would be taken out of the crate. He always blinked in the sudden bright light outside of the shed, and slowly, gravely, yawned with pleasure. No doubt he had been used to being handled and hauled about by Dai Kew, in those two years he kept Lao Kwei on the steamship liners. No doubt, Lao Kwei had been stuffed into one of Dai Kew's duffle bags to be secretly transported from one Alaskan ship to another.

One day, Bobby Steinberg brought lettuce over and said to me,

"What's his name? What do you call that thing?"

"I don't know," I said. "The family just calls it Lao Kwei. Old Turtle."

"It's not a *Chinese* turtle." Bobby Steinberg sounded disgusted. "It's got to have a—you know—British or Canadian name."

He thought a moment, dropping some leaves into the crate.

"Why don't you call it *Hopalong*? Like the cowboy."

"That's United States," I protested. "This is a *Canada* turtle."

"So," Bobby Steinberg snapped, tossing the rotten head of lettuce in the air. Tossing. Catching. Tossing. "Name it!"

"*George*," I said, pausing for effect. "*King* George."

Bobby Steinberg dropped the head of lettuce, and the turtle, neck outstretched, defiantly snapped it in half. It loved the rotten parts.

For two more weeks, King George sat in his crate waiting for me to harness him, pick him up, and take him out into the daylight. On weekends, I began to carry him about the neighbourhood, showing him off, but was always careful to carry him at arm's length. I let King George snap impressively at sticks, snapping some, cracking some, hanging onto others, and all the children in the neigbourhood crowded around Bobby Steinberg and me, wanting to take a turn with the sticks. They even brought food for King George. By late October, I was famous for my turtle.

Then, one Saturday morning, Bobby Steinberg and I were in the back yard; I was chopping up some crates for firewood and Bobby was singing to King George, "*I'm an ole cow hand, from the Rio Grande...*" When I looked up, Dai Kew had stepped out onto the back porch, coins jingling in his pocket.

"Well, *Yee Doy*," Dai Kew called out to me in Toisanese. "How is the Second Son today?"

Bobby stopped singing. He jumped up, respectfully, and Dai Kew noticed King George in his harness, and laughed. Bobby had just heaped a pile of leaves over him. The yellows and reds of the leaves stood out against the dark shell of the turtle.

"So," Dai Kew said, "your father tells me you've taken very good care of Lao Kwei."

He said something more to me, about my "partner's share" or "part of the bowl." Dai Kew was a bachelor-man who spoke a heavier dialect than the one I understood, but I quickly imagined that I would be rewarded with some lucky money for all my work, or maybe even given King George to take care of for the whole of next year.

"Can I keep Lao Kwei a little longer?"

Dai Kew stood over me, unsure. He knitted his thick eyebrows.

"I'm going to build him a winter home," I said, unable to stop. "The family won't let me take him inside the house to live. Poh-Poh says he's too stinky. I read all about this kind of turtle. I'm going to bury King George in thick mud just before the winter comes."

Dai Kew looked strangely at me.

"*King George?*" he said to me. "You named the turtle after the Royal King?"

"Yes," I said, and I pointed to Bobby Steinberg who kept piling on more leaves. "This *low fan doy* here, this foreign boy, said it was a *low fan* turtle."

"Ahh, yes-yes, Jung," the wiry Dai Kew smiled broadly. "Named after the *King...*" Dai Kew seemed to be talking to himself. He frowned, began to hum, and then half-sang some words from *God Save the King*, "...lonnngg livadah King..."

Suddenly, Dai Kew snapped his fingers, as if struck by a revelation.

"*Aaiiyaah!* An omen!" he said. "Today is the day!"

"What's today?" I asked, puzzled.

"Nothing," Dai Kew said, too quickly. And just as quickly he disappeared.

Bobby Steinberg looked at me and said, "That guy's crazy."

I could hear Dai Kew talking with Grandmother, then Stepmother, and finally Father's voice came drifting through the yard. But I was busy chopping up the wood, and now and then, stopping to watch King George watching me. When I looked up, all the family was standing at the kitchen window, faces close to the glass, unsmiling. Dai Kew stepped out of the back door again.

"Here," he said, and handed me a crisp new one-dollar bill. "You take your *low fan* pal with you to a good movie and some ice-cream treat afterwards. I'll take care of King George until you come back. Go on, now."

I had rarely held a large one-dollar bill with the face of King George on it that was my very own to spend. Any lucky money I was given, even coins, was put away for my future by the family. But I could see the family at the window, Stepmother with her hand on her big stomach, and no one made a move.

I took the dollar and told Bobby Steinberg to ask his mother if he could go with me to see a double, maybe a triple bill, at the Lux on Hastings. We gave a cowboy cheer. I bent down and tugged at the rope-harness, and King George slowly turned his yellow-eyed head to look at me. He did not snap, I remember. Just looked. And from his turtle brain he must have seen me and Bobby Steinberg happily running out of the back yard and away, pulling close our windbreakers against the autumn wind.

Perhaps Grandmother was right, as she told me later that October evening: Lao Kwei heard ghost-voices in that autumn wind.

FIVE

"JUNG, it's snowing," Father said. "Go see how Old Yuen is doing," and then he added, lowering his voice, "*before it's too late.*"

I hesitated.

The radio was just warming up; outside, the temperature was dropping. I could hear the late autumn wind pouring down from the North Shore mountains.

"Go now," Father urged. "Hurry. Get the rent money from Old Yuen before he spends it on drink or gambling."

Father reached over and turned off the radio. Stepmother handed me my "best" coat.

"Put this on," she said. "It'll be cold enough today."

Stepmother had patched my wool coat behind the left shoulder, a reminder of its first years spent on Old Yuen's back before the thick charcoal grey coat was finally passed on to me. His only son, Frank Yuen, had turned it down.

"It just needs cleaning," Old Yuen said to Frank. "I wear this, all the crooks think this is rich old sonovabitch China man."

"Not my style," Frank said, holding the heavy coat up against himself. "Too fancy for me. Give it to Jung-Sum for his birthday. Jung wants to be an army captain."

The wool coat was a little tight on Old Yuen, but fitted on me like a loose blanket. Poh-Poh said I would quickly grow into it now that I had turned twelve.

"Stay small," she said, with her ancient eyes registering my recent growth. After eight years of living with her, since I was four, she never stopped appraising me with her faded eyes; her glance, still watchful, searching.

"Jung-Sum is different," I overheard her say to Mrs. Lim one day when I was waiting for a chance to do my daily round of shadow boxing. I walked in on them in the parlour. I was dressed in an undershirt and Boys' Club boxing shorts, and wore a pair of old runners that no longer fitted Kiam. Poh-Poh was demonstrating an embroidery stitch and Mrs. Lim was watching carefully, now and then biting into red melon seeds.

"Of course," Mrs. Lim responded, always blunt. "He has different blood. More handsome than your own two grandsons."

"No, no, not looks," Poh-Poh protested. "*Inside* unusual, not ordinary."

"Very ordinary to me," Mrs. Lim chimed back. "All Jung wants to do is to fight all the other boys. All boys the same!"

"*Different*—that's all I say!"

I usually did a daily fifteen-minute round to keep in fighting shape. I put Father's snake-arm desk lamp on the floor, the green shade turned to face the wall as if it were a spotlight. I clicked on the lamp. My shadow sprawled across the wall. Max said it was important to see how the line of your left and right arm pitched forward, at what angle the shadow lengthened; it was necessary to push your fist with an illusion of weightlessness, pushing into the air like a bullet propelled through someone's skull. That's why Joe Louis always seemed to float, to centre the power of his jabbing fists as if they were no more than an extension of his own shadow, a bomb falling through air.

In front of the two old women, I began to shadow box, taking deep breaths, punching away in the air, my feet skipping, just as Max taught me. I danced about, happily showing off, moving faster than I should, tiring myself out in five, six, seven minutes. My arms began to feel leaden.

The Old One put down her embroidery and turned back to Mrs. Lim and started an old saying, "Sun and moon both round…"

"—yet," Mrs. Lim finished the saying, "sun and moon different."

"I'm the sun," I said, cheerfully, puffing away, breaking into their conversational dance. "I'm the champion!"

"Jung-Sum is the moon," Poh-Poh said.

Mrs. Lim stopped drinking her tea, her eyes as alert as the Old One's. Between her fingers she held a half-shelled melon seed.

"The moon?" Mrs. Lim blurted. "Impossible!"

Mrs. Lim knew the moon was the *yin* principle, the *female*. Mrs. Lim studied me as I went through my paces, jabbing away at the air.

"Impossible!" she said.

The Old One slowly lifted her tea cup and gently focussed on me, her gaze full of knowing mystery.

When I was four years old and brought on the train from a town called Kamloops to this family, it was the Old One at the Vancouver train station who first looked askance at me like a shrewd farmer's wife.

"Too thin," she complained to the dark-suited, solemn Tong Association official, Mr. Chang, who held me up for her to see. As the train noisily chugged away from the station, she squeezed my upper arm and blasted over the noise, "Cost too much to fatten him."

"I feed myself," I shouted, in a *Hoiping* accent. "Mommy lets me feed myself!"

Mr. Chang put me down. I grabbed at my suitcase to run away. The Old One pulled me back by my shirt collar. Mr. Chang stood solemnly on guard, his heavy foot pressed down on my suitcase.

The Old One bent her head down.

"Your daddy and mommy dead," she said, adjusting her Toisanese.

A strand of hair fell over the Old One's narrow eyes and made me think of the cunning Fox Lady my mother had warned me about. The gut-hungry Fox, a demon, took on many shapes and disguises to ensnare little children for her supper. To the Fox Lady, the bony crunch and sweet flesh of small, well-fed children tasted best of all. But any smart child could expose and outsmart the Fox Demon soon enough.

The demon creature loved to take on its favourite disguise of a friendly elderly old lady. Like a helpless grandmother, Mother told me, begging for a small child's assistance to cross a stream or to help her reach into a deep sack to retrieve some candy. When a child could not perceive any danger, the Fox Lady grew full of satisfaction and delight, her teeth dripped with saliva; her furry tail began wagging impatiently, pushing away at her ankle-length black skirt. And that was the clue, Mother warned me: Look for the furry tail waving frantically. *Always look behind.*

The Fox Lady at the train station took hold of my hand and held me in front of her. Her eyes narrowed. I imagined the back of her dress moving, side to side.

"Who feeds you now?" the disguised Fox Lady said, her eyes twinkling, just as I was told they would, though her voice might have been more friendly.

I said nothing. I stared back to hide my growing fear. Her furry tail would poke out from under her skirt and start wagging like crazy. Then everyone at the train station would see it was the Fox Demon and attack her, poke out her gleaming eyes, rip her apart, and cut off her foxtail. The tail would hang on my suitcase like a trophy.

"*Aaiiiyyyah,* the boy's a mute!" the Fox Lady exclaimed to Mr. Chang. Mr. Chang was being totally fooled by the cunning demon. I knew I had to say something.

"I feed myself now," I repeated, loudly, for the Fox Lady always pretends she is very deaf, so you will bring your delicious young head within biting range of her row of razor-sharp teeth. I shouted even louder: "I FEED MYSELF!"

The startled old lady jumped back. People in the station turned their heads to look at us. Perhaps they'd already spotted her fox tail. She let my hand go, but her keen eyes kept appraising me. No one came near us.

"So Jung-Sum thinks he doesn't need anyone," she said to Mr. Chang. I glared at them both. The Old One started moving her lips again.

"Mr. Chang, the boy is fine," the wrinkled lips said. "We'll take him."

I darted behind the foxy old lady to look at the many folds of her skirt. Nothing moved. No furry tail appeared, no wagging motion whatsoever, only the extended long fingers of her old hand, stretched behind her back, offering to take my hand.

"Let's go," Mr. Chang ordered.

I put both my hands on my suitcase and followed them out to a taxi. In the distance, another train whistle blew as its engine chugged away.

"I'm your new Poh-Poh," the old lady said to me in the back of the taxi, as Mr. Chang settled in the front seat. "That's what you call me from now on."

That afternoon, in the house of the Old One, I met a little girl with a moon face, who kept staring at me from behind the Old One's ankle-long skirt. I was only a little taller, but knew I could handle her if I had to. Lady foxes had little foxes. She held onto the head of a Raggedy Ann doll and poked its head at me as if the doll could see, too.

"Jook-Liang is your new sister," the official said. "Your *Sai Mui*, your Little Sister."

Liang slept in a room with her grandmother, Poh-Poh. Everyone spoke with an accent, a tone or two different, though I understood the same dialect.

"Jung-Sum," Mr. Chang said, positively. "You'll get used to

your new family very quickly."

Things change. This is the way things are, I said to my four-year-old self, and accepted that I was not in Kamloops any more, but in Salt Water City.

The man and woman who earlier had seen me at the Tong Association office both smiled at me nervously and said that this was their house, too. This man and the thin, graceful woman beside him were now taking care of me, along with Poh-Poh. I was to call the woman, who wore a pretty print dress, *Stepmother*, and the man *Father*.

"You have a family again, Jung," the man who was my new father said. "Forget everything else."

He reached out to pat my head, but I darted away just in time. *The Head Fox*, I thought to myself. But when the Head Fox, with his slightly balding head and round face, turned back to talk with Mr. Chang, I was disappointed. He had no tail.

Mr. Chang said that I must be well-behaved. I now belonged in this house, belonged with these people. I remember I looked past each of them to see if my mommy and my daddy would suddenly appear.

"He's done that everywhere we've taken him," the Tong official said. "The boy still thinks his own parents will come back for him. It's been six months."

"Let him look," the Old One commanded.

When Stepmother and Father first showed me the rooms in this house, they watched me get down on my knees to catch any moving shadow under the beds. I walked inside the small closets and pushed aside racks of clothes, *nothing there*, and looked behind the large dressers, *nothing*; I peered behind doors and stand-alone wardrobes but the faces of my mother and my father were not anywhere.

That first night in Salt Water City I was given a cot to sleep in, set up in a small room with my new brother, Kiam, who was almost twice my four years and a head taller than me. Stepmother said the adults were going downstairs to have some tea and sweetmeats. Everyone left Kiam and me alone in the small room to first put away my suitcase things. There wasn't much, just a few pieces of underwear and shirts, two sweaters, a toy cowboy that was supposed to be Tom Mix, and a snake with a clay head. The snake had a long accordion body made of black and green paper. Its head hung from a string tied to a stick, so that it curled like a real snake. But the snake's paper body was badly crushed even though its head was intact. There were also three pairs of socks, two with holes in them, and a pair of shoes that didn't fit me any more.

Kiam got to business right away. "Your side of the room stops here," he said, pointing to a red line he had crayoned on the linoleum floor, "except when you have to get your clothes from that dresser over there by the window." He asked me if I knew anything about British football or muscle building and showed me some cuts on his knees from playing football. He thought I was too weak to be *his* brother, a *real* brother, so it was his plan to make me strong and tough. He was going to be eight in two weeks, he said, and wanted me to know his rules, and not being a sissy was one of them. His baby sister Liang did not count for much, but if I was going to be a real Second Brother, I had to put on some more weight. He crossed the red line and punched me in the chest to see if I could take it. I hardly felt anything; I was wondering where I was and how I got here and where my mommy and my daddy were.

"Don't cry, sissy," Kiam said, "or we'll throw you under the Georgia Viaduct with the bums and the dead people."

Poh-Poh, carrying some folded clothes, came into the room and walked deliberately between Kiam and me. She took some clothes off the small pile and handed them to me.

"Put this and this on," she said. "Then come downstairs for some dumplings."

She told Kiam to help Little Brother, and I realized she meant me. Kiam lifted my arms up and pulled my undershirt off.

"Look," he said to the old woman. She looked.

The reddish scars on my back did not surprise her.

"A belt buckle," the old woman said. "We put something on it tonight."

I pushed them away and dressed myself. We went downstairs and I sat through the tea-drinking and chatter. I drank an orange pop and ate three dumplings just to show Kiam how strong I was going to get.

Stepmother had a thin face and pretty eyes, and, as she bent down to brush back my hair, to offer me another dumpling, her flower-print dress smelled of flowers, too.

Kiam asked about my name. Everyone called out my name, *Jung-Sum*, and the man called Father said it meant *loyalty*, one who was faithful, loyal, and he pronounced it in an odd way, a tone of dialect different from the way I had always heard it. For some reason, I suddenly was not afraid of any of them; for some reason, as I lifted up my fourth sweet dumpling, hearing my name over and over again, I knew I belonged. A baby cried, and it was Jook-Liang, my new sister.

Before he tucked himself under his sheets that first night, First Brother Kiam said, "Stay on your side of the room. And don't start bawling or anything."

I looked up at the moonlit ceiling, at the ceiling cracks and shadows thrown up by the streetlamp against the half-drawn window shades and the lace curtains. I peered at the dresser drawer that held my things, the third drawer down. I thought of my crushed snake and my socks with the holes in them, and Stepmother that evening mending them as Kiam sat by the kitchen table straightening out my paper snake. Poh-Poh sat holding the baby girl, rocking her, and Father was ink-brushing words that trailed expertly up and down a long sheet. Mr. Chang's last stern words to me, as he took some signed papers from Father, came back into my head: "This is the way things are, Jung-Sum."

And I knew it was so, and could no longer worry about demon foxes.

"Bet you're crying," Kiam said, in a half-awake voice, but soon he drifted into sleep. From my cot, in a rectangle of bright moonlight cast down from the window, I saw First Brother toss, heard him talk, and envied him his dreams.

I gripped my pillow and not one tear fell from my eyes.

I did not cry that first night, nor any night thereafter, as I did the strange morning a long time ago when someone frantically yanked up the blinds and stubbornly pulled me away from the cold arms of my mother.

I remember groggily pushing myself up in the morning light, pushing away the weight-laden blanket, half-tottering with sleep, half-groping in my pyjamas in fear that I might have wet the bed. In the kitchen, in the blue morning light, I glimpsed my father oddly slumped beside the open oven door; then I walked into the bedroom and pushed Mother, but she would not move. I called her once, then something told me not to say anything more. I adjusted to the semi-dark, the morning light breaking between the pulled bedroom blinds and now pouring in from the kitchen. On the bed mattress that she slept on, at my level of vision, my mommy stared with unshut eyes at the ceiling, her neck a purple colour from ear to ear. I climbed into the bed and lifted her stiff heavy arms, one after another, over me, and slowly crawled under them. Mommy's two arms collapsed on me when I let go, and they felt cold. I stared at the ceiling and thought I should sleep... close eyes... sleep...

I pushed my face between Mommy's arms, against her body's still plush softness; I let my body fall against her: I stayed very still. After that, the pee started leaving me, a soothing warm wetness between my legs. I waited for Daddy to get up from the kitchen floor, half-drunk, waited for him to beat me with his belt. I waited for Mommy to tell him to stop, waited for Mommy to twist against the falling belt and take the blows. I waited.

I stayed very still, long enough for the pee to feel cold, for the acrid smell to reach me, for the staining warmth to fade and the growing chill to numb me. My thumb felt sore from being sucked for the one or two hours I had lain there, unmoving. A boy's voice suddenly shouted, "Mommy! Mommy!" and for a moment I thought it was my voice. Then another voice shouted "Get Mommy! Get Mommy!"

Herby Chin kept calling for his mother, until finally I heard the back door open and a rush of footsteps and voices from the kitchen; a chair fell over, curtains were whipped back, blinds whirled and snapped up. Mr. Chin was shouting instructions. Mrs. Chin called my name. Shadows moved, and bodies, tall and short, shuddered around the room. At the doorway of the bed- room, when she saw me look up at her, Mrs. Chin only hesitated for a second before she rushed beside the bed, shoved aside some pillows and clothes, and warily knelt beside me on the mattress: "*Don't be afraid ... don't be afraid ...*" I felt Mommy's head move.

Mrs. Chin, with her strong farming hands, pulled apart the rigid arms and began lifting me up, up, up, from the dark between my mother's breasts. Wetness clung to my legs. Sheets of wetness pulled away from me.

I was carried away at last, carried into the late morning air to the Chins' heated cabin. Mrs. Chin told me again not to be afraid, put me down in a large chair in the midst of her own four children sitting around the table. Their small faces reflected back to me my own vacant stare.

"Now we have some *jook*," Mrs. Chin said, as calmly as she could manage, putting a bowl of morning gruel in front of me.

They told me later that I ate, that I said nothing. I remember hearing the siren of the police car, Mrs. Chin scrubbing her hands furiously; and when night fell, Mr. Chin sat beside me and told all his four children and myself a story of Old China. There were many words I did not understand, phrases whose meanings were riddles. In the kerosene lamplight, he recited poetry and sang old songs, and slapped his overalls till the dust from his day's labour settled over everyone. I remember the joy and excitement of his storytelling, and the quickening of my heart when he asked me what I would like.

"Tell another story!" I said, and knew suddenly, another's voice, my mommy's voice with its *Hoiping* tones, would never say again "*Long time ago...in Old China...*"

Mrs. Chin passed some pie a neighbour had brought by. The pie was freshly baked and steaming, and smelled of apples and cinnamon. It was made by a white lady named Mrs. Lawrence. She had white hair and wore glasses and had a kind face. She poked her head in and asked, "How is the little boy doing?"

"Good," Mrs. Chin said. "Jung strong boy. Never cry."

A week afterwards, I was taken from one strange home to another. I spent a month or two in one place, a few weeks in another, finally travelling on a train to *Hahm-sui-fauh*, Salt Water City. A Chinese man wearing thick glasses, with a white band for a collar, said to me over and over again. "No use to cry. Big boys don't need to cry."

Kiam told me *Hahm-sui-fauh* was the Chinese name for Vancouver because it was a city built beside the salt water of the Pacific Ocean. Until Kiam told me, I thought it was where all the salt tears came to make up the ocean, just as my mother told me in one of her stories about her own father's coming to Vancouver. And then I told myself, this is the way the world is. I felt I would never need to cry again. Never.

Now, Stepmother took me in her arms when I could not sleep, but it was not the same and I began to push her away.

The Old One said, "Leave the boy alone," and pushed me away from her. "Go downstairs," she commanded. "First Brother is waiting."

My job was to help Kiam start the stove in the morning by banging on the sawdust bin. I helped pour ladles of water into a larger container which sat heating on the stove for all-day winter use. I was given some picture books to learn to read with Liang and was expected to do better since I was two years older. Poh-Poh showed me how to dress myself properly; Stepmother taught me how to make my bed; Father took me to places in Chinatown and boasted of his new son and patted my head. First Brother Kiam became my guardian on the playground and warned everyone not to get smart around me. People gave me lucky money and candy and toys. Women with powdered faces and red lipstick kissed me and pinched my cheeks and went back to playing *mahjong*. I did not always do my chores nor read every book, for there was so much more to discover. Vancouver was bigger than anything I had ever seen. There were blocks and blocks of houses and stores and places to play.

One day, I got a new box of hand-me-down clothes. Everything seemed two or three sizes too big.

Poh-Poh said to me, "Can you feed yourself now?"

"Always," I said, still wondering about her wagging tail.

"Good," she said, tossing me one of the hand-me-down sweaters, "feed yourself until this fits you." She blinked. "Jung-Sum, are you still worried this Old Fox will eat you up?"

In a year, that sweater fitted me. Time did pass, just as the Tong official had said it would. I belonged.

The Depression meant the man whom I now called Father struggled at many jobs to keep everyone at home well nourished. I was never treated differently from First Brother Kiam or Only Sister Liang. But when Sekky was born, and was sickly, Poh-Poh poured almost her entire attention on him. Neither Kiam, Liang nor I minded; in fact, things went easier for all of us because the Old One no longer nagged us as much about our shortcomings or pestered us with old sayings. Liang demanded a little attention now and again, because she was so young.

From Father and Stepmother, we all received equally what clothes or second-hand goods were salvaged or given to us from the Tong Association. As well, the Anglican Vancouver Chinese Mission passed along books they couldn't sell and gave Sekky stacks of magazines to look through before they were bound up for the paper drive.

In the months after I arrived, I nearly forgot my own mother and father, even in my dreaming. As the years went by, they became part of the darkness at night or, on the brightest day, merely shadows.

I came finally to celebrate my twelfth birthday, with friends like Bobby Steinberg and two of the boys from the boxing club at the Hastings Gym.

I had discovered Joe Louis, read everything about him, and taken to boxing. After Kiam's lion dance practice with the Chinese Students' Athletic Club, Frank Yuen took Kiam and me to the Hastings Gym one day. At once I liked the *whack-whack* sound of the punching bag being hammered into a blur.

That day, a lanky Negro was throwing himself at the punching bag, his feet hopping in rhythm with his lightning-fast fists. He noticed me practically hypnotized watching him.

"Wanna try, China boy?" he asked, breathless, then stopped. In the glaring lights of Hastings Gym, the black man took the towel from around his neck and wiped silver beads from his forehead; he laughed and joked as he pulled off his gloves. He inspected a smaller pair on a rack, held them next to my hands, and fitted them onto me.

Frank waved to him and called him Max and told him to go easy on me. Max laughed even harder. I liked him.

Guys at the Hastings Gym took turns with all the equipment and a few, like Max, took it upon themselves to teach the younger boys how to hold their fists, how to swing and fake a punch, how to pull back and lunge forward, how to shadow box.

"Do this," Max said, in the weeks that followed, putting me through my paces. Frank and Kiam thought that was great. Someone else to babysit me while they sat on the bench waiting for weights or whatever, talking about the war and how they would like to join up somewhere.

Max teamed me up with my friend Bobby Steinberg and taught us both how to take a punch, how to absorb the shock. He taught me how to breathe in rhythm to the movement of my arms. "You see, kid," Max said, "the muscles of your arms are pumping up your rib muscles. Bobby, show him."

Bobby Steinberg caught on to some things faster than I did, but soon he couldn't come to the gym any more, unless he sneaked around. His father and mother didn't want him getting into fights.

I joined the junior boxing section and paid my fifteen cents each week for lessons with one of the coaches. But I thought Max was my best trainer. I happily learned how to swear, how to kick if you have to, how to throw back any shit you didn't want to take.

On my twelfth birthday, Frank Yuen brought me a ticket to see three fights with him at Exhibition Park. Max was fighting. As I was staring at the ticket, looking for the name of Joe Louis, he tossed around my shoulders his father's topcoat and held my fist up as if I were Champion of the World. Joe Louis never fought in Vancouver, of course, but if he had, he would have worn a coat like the one Frank gave me.

The second-hand coat from Old Yuen, falling on my twelve-year-old shoulders, felt like armour. It had been worn by Frank's father, for sure, but it was top quality and had been well taken care of.

This charcoal coat, Frank told me, had cost his father, Old Yuen, three straight lucky nights of gambling; otherwise, it would have cost a regular Chinaman more than three months' hard wages. During the Depression and the opening of the war years, you could only buy such a classic coat on Granville Street, in one of those men's stores where a salesman in a black suit sniffed at Chinamen who asked for the *bess-see*—the best—and who proudly pulled out a thick roll of folding money. It was money earned from a labour camp's honest sweat or won from gambling, or from playing a longshot at the Hastings Park races, but it was enough money to have the salesman go to the back room and pull out his best stock.

"Make it like an army or navy coat," I pestered Stepmother.

Father presented me with a set of military-looking brass buttons for the coat. Stepmother washed the coat twice to get rid of Old Yuen's stale tobacco smells. To dry it, she hung the heavy dripping coat for two days on the back porch laundry line.

Afterwards, studying pictures of military men I'd ripped out from old copies of *Liberty* and *Life*, Stepmother stitched up two inches of sleeves; Poh-Poh raised some inches off the bottom, and Mrs. Lim, cutting with sharp butcher scissors, narrowed the two back panels, and Stepmother steadily foot-pumped and turned the wheel of our neighbour Mrs. Chin's Singer every evening for a week.

In exchange for the use of the Singer, Kiam and I carried Mrs. Chin's dump-truck delivery of firelogs and kindling up the slope of her backyard and stacked the wood in her shed for her. The wood had been left in a dumped pile after the turbaned, dark-skinned driver promised Mrs. Chin he would stack the wood for her; instead, he collected his money, dropped the wood, and drove off. It was an annual ritual between Mrs. Chin shaking her fist at the disappearing truck and whoever sold her the firewood, laughing and waving goodbye sucker. Meanwhile, Stepmother ran the Singer under Mrs. Chin's direction. Six days later, on a Saturday, the coat was sewn back together.

Everyone stood around me as I tried the coat in front of our hall mirror, even Kiam, wondering if the coat was worth all that wood-lugging labour.

"Good, good," Mrs. Chin said.

Unbuttoned and loose, the garment sagged shapelessly over my shoulders. I didn't look anything like a champion or an army captain.

Before I could register disappointment on my face, Stepmother looked at me sternly and said, "Not finished yet. We go with Grandmother to visit Gee Sook."

Gee Sook was a bachelor-man dry cleaner and tailor who ran the one-man American Steam Cleaners at Pender and Gore. Despite urgings that he should marry and father many sons, the cleaner claimed he could never afford a mail-order bride and would ask aloud how at fifty-five he could ever have sons and see them grow up. Gee Sook looked years younger, but everyone said that was the steam.

If marriage wasn't part of his plans, Gee Sook seemed neither bitter nor jealous of anyone with children, as some bachelor-men were. He gave generously of his cleaning and tailoring services, and at the lowest fees, to those poorer families like ours who were always making over old clothes.

"I make like new," he always sang in Cantonese, even to the white people who gave him business.

Poh-Poh often camped at the small back room behind the store, just to rest in the midst of her daily Chinatown rounds, to sit back, gossip. Other elderly women dropped in, too. Sometimes the women helped Gee Sook with mending a piece of embroidery or sewing on some buttons. They drank tea poured from Gee Sook's all-day teapot encased in a cloth-quilted jacket. They would urge Gee Sook to sing familiar village ditties and watch him drip with sweat over his steamer. When Liang and I were younger, the Old One had often taken us with her to show us how hard Gee Sook had to work to earn a living. For all Liang and I could make out, Gee Sook did not look like he was working hard at all. He sang Chinese songs and English songs, like *chick-a-ree-chick, cha-lah, cha-lah*, and pressed jackets and suits, while two or three old ladies sat at the back mending and sewing and stitching away happily.

"Such waste!" Poh-Poh would shout in Toisanese over the machinery and Gee Sook's merry singing. "You should buy some papers, some *gai gee*, and send for a bride!"

"Marry me!" Gee Sook sang back, wiping the steam from his glasses. "I'm asking you for the tenth time—marry me!"

"You watch out," Poh-Poh laughed. "I say *yes* and chop you to death!"

Why Gee Sook never did marry was sometimes a topic of conversation at the ladies' *mahjong* tables, but, in truth, many men dared not marry. There might never be enough money to buy more food for another mouth, never a secure job to pay regular rent, never enough decent work to feed the children that would come along.

"Your ancestors must be furious," Mabel Tam told him one day. "It's a natural law that all men should marry!"

Gee Sook winked at Poh-Poh and charged Mabel Tam twice the fee for her cleaning.

"If I get marry," he said to Mabel, "then my fees are double. Thank you."

Yet Gee Sook was not merely selfish, like some of the bachelor-men who lived quite openly with loud and disorderly white or native women, drank and gambled and roamed the streets looking for trouble.

"Mix blood," many of the Chinese ladies told their children, quoting an old saying, "mix trouble!"

There were exceptions, of course. There were Yip Gong and his wife, Nellie, a white woman who had been educated in both China and the United States, lived in New York, and fluently spoke five Chinese dialects, spoke them better than those born into the language. With her perfect unerring district accents, Mrs. Nellie Yip would berate any Chinaman who dared to cross her path or dared to match wits with her. Like Poh-Poh, she could criss-cross into a variety of dialects—pidgin, formal or informal—and snap out a hundred sayings, enough to slaughter any peasant or mandarin attempt at a comeback. She was a legend, but how many Chinese could find a legend to marry?

Nellie Yip was also one of the midwives most trusted to help with the delivery of Chinatown babies. When Stepmother ended up losing the baby during her third pregnancy—not long after Dai Kew reclaimed his turtle from our shed—Grandmother reassured everyone that the very best had been done for Stepmother, especially as Mrs. Yip, as a favour to Father, was in attendance. Poh-Poh said that Nellie Yip knew both white and Old China medicine ways, but she was mainly Chinese in her heart, which was all that mattered. Father and old Mrs. Lim, our neighbour, agreed.

"If Madame Yip cannot save the baby," Mrs. Lim commented later, "then no one can."

After the troubled pregnancy was over, Stepmother seemed to accept that it was meant and felt relieved.

Miscarriages and stillbirths were not uncommon in those days, and no one expected a safe delivery so soon after Stepmother had just had Sekky. Besides, the more practical *mahjong* ladies stressed, how could her man manage another mouth to feed?

The dead baby was strangled by its cord. Stepmother wanted to know if it was a boy-baby or a girl-baby. The dead baby was in a pail at the foot of the bed, a tin pail covered with a folded bedsheet.

"A boy," Mrs. Yip said. After she gently wiped Stepmother's wet forehead and passed the cloth to Poh-Poh, Mrs. Yip cleaned herself, said goodbye to each of us, and went to get a doctor to verify the baby's death.

Poh-Poh came to the door and brought me to Stepmother.

"This is why we were given Jung-Sum," the Old One said, taking me by the hand and holding it tightly and making sure everyone paid attention to me. Stepmother called me over to her bed and hugged me. She smelled of Tiger Balm and sweat, and her hair was matted against her forehead. Liang pressed closer, and Stepmother reached out to hold her as well. Kiam and Father, holding a sleeping Sekky in his arms, and Grandmother stood back and watched.

The three of us, Kiam, Liang and myself, had stumbled into Father and Stepmother's bedroom and heard and seen almost everything of the last half-hour of the birthing. That is, what we could make out from the doorway. We knew we were to keep out of the way, but factual matters about birthing and dying were not secrets kept from children. Births and deaths were part of life. Families went to cemeteries to see graves dug up after seven years, to see bones gently washed and prepared, and wrapped by Bone

Men who hummed blessings as they worked. These bones were to be returned to China, as promised.

Kiam stood matter-of-factly by the door, unafraid to watch everything. Kiam was *First Son*, Poh-Poh had told me, born of First Wife who died in Old China during the famine when he was just three years old. "Those were hard times," the Old One said. "No food, not even enough water to drink." I noticed she had little to do with Kiam, spending all her time with Sekky or Liang or me, but mostly with Sekky.

Ever since Kiam had come to Canada, Third Uncle always told him that, as First Son, he had to behave more like a man than a boy. Father agreed, and together, he and Third Uncle taught Kiam as much as possible how to behave responsibly. Of course, he was expected to stay away from the influence of the women. Kiam belonged more and more to Father, to Third Uncle, to the men of Chinatown who knew the worth of a well-trained and well-mannered First Son. Already, at only ten years old, Kiam was doing odd jobs at Third Uncle's warehouse, and he had shown an interest in helping with the careful business of entering numbers onto long sheets of papers printed with columns. Kiam made Father proud.

Standing tall and quiet by the doorway, Kiam might have imagined by contrast how happy his own birthing day had been back in Old China. *It's a boy!* Poh-Poh had half-whispered when Kiam first pushed his way out of First Wife.

The Old One told us the story again and again, told how she bundled the wet baby boy with suppressed joy, barely whispering Kiam's birth name into his tiny ear.

"Why did you whisper?" Liang asked.

"So the gods would not notice and be jealous," Poh-Poh said. "Kiam-Kim was perfectly shaped, strong and bawling. So I shook my head sadly, as if he were not so."

"What would happen if you didn't?" I asked.

"Why," the Old One said, "the gods from jealousy would strike the baby dead."

The birth of a boy-baby, in Old China, would be announced from bedside immediately to a village crowd at the doorway. The father would be praised, the ancestors' names called out one by one.

Kiam's name was not spoken aloud by Poh-Poh until he, as a baby of Old China, had survived the first month and had his hair symbolically shaved. Whenever Poh-Poh told this story and he happened to be around, First Brother looked indifferent. Kiam only half-listened, if at all, to any of her tales. He was to step into Father's shoes and learn sensible, grown-up things from Father and Third Uncle. Kiam spent more time with the men, and Liang, Sekky and I spent more time with Stepmother and Grandmother. He was the First Son.

The next day, Gee Sook, Mrs. Lim and Poh-Poh, went to the Tong Association Temple to light joss sticks, to give up prayers for the dead baby boy. Liang and I helped to burn paper images of powerful gods, and we set on fire sheets of silver and gold paper, and small paper toys that Mrs. Lim and Gee Sook had folded the night before. Nothing need be done, for the nameless baby had never reached its first breath, but Poh-Poh insisted, and it comforted Stepmother. Then Father Chan came by, read a blessing from his Bible to further comfort all of us. A week later, Liang had a pretend funeral with one of her dolls, and Sekky kissed it and helped Liang to bury it in the backyard.

Poh-Poh went to the herbalist and traded one of Sekky's jade baby bracelets for a priceless root of rare Korean ginseng and a small mysterious packet of black powder.

Father stayed all day with Stepmother and spooned into her mouth a strength-giving soup made of the ginseng mixed with dried orange peel, sugar crystals, crushed fresh ginger and the black powder, which Poh-Poh would only say was "best for woman only." Mrs. Lim insisted on adding the powder of half an aspirin tablet.

Stepmother asked about the baby, what would happen to it. Father said that it would be buried that day in a nameless plot, that Gee Sook had made a burial cloth of special silk, perfectly pressed and sewn, for the dead baby. He showed the small vestment to Stepmother, who approved, and Father took Gee Sook's hand, bowed and thanked him.

In such thoughtful ways, Gee Sook gave away so much of his cleaning and tailoring services, so much of his time at the Free China fundraisers, so much after-hours time reading and writing letters from and to China for those who could not themselves read or write, that the elders said of him, "This man lives in Heaven already."

And Gee Sook so much seemed to enjoy the company of other people's children in his shop that Liang and I took our visits to his kingdom for granted.

Liang and I used to like sniffing the smell of the drycleaning chemicals mixed with the bolts of cloth and bags of material lying everywhere around Gee Sook's shop, and we had fun watching the long blasts of steam shoot into the air as we threw handkerchief-sized rags at the machine and they rose like kites against the large picture window. Sometimes Liang and I just sat mesmerized looking at the fire lit in a ring beneath the water heater tank in the corner of the room. Gee Sook could make the flames dance up and down and hiss at will.

When we grew into our six and eighth years, Liang and I stood on a stool and a wicker chair to help Gee Sook shelve the wrapped packages of cleaning waiting for his customers' claim tickets. We learned the order of the numbers as we did so. It was a job Kiam had liked to do, too, when he was the same age. Gee Sook also had treats, like dried fruit, sticky plums, sugar-glazed ginger, burnt crackling pig's skin, thick dumplings with plush red bean centres, or an Orange Crush for Liang and me to share.

When Liang and I grew too old to hang around with Poh-Poh,

it was Sekky's turn to follow her on her rounds, though, as she got older, she began to roam alleyways as well. And when I went back that day to American Cleaners to be fixed up in my "new" coat, I felt at ease in the old way, as if I might toss cloth patches into the streams of steam and watch them float down.

But now I was twelve years old, too tall and grown up to be patted on the head by Gee Sook. At his cheerful greeting, I shook his hand and stood patiently still while he expertly checked the inside of the coat now lined with the navy-dyed cotton twill Poh-Poh insisted was *bess-see* for long-lasting wear.

"Good job," the tailor said, and quickly threw the coat over my shoulders and brushed over it, dusting away loose threads. At last, Gee Sook raised the garment onto the massive steam-pressing machine that he worked with a wide foot pedal; he began raising and lowering a metal panel, pulling it down with one hand, as he wiped the fog from his wire-rimmed glasses with his other hand.

Luxurious blasts of steam penetrated every fibre of the coat. The machinery hissed and sang; the flames danced blue and red in a ring beneath the water heater. The wool material stiffened "like new" in the mix of chemicals and steam. The brass buttons began to gleam in the sunlight pouring from the store window. Gee Sook pulled the last panel through the steam and then swung the heavy, now quite stiff topcoat majestically off the machine. Everyone stood back in the narrow work space of American Steam Cleaners.

Gee Sook slowly draped the coat over me.

"Jung looks like the young Generalissimo Chiang Kai-shek," Mrs. Lim said, clapping her hands. "We should take a picture."

"This is a man's coat," Gee Sook grandly announced. "All of you women stand back."

I felt intense heat embrace my shoulders, then curve over my back and drop upon my chest. I felt like a young warrior receiving the gift of his bright armour, a steely-grey coat born from fire and steam.

The coat felt and smelled like new. I wished Frank Yuen could see me. Stepmother smiled at her work, at me standing so proudly before all of them. Only the smallest outline of a stain could be seen on one sleeve. It was a happy flaw, I could sense her thinking. For the gods would not be jealous and take away any more of her sons, however they came to her.

When I pushed my arms through the hot sleeves, the reincarnated coat fell on my bony shoulders with military precision. I could feel my cheeks redden with pleasure.

"Yes, yes," Gee Sook said. "Look how Jung stands like a man today."

"Now this," Poh-Poh said, and hobbled over and held out to Gee Sook the last task to be dealt with: the stitching back of the coat's original trademark label.

"Inside here," Poh-Poh instructed.

Poh-Poh had saved the label once attached to the old satin lining. The three-inch *Genuine British* label depicted an old windjammer under sail in a stormy sea. It was always this same label that had caught my eye when I hung up the coat for Old Yuen on his visits to our house. Poh-Poh had noticed.

Poh-Poh said that a long time ago before boats were powered by the breath of steam dragons—that is, before all the ships were named *Empress*—the first Chinese came to Gold Mountain huddled in the smelly cargo hold of old sailing vessels like this ancient windjammer.

"The journey took three sea-sickening months," Gee Sook said. "The elders still talk about that."

"Many die," Mrs. Lim said. "Die like fish or pigs to market."

"But you, Jung-Sum," the Old One told me, "you came over by steamship, long past the wind days."

Poh-Poh told everyone, once again, the story of how I was already in my First Mother's tummy when she set sail to join my First Father in Victoria. "Jung-Sum born in B.C. town. Family move to Kamloops. *Aaaiiiyah*, too many years ago! I die soon!"

Once again, they all nodded their heads.

For as long as I could remember, Poh-Poh always said she was going to die soon, so that the gods, hearing her pronouncement, would not waste their time and she would fool them into leaving her alone to live another day.

"You live to one hundred!" Mrs. Lim, who was decades younger, quickly said. "I die first!"

Familiar stories, familiar phrases, comforted the Elders of Chinatown.

"What were my mother and father like?" I asked.

"Like everybody else," Poh-Poh answered, and turned me around to remove some two-inch pins Gee Sook had stuck in for the pressing. "Better you forget. Look."

Everyone stood back. Gee Sook's full-length tailor's mirror framed me perfectly. I felt reborn.

"Not too ugly," Poh-Poh said.

I marched home proudly, stopping now and then for everyone to catch up with me. I wanted to see myself in the mirror at our house, in the familiar light of home.

SIX

not him interesting

I LOOKED in the hall mirror. The heavy coat was now a year older; I was thirteen, taller, and fifteen pounds heavier, gaining the weight I needed to box in a higher class at the Hastings Gym. A small bandage covered a cut above my left eye, a cut caused by a loosely laced glove during a barely missed upper left hook. Max said I could have lost an eye. I liked the way the bandage looked. Joe Louis had one in a photo in the *Province* newspaper this morning.

I turned to see if the patch on my shoulder that Stepmother had fixed was too prominent. It was barely noticeable, unless you knew what to look for. Old Yuen's coat fitted beautifully. The engraved brass buttons barely shifted.

"See?" the Old One said, breaking into pidgin English, "Still likee new and fit perfect good."

"Tell Old Yuen," Stepmother said, "the Tong is planning to move him out of the hotel next week."

The door shut behind me. I was to rush to Old Yuen's rooming house and pick up the rent for the Tong Association office.

I wanted to stay home that Sunday afternoon to listen to *The Shadow* with Orson Welles and Lamont Cranston; but I knew what Father meant when he lowered his voice in warning, just like Lamont Cranston, "*before it's too late.*" Someone had to get the rent money from Old Yuen before he drank or gambled it all away.

Old Yuen was only in his early forties, just a few years older than Father, but had been made older by years of crippling camp labour, his drinking and gambling, and his bad luck.

Old Yuen's bad luck was legendary. Chinatown gossips still talk about the time Old Yuen took his joss stick and burned seven winning spots on a lottery ticket, on a "bad water" day when the *fung-suih*, the wind-water energies, were in disharmony, only to hear that the numbers-man had been killed by a runaway horse pulling an ice wagon. When the police and ambulance finally arrived, the wagon was dripping with water—"Oh, such ill waters," Mrs. Lim wailed when she heard that the water had soaked into the tickets the lottery runner was clutching. The sopping illegal mass had been seized by the police as evidence of wrong-doing. How could Old Yuen dare go to the police to claim his ticket, and what could he claim? The melting ice had soaked all the flimsy, tissue-thin tickets into illegible pulp. Such bad luck, after years of faithfully playing them, all those numbers coming up at last.

Those special numbers had come to Old Yuen's wife once in a dream she had, long before she gave birth to their only child, Frank. Mrs. Yuen told Stepmother a ghost told her the numbers. Old Yuen faithfully played those numbers for a year, but too few of the numbers came up to win anything. He went home and beat up Mrs. Yuen and she did not cry. But he kept playing them, nevertheless, and beat her at his whim. It maddened him that she never cried, only whimpered as she backed away from him.

"Too bad she won't cry," Poh-Poh said to her friend Mrs. Lim, the gossip.

"Too bad?" Mrs. Lim was perplexed.

Kiam said he thought Poh-Poh was crazy. After all, if Mrs. Yuen cried, she would be weakened.

"Yes, yes," Mrs. Lim agreed. "Her dog's turd of an ill-fortuned husband would beat her even more."

"Why should she cry?" Kiam asked, when he knew he was supposed to pretend he'd heard nothing.

"Tears..." Poh-Poh told Mrs. Lim, as if her friend instead had asked the question. "...tears save us from damnation."

It was another one of Poh-Poh's old sayings; she and her generation were full of ancient words. Dai Bak, the grocer, and Mrs. Lim always traded sayings with her. Father knew these sayings but wanted to be more modern.

"Just old poetry," Father said, when Kiam asked him about the tears. There was an old story about that saying, but Father could not remember all the details, except something about the tears of gods falling to earth and turning into precious jewels.

Tears or not, Old Yuen's bad luck was irreversible. The gossips told Gee Sook at American Cleaners the story of the lottery ticket and Old Yuen's misfortune.

"I can change his luck," Gee Sook exclaimed. "Everyone knows that I was born the tenth day of the tenth month."

Gee Sook asked Old Yuen for his lottery numbers. Gee Sook told the new runner to take a cigarette and burn every other number into the ticket. Then the laundry man added his own lucky numbers. On fifty cents, Gee Sook won almost seventy dollars. He bought Old Yuen a bottle of Tiger Bone Wine and did a free load of dry cleaning for Mrs. Yuen. It did not help. Old Yuen got drunk on Tiger Bone and then threw up over the clean laundry.

Later, when Mrs. Yuen, in a small mining town, gave birth to a son, and it survived its first month, Gee Sook sent the child a ceremonial bonnet with gold-embroidered lucky words. The baby boy's head was shaved to symbolize its first Chinese birthday. Perhaps the son, Frank Yuen, was lucky, but his father's luck did not change.

First Brother told me that when Frank was three years old, Old Yuen gambled big at *pai kew* and won big, then lost everything to a red-headed woman who drank with him and slept with him at the Winter's Hotel; she stole all his money and disappeared. Mrs. Yuen told Mrs. Lim how Old Yuen took the last of her jade pieces and tore the gold bracelet from her arm and pawned them to buy milk and groceries and pay rent. When Mrs. Lim told Poh-Poh how things were, Kiam said the Old One nodded her head, and said, "Nothing one can do about bad luck."

Then Poh-Poh told Mrs. Yuen to think of her son, to endure, to survive for the boy. Father spoke to the Tong Association, and a parade of elders spoke to Old Yuen about his bitter and fermenting shame, about his losing face. Old Yuen stayed sober for a while, worked hard as he always did when his hand was steady. But he grew mean and cursed his rancid ill luck.

There was more Chinatown talk in the next five years: Old Yuen went back to drinking and took to beating his wife for her nagging, for her simple-minded ways, for her avoidance of him when he came home from his seasonal work at the lumber camps. He slapped her for the baby's crying, for his losing this job or that job, for his gambling debts, for his bad luck. Then Old Yuen's wife finally deserted him, took five-year-old Frank with her and begged to stay at the Tong's rooming house.

When Kiam sat down to tell me all this, he said to me, "Jung, you were lucky to become part of our family. Imagine if you had been given to someone like Old Yuen."

I had asked Kiam about my own parents, who faded from my life when I turned four, but there was no history to be told.

"Too long ago," Stepmother said.

"Old history," Father said, when I asked about First Father.

"Too much talk," Poh-Poh said, and pushed me out of her tiny room.

But when I asked about Frank Yuen, Kiam said, "That's different. Everyone knows about Frank's parents."

The Tong Association had to take a vote before Mrs. Yuen was permitted to stay in the three-storey building that served as the Tong headquarters and also as a place for all the bachelor-men to room. There, Mrs. Yuen cleaned out the toilets on each floor and swept the communal rooms with their rows of cots and night tables and brass spittoons. She pushed and harried the bachelor-men who coughed too much and smoked their water pipes, who swore—*eel-ka-ma!*—and talked cunt-talk and penis-talk, who spat into brass bowls and missed, and who washed their feet every other night in the same porcelain and tin basins in which they soaked their facecloths.

In a tiny room at the very back of the building on the second floor, Mrs. Yuen's son sat alone, wondering when his father would come for him. Some of the bachelor-men brought him toys, made him a shuttlecock and showed him how to kick it, taught him ancient words and took him to the Chinese Opera and delighted in his amazement at the noise and lavish colours. No one ever noticed that the boy, still only a child, never cried.

One of the men took Frank into a dark place in the building, gave him candy, hugged him, calling out the name of his own son back in China, and would not let him go for a long time.

Mrs. Yuen coughed into the night, began to spit blood and told her son not to tell anyone about the red smear she would wipe from her lips. One morning Mrs. Yuen could not get up from her cot. She lay there, not even coughing. Frank got in beside her. That evening, when he was barely awake by his mother's side, his father lifted him in his arms and took him away.

Now Old Yuen himself was gravely weakened by his work injuries, the alcohol, and the bad luck.

The only luck he had left was his son, Frank, the boy he took with him to the lumber camps and raised: the father taught the boy how to survive, how to fight, how to labour in the mills, how to avoid bad luck.

Frank grew older and waited and watched, went from school to school, fought on every playground, lived from rooming house to rooming house, until he was old enough to start work, old enough to stay away, old enough to call his father *Lao Yuen*—Old Yuen—as everyone else did, in a kind of mock respect for a man who had aged before his time but never grown wise.

The son would not desert the father, as the father had not deserted the son when the mother died; but the son did not linger with the father beyond a cursory greeting and the counting of the paper money he placed in his father's gnarled hand.

Old Mrs. Lim told Poh-Poh there was no reason for Frank to stay around.

Frank himself said: "Why stay around bad luck?"

Yesterday was payday.

Frank Yuen, grown up, would bring home a money packet from one of the lumber camps, leave his father a portion for two months' rent and food, then take off again to gamble or drink. Like Old Yuen always did, but Frank Yuen was lucky.

Frank told Kiam he visited the East Hastings rooming hotels, where men smelling of sweat and dirt from fishing and lumber camps paid weekend rates. The labourers now competed with men in military uniforms; fights often broke out over which of them would sleep with this woman or that woman, in this room or that room.

Kiam and his teenage friends were eager to hear all the details; Frank enjoyed the audience of Kiam's teenage friends only a half-dozen years younger than he was. They hung out in a Chinatown alleyway, back of the Blue Eagle, always smoking and arguing about the war in China or England. Frank shared his tobacco with them, and sometimes a swallow from his bottle of Johnny Walker, which he kept in a brown paper bag.

And Kiam came home and sometimes told me things, just so that I would not grow up stupid about luck or women or life. Kiam did not want me to grow up taking in too much of what he considered the Old One's superstitions about fate and jealous gods. "Just Old China village nonsense," he assured me, sounding more like Third Uncle than he realized. But I listened to every word about Frank Yuen; he was someone to admire, a survivor.

So, whenever I had a chance to collect the rent from Old Yuen for the Tong Association, I always hoped to meet up with Frank Yuen.

Once, Old Yuen pulled on my sleeve as Frank hurried away from him.

"Stay," he said to me. "You be my son."

"I can't," I said, thinking of Poh-Poh waiting on the street for me to pick up the rent money and take it to the Tong official with her. I took the three bills plus the coins that I was instructed to remove. Old Yuen smiled at my counting ability.

"Your papa lucky. He has three sons and I have none."

"You have Frank," I said, and hurried away.

I was thirteen and envied Old Yuen's only son for his unfeeling independence; the history of his family troubles, however bad, was a history I did not have. I marvelled that Frank found girls so interesting, just as Kiam did, now that Kiam was starting to date Jenny Chong and even jitterbugging with her at the Y dances. Kiam hardly stayed home, except to work on the account books Third Uncle asked him to do at the end of every month. The Old One said he would soon go blind from working so hard with numbers. Kiam ignored her, his mind on balancing the books or on Jenny.

At our house sometimes, Frank and Kiam talked about the war back in China. I imagined that Frank, with his short hair and high forehead, his wiry body, would be a superior soldier, as tough as any U.S. Marine, tougher than John Wayne himself.

No one crossed Frank Yuen. He was nearly a decade older than my own thirteen years. At four I had lost my mother and father; he had also lost his mother and, in a way, too, lost his father to alcohol. At least, Old Yuen, aged by worry, by drink and gambling, by a dark unhappiness and unlucky streak that was relentless, still came back for him, took Frank wherever he could, sat the boy in the gambling halls, sat him outside beer parlours. "My boy Frank," he told everyone who walked by, his arm on his son's shoulders, as if Frank's being there were enough to win some respect for himself.

One day I saw Frank Yuen at Hastings Gym. He was not a boy like First Brother but a wiry, sharp-eyed man, earning big money at lumber mills and paying for his own father's upkeep.

"Kiam tells me you're getting pretty good at boxing," he said, and started to shadow box like an expert.

"You like the Brown Bomber?" I asked.

"People say I fight like him."

I doubt it, I thought. But after a few more meetings, he changed my mind.

Frank Yuen spat with deadly accuracy and cursed in a variety of languages and dialects and took on all comers in bars and street fights. Sometimes he came to our house with a black eye or wrenched shoulder and boasted to Poh-Poh how she should have seen the other guy. Frank liked the Old One's ways with herbs. She soaked large leaves and put them over his eye and swore back at him for swearing so boldly. She happily took the packages of dried mushrooms and bark he gathered for her from the forest. Stepmother stood back and told Liang to stay out of Frank Yuen's way.

Frank had grown up in work camps, been taught much by his father, who slaved beside him, and his fellow labourers. They were natives, Hindus, and runaway city men of all sorts, depression-broke and desperate. From them, Frank Yuen learned to carry a long knife in a carved leather holster, dress in torn workpants or soiled overalls, wear loud plaid shirts so that, at least in the lumber camps, he would not be mistaken by hunters for wild game; and in the city, he would not be mistaken for a country hick ready to be robbed blind. And they taught him how to box: his fists danced, clenched like two grenades waiting to explode.

I wished my best friend Bobby Steinberg could see this man shadow box. Bobby and I had set up a boxing ring in his shed and got a bell we rang to start each round of pretend-boxing. We took turns playing the announcer, took turns being Joe Louis. And here was Frank Yuen shadow boxing the way the Brown Bomber shadow boxed in the News of the World. When I started boasting about Frank Yuen, Poh-Poh refused to listen to anything about him. She was like most of Chinatown; they already knew too much about Frank Yuen.

The Chinatown elders, especially of the merchant class, were offended by Frank Yuen's openly "hoodlum" gambling ways, shooting dice with a mix of *fan quo* and *kai doi* low life. Chinatown expected no more from Old Yuen's only son than the young man's early death. In fact, Kiam was constantly warned to not get too close to him. Father was relieved when Kiam's girl-friend, Jenny Chong, also insisted that he spend less time with Frank and more time with her.

No one realized that I still saw Frank Yuen.

No one realized that he would take an interest in a thirteen-year-old.

I was always hoping for a chance to run into Frank Yuen. I liked to see him spit and swear and have him show me how to fight properly. Some of my friends got to meet him, too, but Frank tended to have a temper and a mixed-up kind of English and Chinese, so that there were misunderstandings, I guess. He wasn't easy to get along with.

"Tell your bratty pals to stay away from me, okay?"

I guess if it weren't for the fact that Kiam was my brother and I sometimes ran errands for his father, Frank would probably have pushed me away, too.

He bought me a pair of second-hand boxing gloves, which we both wisely decided to keep at Bobby Steinberg's shed so that no one at home would know.

Many times when I visited Old Yuen to deliver his Chinatown newspaper or some herbs he needed or to collect his rent money, I met Frank Yuen. If he happened not to be busy, we would go to the Tong's assembly hall room, which was always empty in the afternoon.

"Okay," he would say, "put up or die."

Then we would take off our coats and sweaters, shirts, too, if it was warm enough. Like Max, Frank showed me how to hold my elbows in; how to take a dive, his way; how to propel my fists with fake jabs; how to duck my head and aim my right into my opponent's glass jaw.

The assembly hall smelled of dust and burnt rope. A line of Chinese carved chairs stood on both the far sides of the room, and the walls were hung with scrolls of calligraphy. At one end of the room, three large five-foot porcelain gods of fortune stood guard, with incense pots beside each one. They looked fierce and cast long shadows on the back wall, doubling their size. At night, Poh-Poh told me, they came alive and worked as guardians for the Tong members and fought back evil spirits. When I told Frank what the Old One said, he laughed.

One day when I'd picked up Old Yuen's rent money from his room and was leaving, crossing the empty assembly hall to get to the outside stairs, I ran into Frank, who was in a foul mood. There was the sour smell of whisky on his breath. He stepped in front of me.

"I have to go to the Blue Eagle and meet First Brother," I told him. It was snowing outside, and I wanted to go to the Blue Eagle for a cup of hot chocolate to warm up.

Frank said he knew that and burped in my face. I felt uneasy and wanted to get away, even though I was a bit early for meeting First Brother. Confronting Frank Yuen, a head taller than me, I felt shy. With his leather jacket half-opened, his zoot pants tight at the ankle, Frank Yuen was tough-looking, all right.

"Let's see if you can really fight," Frank Yuen said to me, switching on one bank of spotlights at the far side of the hall. "Show me," he sneered. "Take off your coat, if you're not too chicken-shit."

I measured my height against his: the top of my head came up to his chin. The three spotlights, which were only used for staging lion dances, operas and fund-raisers, threw our shadows against the wall. Old Yuen had told me once, as I counted out his rent money, that a great Chinese warrior in 1911 was lit by similar lights. His name was Sun Yat-Sen, the man whose China we pledged allegiance to in Chinese school. I felt my warrior arms grow stronger. My warrior coat slipped from me. I was not paying attention, distracted by the fierce faces of the gods lit up at the other end of the hall.

As I turned around, Frank Yuen swung his leg up in slow motion, aiming at my head. I ducked. His loose leather jacket went flying about him.

"Take off your sweater," Frank ordered.

I did.

I pulled my sweater off over my head and his right foot went up again, just missing the left side of my head. He pushed me aside like a piece of nothing.

"A sissy punk like you," he challenged, "wants to *fight*?"

He jumped away from me, kick-boxed, yanked off his jacket, yelled bloodthirsty curses; his fists jabbed away at each side of my head; his lethal left foot snapped into the air. His shadow danced around the room. Frank Yuen narrowed his eyes and looked at me menacingly. He looked like one of the porcelain gods. His pant leg danced up and I saw a lump with a handle bulging inside his sock.

"What's that?"

"Wanna see?"

He stopped, bent down and lifted up his leg to show me an ebony handle sticking out of a leather holster strapped around his stocking. He unsnapped it; six inches of glistening blade slid out, razor-sharp. The knife could easily slit a man's throat with a single swipe or, with a well-aimed thrust, pierce through bone.

"Honed German steel," he said. "World War One. You could shave with it, if you weren't still a baby."

The blade glided back down into its leather holster.

"In a fight, I always win," he said to me, snapping shut the strap that held the knife in place. "My lion friend here helps me out now and then."

Frank Yuen would not let his conviction go unheard.

"Always fight to win or ... *die*."

"Die?"

I always thought you only died in movies. In real life, no one fights to the death. If you knock the other guy down, you win.

"If you don't win," Frank spoke as if the truth were obvious, "you don't deserve to live."

For some mad reason, I thought I could catch Frank Yuen off guard, show him I was every bit as good as he was. For some reason, I wanted to win his respect.

Following his example, I swung my foot into the air; the tip of my boot barely reached his chest. His left foot swiftly kicked up, hit my own foot mid-air and sent me crashing like a knocked-down bowling pin. I thought I heard porcelain laughter.

"No fair," I said, getting halfway up. "You're bigger than me."

"Mukka hai," he swore, and with his right fist sent me slamming back down to earth. The immediate intense pain took my breath away. Tears welled up in my eyes; the skin on my face stiffened in shock.

"You think no man is going to beat up a little fuck-ass bastard kid like you, eh?"

He danced around me, his left foot suddenly whizzing past my right ear. He laughed: "You want *fair?*"

I froze.

"Stupid asshole," he said, his fists came closer and closer to my face. "Don't you know hotshots like you make perfect punching bags?"

He stopped dancing, stood high above me, breathing hard.

"You sure you like to box?"

I nodded my head. He opened his fist and slapped me hard across my right cheekbone. It sent me sprawling. I knew he expected me to cry or yell stop. Some wildness in him was unleashed; his eyes looked through me. He rushed closer to me, waiting for a sign of weakness, a gesture of surrender. I pushed myself up off the floor. His other hand slapped my left cheek. The sound echoed in the hall. My face burned.

I consciously stood my ground, but that enraged him, pushed him to hitting me again, only harder. A deep burden began to lift inside me, but no words came out, only a rising sound, a keening, half-animal, half-human sound. Another part inside me instinctively went cold, said, *"Win!"*

In spite of my bravura, the hot pain on my cheeks burned; my eyes began to water. I willed myself not to cry, not to break down. I willed myself to think … react … *fight to win or die.*

"Jesus," Frank Yuen said, disgusted. "You're just a goddamn chicken-shit punk!"

An intense icy resolve came over me, a clarity about what to do next. I dropped down, bolted sideways, and grabbed at Frank Yuen's leg. Startled, he tried to pull away, resist. I quickly pushed up his trouser cuff and clawed with my fingers until the lethal German blade slipped out of its holster. And just as Frank Yuen's disbelieving eyes began to understand, I grabbed the weapon. His open-shirted throat stood naked just above my face.

I clutched the ebony handle, felt for a split second its odd, dead weight; then, with the speed of a rattler, taking only half a breath, I thrust the knife point-blank at his bobbing Adam's apple.

Frank Yuen jumped back, not a second too soon, his arms flailing away from the knifepoint coming up at him like a spear. The thin material of his shirt tore, *hissed* apart, as the blade slit upwards.

"*Stop!*" he said.

A sharp pain burst into my fist and my shoulder. My fingers flew apart; the knife flew away.

Frank's left foot had connected. The steel knife skittered across the assembly hall like a small frantic animal.

I fell back down, harder than before.

"Shit," he said. "You were going to kill me."

I was on my knees. The tears began to fall. My chest began to heave.

"Okay, okay," he said. "C'mon, catch your breath." He knelt down to see how I was.

Frank's shadow fell across me. Long shadows on the wall moved as we moved.

The pain burned across my shoulder.

A memory came to me, of something hard hitting my back, its metal sharpness ripping flesh; a strap whipping lines of fire across my back. Words began to tumble out of my mouth, in a voice that was childish, panic-stricken, in a dialect that I had forgotten: *"Bah-Bah, don't hit me ... don't hit me ..."*

I curled up on the floor. My child's voice could not stop its pleading. Frank Yuen, kneeling, bent forward and pressed my babbling head against his torn shirt. He began to rock me, and the slow rhythm of his rocking, back and forth, caught me off guard. I closed my eyes and moved with him, a child being cradled, back and forth. There was the smell of Frank's sweat and his tobacco; his rapid breathing sounded as loud and ragged as my own. We were collapsed together on the floor. The porcelain gods gazed down on us from the far end of the hall. Minutes passed. Frank's lips brushed my forehead, settled for a second, then lifted.

But Frank Yuen could not comfort me forever. He sighed deeply, began to let me go, to let some darkness gently go.

I felt his arms withdrawing, the strong warrior hands leaving me. Frank got up and walked away to pick up his jacket and sweater.

As I, too, moved to get up, my whole body suddenly lit with an unbidden, shuddering tension; a strange yearning awoke in me, a vivid longing rose relentlessly from the centre of my groin, sensuous and craving, rising until my hands unclenched, throwing me forward, soundlessly, until my fingers tingled and stretched to grope the raw tactile air.

I closed my eyes, tasted salt and smelled the dust in the air. A roar came into my ears. Outside, a car drove past, its engines gunning.

"Jung," came a voice above the roaring, "are you okay?"

I opened my eyes and looked up and was astonished at the depth and height of the vast shadowy ceiling looming over Frank's head. He stood in silence above me, like one of the temple gods. For a moment, we stared at each other. He spoke, and I was surprised at how ordinary his voice sounded.

"Are you okay?"

"Yeah," I said. My cheeks were wet. "You?"

Frank put his hand through his slashed shirt and waved.

"Nearly killed me, you little bastard," he said and grinned.

I broke into a smile, then flinched with the pain that stabbed my shoulder. He reached into his pocket and gave me a clean handkerchief.

"Honk," he said. "Keep it."

I wiped my cheeks and blew my nose.

"So where the fuck's my knife, Champ?" Frank said, looking around

"Under that chair," I said.

I stood up. He'd called me Champ. Champion.

Frank walked over and picked up the knife and snapped it back in its sheath. He threw me my sweater and reminded me that Kiam and Jenny Chong were waiting for us at the Blue Eagle.

I pushed my arms through the sleeves, careful not to show how badly he had hurt me. Frank switched off the lights. Our shadows disappeared.

After that time I fought Frank Yuen, I never felt the same about anything.

Frank Yuen is the sun, I remembered thinking, and I remembered also the Old One telling Mrs. Lim, "Jung-Sum is the moon."

Yes, I said to myself, as I finished putting on my coat, my armour, *I am the moon*. As I walked briskly to keep up with Frank on our way to the Blue Eagle, the Old One's words followed me, followed me all the way along the snow-dusted streets of Chinatown.

SEVEN

A YEAR after I first met him, Frank said he was going to Seattle to sign up with the U.S. Marines. They were welcoming English-speaking Chinese. Max, the Negro coach at the Hastings Gym, and the gang gave a goodbye party for Frank. Kiam and Jenny Chong went to it, and Frank insisted that I join them, too. First they had a ten-course dinner at the W. K. Gardens, where people passed around a bottle hidden in a paper bag and poured "tea" into the tea cups. I got some cherry pop in mine, and Frank picked up his chopsticks and gave me the best pieces of chicken and duck and pork.

After the meal, it was only about seven-thirty. All the guys, about twelve of them, went back to the gym to get in some early drinking in the back room. I went along too. The three women, including Jenny Chong, went first to her place to "freshen up." Frank got a little tipsy, made a big deal of looking at his watch for the time. It was the gold watch Old Yuen had given him to take away for keeps. In front of everyone, Frank made a big show of handing it over to me.

"It's yours, Champ, if I don't make it back," he half-joked.

Ever since that time we had tangled in the Tong assembly hall, Frank had been calling me Little Brother and Champ and Killer.

He let me hang out with him sometimes, and when Kiam and he went to boxing matches or rugby games, I was allowed to tag along. He had let me hold that gold watch now and again, just to time a match or check how long it took him to do ten push-ups.

Frank was a little drunk and he put his arm around my shoulder, proud of me. I was beginning to win some of my exhibition fights, just like Max said I would. Frank kept holding onto me.

I felt a little queasy, maybe it was from the two or three swallows of beer that Max, just a few minutes ago, had allowed me to guzzle from his bottle.

"Whoa!" Max said. "Don't hog it, just drink it!"

I thought it was great to get away with a gulp or two. Frank, laughing, pulled me even closer to his chest and pressed me harder against himself.

In the joy of his affection, secure and clownish, he gave me a kiss-smack on my forehead, cheerfully shouting to his gang of friends, "Hey, all you bastards! This is my Little Brother, Jung-Sum—the CHAMPION YELLOW BOMBER!"

At first I blushed, then laughed with everyone. Then all at once I felt the centre of my body go weak. I began to push Frank to break away from him. He let me go. Maybe he thought he was acting too crazy and embarrassing his Champ. But he wasn't. I was getting scared.

I wanted him to hold me again, wanted him to press against me, even harder and closer. But I pushed him away. I pushed him away. A warm, sensual shiver started inside me, rising from my groin and threading up my spine. The same feeling had come over me that time when Frank held me, rocking, back and forth, on the assembly hall floor.

My mind reeled with distorted, sneering faces, including Frank's and Kiam's. I thought someone would see inside me. I waited for someone to expose me. I waited for Frank to turn on me, to spit in my face. Across the room, a camera flashed. My hands desperately tightened around the gold watch, the metal still warm from being next to Frank's body.

Nothing happened. Three of the guys raised more bottles of beer and shouted "Bon voyage!" and then someone started everyone singing "For he's a jolly good fellow..." The camera flashed again.

Minutes later, everyone was quietly watching Frank at the other end of the room, reading out loud his farewell messages from a big card that Jenny Chong got from Woodward's.

Frank laughed, threw his head back to drink more beer.

My eyes suddenly focussed on the smallness of his ear, the curve of his neck; I thought I could smell again the sweet soy, the salt of his body. I stepped back, thirsting for the sensations that were already leaving me.

Sometimes a lightning bolt strikes the darkness, making visible for miles a frieze of housetops, trees and mountains carved against the sky, and you see at the same time your smallness against the immensity of the world. As Frank turned his muscular body to smile for the camera, he waved to me.

Fear abruptly turned my spine to water. My fists began to shake. What if Frank caught on? Would I still be his Little Brother? Would I still be the Champ? A hand touched my shoulder from behind. It was Max's hand, dark and shining in the gym light that spilled off the boxing ring. He neatly gripped my shoulder. Everyone's attention had turned again to Frank, who was singing some bawdy song about girls in the back of cars. Only that ebony hand could feel me trembling.

"It's okay, Jung," Max whispered in my ear, a whisper not of warning but of deliverance. "It's okay."

He didn't smile at first, not until I looked him in the eye, not until I stopped trembling.

"Good boy, Champ," Max said. "Here."

He put the bottle in my hand and let me throw back some more of his beer. Then he took the bottle from me, and without looking back, walked into the crowd and joined the applause that ended Frank's yowling.

I was the youngest there. All the guys and the three girls,

including Jenny Chong, wanted to go dancing in the back room of the Jazz Hut. Kiam said I should say goodbye to Frank and go home; it was getting late.

I made my way through the crowd. I shook Frank's hand and wished him well. He gave me another sloppy kiss on my forehead. Everyone cheered and laughed. Then Max said he'd walk me, the Champ, back to the lockers, because he had the key to the room where we kept our coats and things.

On the way there, we hardly talked, Max and I, except to joke and wonder how many bad guys Frank would kill. When he unlocked the storage door, Max unfurled my coat and draped it on my shoulders, like I was a Champion.

"Have courage, kid," Max said.

"Thanks, Max," I said, and pushed my arms through the coat.

Max stood at the gym door and watched me until I disappeared down the stairs.

I walked home fingering Frank's heavy watch in my coat pocket. I stopped under a street lamp, thinking. I took the timepiece out, looked at its gold case and saw my face reflected from the curved glass. I played with the watch stem and turned it between my fingers. There was a November chill hitting against the warm metal.

The old watch had a cut-out, upside-down crescent under the numbers, and in the semi-circle the face of an antique sun rose and fell, and then the moon took its turn. I kept thinking things over and over. Just thinking. I don't know how long I stayed there. Maybe just a few minutes, but I don't know.

In the halo of the street lamp, the old watch gently chimed eight times. I said Frank's name, in a half breath, my lips barely moving. I tried to feel again his muscled arm pressing around my shoulder.

Max had whispered to me to have courage, but it was not courage I desired most at that moment. It was Frank Yuen.

When I got home, it was only a little after eight-thirty but it felt like midnight. Everyone was home and sitting around the parlour. They admired the gold watch and said how spoiled I was, and Stepmother said I must put it away in some safe place until Frank got back. Of course, he'll be back, Father said.

"And he'll come back with medals," Sekky said, cheering me up.

"Frank Yuen will look really handsome in that army uniform," Liang said, and looked at her *Screen Stars* magazine at an American actor standing proudly beside a tank.

I carefully studied the moon in the blue crescent of the gold watch and asked Poh-Poh what else the moon was besides the *yin* force. She said the moon was the sign of the dark storyteller. In Old China, this was the one who told of hidden things not seen in the glare of daylight. Moon people *felt* things, as she did, things that others did not name. I could see Father shaking his head at his desk, wanting to interrupt her Old China nonsense.

That same evening, Poh-Poh decided to show Liang and me and Sekky some of her jade amulets and charms. She carefully removed each piece from its small envelope of silk.

"Here is a moon piece, Jung-Sum," she said, holding up a circlet of jade. "See how it glows, pale as a ghost?"

Poh-Poh reached over to me, took my finger and glided it over the rim of the jade circlet, and then she smiled.

"Each piece is different," she said. "Each is precious."

Liang shifted closer to Poh-Poh. She put down her *Screen Stars* magazine and picked up a slender jade stick, one of Poh-Poh's favourite hair ornaments.

"Tell us again," Liang demanded, "the story of this piece."

Grandmother told that story, and then another, each story brief and sad and marvellous. There were seven pieces of jade, carved in the shape of ancient symbols. The one she held most dear, we knew, was a coin-sized one, an exquisitely carved peony of translucent white and pinkish jade; its petals were outlined in a simple, carved relief against a perfect round of stone. Its underside was smooth and flawless.

Grandmother said that life itself was loss and pain and suffering. Who would deny this, she exclaimed, was a fool. Then she recited some Chinese sayings, about the bitter and the difficult, which Father smiled at.

"Half the jade in Chinatown is made from bits of bone and flesh," she said, gathering up her pieces.

"And the other half?" Liang asked, flipping open another movie magazine.

"The other half," Poh-Poh said, "is made of blood."

Liang sat up. Father, who was working on another editorial essay about China and the Japanese invasion, laughed out loud. He was more worried about the rent for next month. He had spent some of Old Yuen's rent for groceries and had to make that up, too, before Monday. He didn't want to ask Third Uncle for another small loan.

Poh-Poh handed me a silk envelope that she said I could have to keep Frank's watch in.

"This silk bag used to hold a good piece of lucky jade," she said. "But I gave it to Old Wong Suk—*aaiiiyah*, too many years ago! I die soon!"

"Stop all this *die* nonsense," Father said. "Your old ways are not the new ways. Your grandchildren have to live the new ways."

"Why?" I protested.

"Why?" Father repeated. "Because, Jung, I have to worry about what will happen to you three boys after this war is over. What will happen to Liang?"

"When I fight for Canada—when I join up, I mean," Kiam said, putting down an invoice he was entering into Third Uncle's account books, "I'm going to call myself *Ken*. Do you like that, Liang?"

"Jenny Chong will like that," Liang said. "Jenny says we should all have real English names. When we're outside of Chinatown, we should try not to be so different."

The Old One shrugged and held up the round jade peony for

little Sekky to see, just as she once had held it before each of her small ones, slowly turning the talisman as she spun out a story of her life in Old China.

She held it high against the ceiling light, encouraging Sekky to make out the shifting swirl of pink in the stone's moonlit centre. Sekky raised the toy plane in his hand as if it would fly, enchanted, on its own. I picked him up and play-tossed him in the air.

"Enough, Jung-Sum," Poh-Poh said. She tapped Sekky on his head. "It's time, Little One. We go upstairs to do our own work."

Kiam and Father looked at each other and shrugged. Father sighed, not too loudly. It seemed that only Third Uncle's frown was missing, and the three of them could have sighed together. But I still belonged with Poh-Poh, belonged to her stories and her ghosts, just as Liang and Sekky did.

I helped her slip each piece into the silk envelopes, and she started putting everything away in her large jacket pocket. One piece was missing.

"Will this one be mine one day, Grandmama?" Sekky asked, greedily clutching the last piece. "Will this one be mine?"

"Why not," the Old One said, laughing, and took the small, round stone from Sekky's hand as she walked into the gloom of the hallway to start work on the windchime she had promised him.

PART THREE

SEK-LUNG, THIRD BROTHER

→ Jade peony passed on to him when
Poh-Poh dies.

→ Jade Peony = old china's culture + traditions

→ when Sek Lung gets it he develops more
of Poh-Poh's characteristics

→ retention of cultural roots

→ Sek Lung becomes overwhelmed, retreats into
himself, obsessed w/ war games

Sekky's chinese b-sitter + Jap boy = forbidden Rel.

Sekky ignores ridicule of his brother's + collects
trash w/ Gma, then plays war games to "fit in"
- embrace fem side instead of
over compensating like Jung.

How do males negotiate boundaries? - cultural, racial,
sexual
- Sekky's friendship w/ Meyling

→ He is the one who truly transcends
boundaries - accepts Meyling, Japanese, takes
Meyling's place in rel. w/ his mother.

EIGHT

w/o boundaries

IN 1939, when I was six years old, the whole family—my two brothers and my sister, and all our relatives—considered me brainless.

"*Mo no!*" Stepmother used to say in Cantonese, pointing to my head. "*No brain!* Wait until your Auntie Suling comes to Canada. She'll give you a brain!" I looked upon Stepmother's best friend, Chen Suling, as my enemy.

Everyone knew why I was brainless. A stubborn lung infection was keeping me out of the Vancouver public school system. My family, however, focussed on the way I stumbled over calling my adopted *Gim San gons* (Gold Mountain uncles) their proper titles. I would say "*Third* Uncle" instead of "*Great* Uncle."

Whenever I called a visitor by the wrong title again, Stepmother shook her head, apologizing for the blunder. Then she would sing in her *Sze-yup* dialect, "*Suling, Suling,* come to Gold Mountain, give my boy Sek-Lung—*a brain, a brain!*"

Suling was Stepmother's age, a woman who had given up her own family's wealth to become a Christian teacher in Old China. Stepmother worshipped the bamboo-framed photograph of Suling and herself standing before a moon gate when they were young together and everything seemed possible.

"The street photographer, an old man, thought Suling was so pretty!"

Chen Suling, clutching a thick Bible in her hand, had discovered the Christian God in the spring of 1920, or as Stepmother told it, "The Christian God picked her."

"Suling gave me that beautiful silk scarf with gold flowers," Stepmother said, pointing. "See how it falls over my shoulders."

The two young girls in the picture were stiff, barely smiling. Suling looked righteous, like Miss MacKinney, my Grade One teacher at Strathcona School. Miss MacKinney had a wooden ruler with a steel edge, unbending. She slapped it on your desk if you didn't pay attention in class. Miss MacKinney had not called me Sek-Lung, but "Sekky," because, she smiled, it was "more Canadian."

I looked at the picture of Stepmother's girlhood friend. She looked so stern, I thought she should have a steel-edged ruler in each of her hands. Instead, there was an embroidered sharp-clawed dragon slinking down Chen Suling's wide sleeve. Stepmother noticed me staring at it.

"Isn't that a beautiful jacket? Suling and I picked it out together. When she comes to Canada, Sek-Lung," she paused to imagine that happy day, "I will wear the same flowered scarf she gave me, like the old days."

The dragon on the sleeve looked powerful, forbidding; Chen Suling's long *cheong-sam* hid everything but her dour face.

Because Stepmother's vanity wouldn't let her wear glasses, she insisted that she could not make out the writing in the letters Suling sent from China, so Father read them aloud: "Today, the farmers tell us landlords and Christians are being arrested in the Outer Districts near Tsingyuan. Some are beheaded. It is difficult to write. Pray for us." Suling's own First Mission Group barely escaped death; then the Japanese pushed deeper into South China and we scarcely heard from her.

Even so, Stepmother believed Suling would someday come to Canada. Rich Chinese merchant families, students and baptized

Christians were arriving every three or four months.

"Why not?" she said to Mr. Tom, the fresh vegetable vendor, "Even if the Chen family deserts her, Suling has her God to help her. And my *mo no* boy needs her brain."

she's his actual mom

Family rankings and Chinese kinship terms gave me a headache. For example, Stepmother was the birth-mother of both my sister Liang and myself. She had been brought over to Canada from China to become a family servant or concubine, a kind of second-class wife, after Father's first wife died in China. Kiam was the son of Father and his first wife, and Jung was adopted.

"Step" = Poh Poh's idea

Grandmama decided it was simpler for everyone to refer to Father's second wife as "Stepmother."

"In Canada, one husband, one wife," Grandmama said. Because of her age, the wiry ancient lady was the one person Father would never permit any of us to defy.

When Third Uncle told me that "Stepmother" was a ranking much more respectable than "family servant," more honourable than "concubine," but never equal in honour or respect to the title of First Wife or Mother, Stepmother remained silent.

Rank worth

Every Chinese person, it seemed to me, had an enigmatic status, an order of power and respect, mysteriously attached to him or her.

"Isn't a *boy* baby better than a *girl* baby?" I asked Father one day, with specific reference to myself and to my sister Liang.

"The older one," Liang butted in, "is always better than the younger one."

Liang was ten; I was six.

Liang was always jealous that Grandmama, whom she called Poh-Poh, treated me better; I was the one the Old One had spent the most time caring for since I was a baby, and sickly. And I was a boy.

My two stepbrothers naturally felt superior. Kiam was fifteen and was getting all *A*'s at King Edward High; Jung was twelve and was learning how to box like Joe Louis at the Hastings Gym.

One afternoon, over small cups of wine with Third Uncle and Father, Uncle Dai Kew changed his tone of voice and referred to Father and Father's First Wife and "the others."

"What others?" I asked, for I knew that Father's Number One Wife had died in China.

The three men drank their medicinal wine, looked at each other, and shut up.

"Keep it simple," Father said. "We in Canada now."

"Simple best," Grandmother said, sternly, tapping her finger on the kitchen table, ignoring Liang and taking me into her arms. Liang made a face at me.

I always wanted to keep things simple, just as Father advised, and that made things worse.

The Chinese rankings for acquaintances and relatives were overwhelming. There were different titles for those persons related to us according to the father's age, the mother's age, and even the ages of the four grandparents, and according to whether they were from the mother's or father's side—never mind if you threw in a *step*mother and *her* best friend. And if these persons were also tied to us by false papers to obtain immigration visas, they became "paper sons" or "paper uncles," heirs to a web of illegal subterfuge brought on by laws that stipulated only relatives of official "merchant-residents" or "scholars" could immigrate from China to Canada. Paper money could buy paper relatives. But whose papers were connected to whose relatives? My head pounded.

First Brother Kiam showed me a few kinship terms you could look up in an English-Chinese missionary dictionary. For every one term in English, like "First Cousin" or "Aunt," there were ten Chinese terms. Jesus, for example, had something like eleven brothers and sisters whose Chinese kinship terms, as a footnote, took up half the page. I could only think that Chen Suling was very smart, and Jesus needed her in China.

"Lucky Jesus wasn't Chinese," I said, seriously.

"These rankings," Kiam agreed, "they're more confusing than Confucius!"

•

One day, after shopping with Grandmama and studying the Chinese flag and the Union Jack and the Buy War Bonds posters hanging in Chinatown store windows, I had a burning question. I came home and interrupted Stepmother, who was busy learning how to knit socks for the soldiers in China.

"Am I Chinese or Canadian?" I asked Stepmother.

"Tohng Yahn," Grandmama said, collapsing in her rocking chair and setting her grocery bags down on the floor. *"Chinese."*

"When Chen Suling comes to Canada," Stepmother said, caught between a missed row, "she will teach you the right way to be Chinese."

Father reached out to touch her hand, but she withdrew from him. Stepmother did not like my spending so much time with Grandmama. They must have had words again about it: "The Old One spoils the boy! Everyone says so!".

"We are also Canadian," Father said.

After a long pause, Stepmother gave him her hand, and he held it for a moment. She would not smile, and he went back to sorting out his Chinese newspaper cuttings spread out on the floor.

I knew just enough Chinese and English to speak to people, but not always to understand the finer points; worse, each language was mixed in with a half-dozen Chinatown dialects. I never possessed enough details, in either language, to understand how our family, how the countless cousins, in-laws, aunts and uncles, came to be related. Behind their wrinkled hands, the few old women and the old bachelor-men, the *lao wah-kiu,* whispered their guarded knowledge of bloodlines, of clans claimed or deserted, of women bartered for silver coins, of indentured children bought or sold to balance family debts or guarantee male heirs.

Each *lao wah-kiu,* each Chinatown old-timer, had been driven out of China by droughts, civil wars and famines. They put their marks on foreign labour contracts and ended up in Gold Mountain engulfed by secrets.

English words seemed more forthright to me, blunt, like road signs. Chinese words were awkward and messy, like quicksand. I preferred English, but there were no English words to match the Chinese perplexities. I sometimes wished that my skin would turn white, my hair go brown, my eyes widen and turn blue, and Mr. and Mrs. O'Connor next door would adopt me and I would be Jack O'Connor's little brother.

"Sekky's driving himself crazy," Liang complained.

"Simple, please," Father urged everyone.

"Sek-Lung will never get things right," Stepmother said. "Even my friend Suling may not be able to help."

"Different roots, different flowers," Grandmama said, chopping a head of cabbage. "Different brains."

Everything was a puzzle to me. Everyone was an enigma.

When Grandmama, still strong in her eighties, and our neighbour Mrs. Lim, younger at fifty-something, sat together on our porch, they talked in private riddles and spoke in a servant dialect, using a kind of clipped and broken grammar they had in Old China. And this was only one dialect of the many Chinatown dialects they knew in common. Each dialect opened up another reality to them, another time and place they shared.

Old-timers knew about survival. Mrs. Lim exclaimed to Grandmama, "*Aaiiiyaah!* The tea is bitter, but we drink it."

And they raised their cups to each other, laughing.

"*We are all Chinese,*" Mrs. Lim said. "*Daaih ga tohng yahn.*"

Grandmama nodded agreement, for to think anything else was betrayal. And betrayal meant that one could still be shipped back to China, be barred from Canada, taken away from Gold Mountain, exiled, shamed, removed from the privilege of sending a few dollars back to the family-name clan starving in war-torn, famine and drought-cursed China. And always came the pleading letters from village and city: "Send more money, send more, send more."

And other letters came, like Chen Suling's: "Can you help me, dear Lily? I must come to Gold Mountain and see you once more." Surely, once in Canada, one was safe.

But born-in-Canada children, like myself, *could* betray one. For we were *mo no* children. Children with no Old China history in our brains.

"Who are you, Sek-Lung?" Mrs. Lim asked me. "Are you *tohng yahn*?"

"Canada!" I said, thinking of the ten days of school I had attended before the doctor sent me home, remembering how each of those mornings I had saluted the Union Jack, had my hands inspected for cleanliness, and prayed to *Father-Art-in-Heaven*.

But even if I was born in Vancouver, even if I should salute the Union Jack a hundred million times, even if I had the cleanest hands in all the Dominion of Canada and prayed forever, I would still be *Chinese*.

Stepmother knew this in her heart and feared for me. All the Chinatown adults were worried over those of us recently born in Canada, born "neither this nor that," neither Chinese nor Canadian, born without understanding the boundaries, born *mo no*—no brain.

*Mo no*s went to English school and mixed with Demon outsiders, and even liked *them*. Wanted to invite *them* home. Sometimes a *mo no* might say one careless word too many, and the Immigration Demons would pounce. One careless word—perhaps because a *mo no* girl or a *mo no* boy was showing off—and the Immigration Demons would come in the middle of the night, bang on the family door, demand a show of a pile of documents with red embossed stamps. Then the Immigration Demons would separate family members and ask trick questions. Then certain "family" members would disappear. Households would be broken up. Jobs would be lost. Jail and shame and suicides would follow.

"Keep things simple," Father expounded.

Beneath the surface, of course, nothing was simple: I was the Canadian-born child of unwanted immigrants who were not allowed *will this get resolved?*

to become citizens. The words RESIDENT ALIEN were stamped on my birth certificate, as if I were a loitering stranger.

stepmother seems removed

Sometimes I found Stepmother sitting in Father's large wicker chair. She looked far away, and I knew she was thinking again of her girlhood in China and the family she had left behind, and the history that was hers, her ghost-whispering history. Balanced on her lap there were two precious things: the old bamboo-framed photograph of two women standing by a moon gate, and a large, delicately carved sandalwood box. Within its sweet, mysterious scent, Stepmother kept her own family photos and all the letters and the few photos sent by Suling.

Once Stepmother said to me, as if she were stranded on an island, "Suling is my only friend who knows *my* family stories. Not the stories Poh-Poh tells you."

I picked up one of the heavily stamped envelopes and slipped out a sheaf of thin-as-water onionskin papers. Holding a single sheet up, you could see the faintest cloud-haunted blue colour. Stepmother took the papers from me and carefully unfolded them.

"See how beautiful her calligraphy is," Stepmother said. "Maybe when Chen Suling comes to Gold Mountain she will teach you how to write as beautifully."

I saw a steel-edged ruler slapping down on my hand.

"Like a g-i-r-l!?!" I sneered and flew a Spitfire over a wooden village, noisily dropping bombs.

"You're right," Stepmother said, "it will be enough work to teach a *mo no* like you to address your uncles properly."

To my child's mind, the matter was simple. In English, I would have been secure with "Uncle," "Sir," or even "Mister." Three basic choices instead of ten dozen Chinese brain-twisters.

"I'm going to speak and write only English!"

Stepmother smiled.

"Suling once won a prize for her English," she said. "If only Suling were here…"

I hated Chen Suling. But maybe when she got here, she would work like Stepmother in one of those basement factories, machine-sewing parts for military knapsacks and uniforms. Maybe Suling would work double shifts, come home too exhausted to bother with me, like Father. After working twelve- or fourteen-hour days any place they were hiring (but rarely any place outside of Chinatown's restaurants, laundries, stores and offices), Father—hardly managing to stay awake—left me alone. So did everyone but Grandmama.

Finally, Chen Suling's family gave her the money to come to Gold Mountain. We also obtained a piece of paper, verified in China by three officials, that said she was the oldest daughter of Third Uncle, Merchant Class. Now, we would be able to sponsor her, through Third Uncle, to come to Canada.

Chen Suling in Canada.

The thought was horrifying.

She probably had a bigger steel-edged ruler than Miss MacKinney. Grandmama was always telling me that Old China had bigger and better things than anything in Canada. For example, Vancouver had that sea wall in Stanley Park, which we walked once until I had to be carried by Kiam.

"Don't you know about the Great Wall in China?" Grandmama said. And the Old One told me everything. How you would need ten lifetimes to walk it just once. Of course, I reasoned, Suling must have walked the Great Wall twice by now and measured every inch with her yardstick!

My mind set to work, to plan Suling's downfall. I knew enough to understand the person named Chen Suling would have "delicate" papers, trumped-up papers, at best, half-true papers.

Oh, I thought, *what if I called her by the wrong title at the very first meeting at Customs?*

Any slip in our very first greetings to her, and the White Demon immigration officers and their translators would pounce. Ship her back on the very next steamer, steel-edged ruler unpacked. But Stepmother wanted to be with her best friend again … I didn't care … I made up my mind: I would call Chen Suling by the wrong name—*on purpose.*

At Sunday dinner, I interrupted Third Uncle talking about the documents being completed for Stepmother's girlhood friend,

"When Suling comes to Gold Mountain," I asked in my limited *Sze-yup* dialect, "will she be Father's Number Three Wife or Father's Number One Concubine?"

I was playing with my rice, but looked up when there was no answer from Third Uncle. He looked startled and said, firmly, "Not my business."

Everyone laughed.

"*Mo no,*" Stepmother said, shaking her head at me. "Suling will teach you proper Chinese," Stepmother said to me. "Suling is a teacher in the Mission House in China."

Stepmother's *Sun Wei* village accent, blunt and final, burned into my ears while she sizzled the late night stir-fry, "*Mo no… mo no… no brain… no brain!*" Then I would hear Father sighing in the next room. He was exasperated with Stepmother's stubbornness.

Against Stepmother's pointing chopsticks, against Father's heavy sighing, I was driven to prove them wrong: *I did, too, have a brain!* There was nothing Suling needed to teach me!

When I got into English school at last, I would push myself. If Chinese was impossible to know correctly, I would conquer my Second Language. I would be a Master of English, better than Chen Suling, even if Miss Chen had ten thousand prizes!

I already had real English books to learn from. I didn't have to struggle for English the way Suling did. "Like a scavenger," Stepmother told me.

Chen Suling had to write down her copy book the English words she searched for on billboards and war posters, had to pick up old British magazines discarded in heaps behind the Foreign Compound. Stepmother said that Suling fought with her father, for he was angry at the way she was taking in the Demon words and was horrified to see her believe that eating the flesh and blood of someone called Jesus was the only possible way to go to Heaven. Suling would light incense to the family ancestors but would not bow three times before their images. Suling's father expelled her from the family, said to the village he had no such daughter.

"She fled her home like the Sky Dragon," Stepmother said.

Chen Suling had moved into the First Mission Church. Suling and Jesus were now best friends.

"In the Mission Church," Stepmother emphasized, "Chen Suling learned First Class English."

I wished someone would expel me and I could live somewhere else. That would be fun. Instead, I pretended it was dangerous to learn English in Canada. I slyly picked up mysterious old books and magazines from the back of Strathcona School. I cut out war pictures and kept them in a wooden, tin-lined shipping crate Uncle Dai Kew got me from the docks. It smelled of sweet marjoram. On the lid I crayoned KEEP OUT!!!

I even took to reading the scraps of English newsprint that wrapped up our groceries, and I bugged my two brothers for definitions.

No one laughed at my efforts to learn English. Education, in whatever language, was respected. Around me were "uncles" who had gone to universities in the 1920s and '30s but remained unemployable because only Canadian citizens could qualify as professionals. For if you were Chinese, even if you were born in Canada, you were an educated *alien*—never to be a citizen, never a Canadian with the right to vote—"an educated fool" in the words of some old China men, or a "hopeful fool" in the words of those who knew the world would soon change.

"Furnish your mind," Father said to us. "You don't have to be poor inside, too."

"Look at your son," Sam Gon, one of the old uncles, said to Stepmother, who was setting the table. She pushed my picture book off the table onto my lap.

"He reads books as if he is a scholar," Stepmother said. "He loves to read, just like my friend Chen Suling."

"But he doesn't know what to call me when I visit," Sam Gon persisted. "All those *low fan* words, those foreign words, and no Chinese! What a waste!"

I slammed my book shut and glared at Sam Gon. In my best Chinese, I said loudly, "What's the difference what *you're* called! My *huhng-moh gui,* my red-haired demon friend, says if you drop a plate in a restaurant, a dozen Chinks will answer!"

Sam Gon's eyes opened wide as saucers. Stepmother dropped a large plate. Grandmama walked out of the room. That evening, there was no supper for me. Stepmother could hit hard, but when Father came home from working at the restaurant, he hit harder. He walloped me with a wad of folded *Chinese Times.*

I was sent to my room and grew even more to hate the Chinky language that made such a fool of me. I hated the Toisan words, the complex of village dialects that would trip up my tongue. I wished I were someone else, someone like Freddy Bartholomew, who was rich and lived in a grand house and did not have to know a single Chinese word.

One day, when I was stuck at home because I was wheezing badly, and everyone was out except Stepmother and myself, the postman had an important piece of mail for us. Stepmother, who was wary of any strange documents, called me to the door. "What does this White Demon want?" I could see she wished Suling were here, with her perfect English.

The bearded postman explained to me he needed a signature; he held out a parcel, as if to tempt us. Stepmother looked at the package with our address in English and some Chinese writing cascading alongside the block-print words: FROM CANTON. INSPECTED / INTERNATIONAL ZONE.

"Just tell your mom to make an *X*," the man said, drawing in the air. I told Stepmother she must sign for it.

Stepmother took the postman's pencil, and he pointed to the

LANG ✗

IRONY:
he provides
bride

document in his hand. Carefully, Stepmother drew two lines, one crossing over the other. She could have written her name in Chinese ideograms, but the man only wanted an *X*. It was the first time I saw Stepmother write anything in English. *X.* She did not like the way the postman smiled at her.

"Sek-Lung, tell the White Demon to give me the box."

"Sir," I said, "my mama wants the box right away."

"You're a smart young fella," he said, putting the box in her hand. He saluted Stepmother and slapped his receipt book shut and left.

"Did you hear that?" I said. "He called me *smart*."

"Smart English not smart Chinese," Stepmother said.

I followed her to the kitchen table. With a sharp cleaver held expertly in her hand, Stepmother cut the twine in two. I tore open the brown wrapping paper.

Stepmother hesitated a moment, then reached in and lifted out a quilted green silk jacket. When she gently, very delicately, unfolded it, we discovered a thick, water-stained Chinese-English Bible, three photos—one exactly matching the photo in the bamboo frame—and an official *Mission Hospital* envelope.

In silence, Stepmother touched the stained dragon crest on one sleeve of the jacket. Dragon claws gripped my stomach. Giant wings pushed against my ribs.

Stepmother took out a sheet of onionskin from the envelope and looked blankly at the two small paragraphs of typewritten print; the Demon language stared blankly back at her. She put the paper in my hand.

"What does this paper say?" she asked in a low voice. "Hurry, Sek-Lung, tell me!"

I silently read the typewritten message and began tumbling them into my broken, *mo no* Chinese:

"... a bomb ... Miss Suling Chen ..."

When I finished, to avoid Stepmother's eyes, and to not hear the silence that was now louder than any noise, I put down the letter and opened up the well-worn Bible. Something was hand-written on the inside of the cover. It faced a decorated page that said this book was presented as a First Prize for Language Achievement. Stepmother pointed her fingers at the handwritten English words.

"*Read,*" she commanded.

I read.

> TO SEK-LUNG, SUN OF LONGTIME FRIEND
> LILY. I NEVER TO FORGET HER. LEAF
> JACKET AND BOOK WITH GOD.
> BLESSINGS.
>
>   —CHEN SULING.

As she listened, Stepmother strained to read the two columns of hand-brushed Chinese words beside the English words. She nodded her head. Yes, the same meaning. Yes, this was her best friend's very hand. Yes, even if the ideograms were shaky, even if there were ink blots here and there, hesitations as if strength or faith were ebbing.

Stepmother took the Bible from me. "See her excellent English, Sek-Lung? She used to win prizes. Did I not tell you Suling was best?"

I said nothing.

Stepmother closed up the thick book, held it a moment, and put it back in my hand. The dragon in my stomach unclenched—twisted once—and flew away. She folded up the jacket and quickly picked up everything, and silently went up to her room.

I never heard Stepmother mention Chen Suling's name again.

NINE

WHEN Grandmama died in 1940 at eighty-three, our whole household held its breath. She had promised us a sign of her leaving, final proof that her life had ended well. My parents knew that without any clear sign, our own family fortunes could be altered, threatened. Stepmother looked every day into the small cluttered room the ancient lady had occupied. Nothing was touched; nothing changed. Father, thinking that a sign should appear in Grandmama's garden, looked at the frost-killed shoots and cringed: *No, that could not be it.*

My two older teenage brothers and my sister, Liang, were embarrassed by my parents' behaviour. What would white people in Vancouver think of us? We were Canadians now, *Chinese-Canadians*, a hyphenated reality that our parents could never accept. So it seemed, for different reasons, we were all holding our breath, waiting for *something*.

I was nearly seven when Grandmama died. For days she had resisted going into the hospital ... *a cold, just a cold* ... and instead gave constant instructions to Stepmother on the boiling of ginseng root mixed with bitter extract. At night, between racking coughs and deadly silences, Grandmama had her back and chest rubbed with heated camphor oil and sipped a bluish decoction of an herb called Peacock's Tail. When all these failed to abate her fever, she began to arrange the details of her will. This she did with Father, confessing finally: "I am too stubborn. The only cure for old age is to die."

Father wept to hear this. I stood beside her bed: she turned to me. Her round face looked darker, and the gentleness of her eyes, with the thin, arching eyebrows, seemed weary. I brushed a few strands of grey, brittle hair from her face; she managed to smile at me. Being the youngest, I had spent nearly all my time with her and knew that she would be with me forever. Yet when she spoke, and her voice hesitated, cracked, the sombre shadows of her room chilled me. Her wrinkled brow grew wet with fever, and her small body seemed even more diminutive.

"You know, Little Son, whatever happens I will never leave you," she said. Her hand reached out for mine. Her palm felt plush and warm, the slender, old fingers bony and firm; so magically strong was her grip that I could not imagine how she could ever part from me. Ever.

Her hands *were* magical. Long, elegant fingers, with impeccable nails, a skein of fine barely visible veins, and wrinkled skin the colour of light pine. Those hands were quick when she taught me, at six, simple tricks of juggling, learnt when she was a village girl in southern Canton; a troupe of actors had stayed on her father's farm. One of them, "tall and pale as the whiteness of petals," fell in love with her, promising to return. "My juggler," she said, "he never came back to me from Honan … perhaps the famine …" In her last years, his image came back into her life. He had been a magician, an acrobat, a juggler, and some of the things he taught her she had absorbed and passed on to me through her stories and games.

Most marvellous for me was the quick-witted skill her hands revealed in making windchimes for our birthdays: windchimes in the likeness of her lost friend's parting present to her, made of bits of string and the precious jade peony, a carved stone the size of a large coin, knotted with red silk to hang like a pendant from the centre, like the clapper of a sacred bell. This wondrous gift to her had broken apart years ago, in China, but Grandmama kept the jade pendant in a tiny red silk envelope, and kept it always in her pocket, until her death.

Hers were not ordinary, carelessly made chimes, such as those you now find in our Chinatown stores, whose rattling noises drive you mad. But the making of her special ones caused dissension in our family, and some shame. Each one that she made was created from a treasure trove of glass fragments and castaway costume jewellery. The problem for the rest of the family lay in the fact that Grandmama looked for these treasures wandering the back alleys of Keefer and Pender Streets, peering into our neighbours' garbage cans, chasing away hungry, nervous cats and shouting curses at them.

"All our friends are laughing at us!" Second Brother Jung said at last to Father, when Grandmama was away having tea at Mrs. Lim's.

"We are not poor," First Brother Kiam declared, "yet she and Sek-Lung poke through garbage as if—" he shoved me in frustration and I stumbled against my sister "—they were beggars!"

"She will make Little Brother crazy!" Sister Liang said. Without warning, she punched me sharply in the back; I jumped. "You see, look how *nervous* he is!"

I lifted my foot slightly, enough to swing it back and kick Liang in the shin. She yelled and pulled back her fist to punch me again. Jung made a menacing move towards me.

"Stop this, all of you!" Father shook his head in exasperation. How could he dare tell the Old One, his ageing mother, that what was appropriate in a poor village in China was shameful here? How could he prevent me, his youngest, from accompanying her? "She is not a beggar looking for food. She is searching for—for . . ."

Stepmother attempted to speak, then fell silent. She, too, was perplexed and somewhat ashamed. They all loved Grandmama, but she was *inconvenient*, unsettling.

As for our neighbours, most understood Grandmama to be harmlessly crazy, others conceded that she did indeed make lovely toys, but for what purpose? *Why?* they asked, and the stories she told to me, of the juggler who had smiled at her, flashed in my head.

Finally, by their cutting remarks, the family did exert enough pressure that Grandmama no longer openly announced our expeditions. Instead, she took me with her on "shopping trips," ostensibly for clothes or groceries, while in fact we spent most of our time exploring stranger and more distant neighbourhoods, searching for splendid junk: jangling pieces of a broken vase, cranberry glass fragments embossed with leaves, discarded glass beads from Woolworth necklaces. We would sneak them all home in brown rice sacks, folded into small parcels, and put them under her bed. During the day when the family was away at school or work, we brought them out and washed the pieces in a large black pot of boiling lye and water, dried them carefully, and returned them, sparkling, to the hiding place under her bed.

Our greatest excitement occurred when a fire gutted the large Chinese Presbyterian Church, three blocks from our house. Over the still-smoking ruins the next day, Grandmama and I rushed precariously over the blackened beams to pick out the stained glass that glittered in the sunlight. Her small figure bent over, wrapped against the autumn cold in a dark blue quilted coat, she happily gathered each piece like gold, my spiritual playmate: "There's a good one! *There!*"

Hours later, soot-covered and smelling of smoke, we came home with a carton full of delicate fragments, still early enough to smuggle them all into the house and put the small box under her bed.

"These are special pieces," she said, giving the box a last push, "because they come from a sacred place."

She slowly got up and I saw, for the first time, her hand begin to shake. But then, in her joy, she embraced me. I buried my face in her blue quilted coat, and for a moment, the whole world seemed perfect.

One evening, when the family was gathered in their usual places in the parlour, Grandmama gave me her secret nod of warning: a slight wink of her eye and a flaring of her nostrils. There was *trouble* in the air. Supper had gone badly, school examinations were approaching. Father had failed to meet an editorial deadline at the *Chinese Times*.

A huge sigh came from Sister Liang. "But it is useless, this Chinese they teach us!" she lamented, turning to First Brother Kiam for support.

"I agree, Father," Kiam began. "You must realize that this Mandarin only confuses us. We are Cantonese speakers ... "

"And you do not complain about Latin, French or German in your English school?" Father rattled his newspaper, a signal that his patience was ending.

"But Father, those languages are *scientific*." Kiam jabbed his brush in the air for emphasis. "We are now in a scientific, logical world."

Father was silent. He wanted his children to have both the old ways and the new ways.

Grandmama went on rocking quietly in her chair. She complimented Stepmother on her knitting, made a remark about the "strong beauty" of Kiam's brushstrokes which, in spite of himself, immensely pleased him.

"Daaih ga tohng yahn," Grandmama said. "We are all Chinese." Her firm tone implied that this troubling talk about old and new ways should stop.

"What about Sek-Lung?" Second Brother Jung pointed angrily at me. "He was sick last year, but this year he should have at least started Chinese school, instead of picking over garbage cans!"

"He starts next year," Father said, in a hard tone that immediately warned everyone to be silent. Liang slammed her book shut.

The truth was, I was sorry not to have started school the year before. I knew going to school had certain privileges. The fact that my lung infection in my fifth and sixth years gave me a reprieve only made me long for school the more. Each member of the family took turns on Sunday, teaching me. But Grandmama taught me most. Tapping me on my head, she would say, "Come, Sek-Lung, we have *our* work," and we would walk up the stairs to her small crowded room. There, in the midst of her antique shawls, the ancestral calligraphy and multicoloured embroidered hangings, beneath the mysterious shelves of sweet-smelling herbs and bitter potions, we would continue making windchimes.

"I can't last forever," she declared, when she let me in on the secret of the chime we had started this morning. "It will sing and dance and glitter." Her long fingers stretched into the air, pantomiming the waving motion of her ghost chimes. "My spirit will hear its sounds and see its light and return to this house to say goodbye to you."

Deftly, she reached into the carton she had placed on the chair beside me. She picked out a fish-shaped amber piece, and with a long needlelike tool and a steel ruler, she scored it. Pressing the blade of a cleaver against the line, she lifted up the glass until it cleanly snapped into the exact shape she required. Her hand began to tremble, the tips of her fingers to shiver, like rippling water.

"You see that, Little One?" She held her hand up. "That is my body fighting with Death. He is in this room now."

My eyes darted in panic, but Grandmama remained calm, undisturbed, and went on with her work. I got out the glue and uncorked the jar for her. Soon the graceful ritual movements of her hand returned to her, and I became lost in the magic of her task: she dabbed a secret mixture of glue on one end and skilfully dropped the braided end of a silk thread into it. This part always amazed me: the braiding would slowly, *very* slowly, unwind, fanning out like a prized fishtail. In a few seconds, as I blew lightly over it, the clear, homemade glue began to harden, welding to itself each separate silk strand.

Each jam-sized pot of glue was treasured; each large cork stopper had been wrapped with a fragment of pink silk. We went shopping at the best stores in Chinatown for the perfect square of silk she required. It had to be a deep pink, blushing towards red.

And the tone had to match, as closely as possible, her precious jade carving, the small peony of white and light-red jade, her most lucky possession. In the centre of this semitranslucent carving, no more than an inch wide, was a pool of pink light, its veins swirling out into the petals of the flower. *made of blood*

 anthropomorph

"This colour is the colour of my spirit," Grandmama said, holding it up to the window so I could see the delicate pastel against the broad strokes of sunlight. She dropped her voice, and I held my breath at the wonder of the colour. "This was given to me by the young acrobat who taught me how to juggle. He had four of them, and each one had a centre of this rare colour, the colour of Good Fortune." The pendant seemed to pulse as she turned it: "Oh, Sek-Lung! He had white hair and white skin *to his toes*! It's true—I saw him bathing." She laughed and blushed, her eyes softened at the memory. The silk had to match the pink heart of her pendant, for the colour was magical for her: it held the unravelling strands of her memory.

Six months before she died, we began to work on her last wind-chime. Three thin bamboo sticks of varying length were steamed and bent into circlets; twenty exact lengths of silk thread, the strongest kind, were cut and braided at both ends and glued to pieces of the stained glass. Her hands worked on their own command, each hand racing with a life of its own: cutting, snapping, braiding, knotting. Sometimes she breathed heavily, and her small body, growing thinner, sagged against me. *Death*, I thought, *is in this room*, and I would work harder alongside her. For weeks Grandmama and I did this every other evening, a half-dozen pieces each time. The shaking in her hand grew worse, but we said nothing. Finally, after discarding a hundred, she told me she had the necessary twenty pieces. But this time, because it was a sacred chime, I would not be permitted to help her tie it up or have the joy of raising it.

"Once tied," she said, holding me against my disappointment, "not even I can raise it. Not a sound must it make until I have died."

"What will happen?"

"Your father will then take the centre braided strand and raise it. He will hang it against my bedroom window so that my ghost may see it, and hear it, and return. I must say goodbye to this world properly or wander in this foreign land forever."

"You can take the streetcar!" I blurted, suddenly shocked that she actually meant to leave me. I thought I could hear the clear chromatic chimes, see the shimmering colours on the wall: I fell against her and cried, and there in my crying I knew that she would die. I can still remember the touch of her hand on my head, and the smell of her thick woollen sweater pressed against my face. "I will always be with you, Little Sek-Lung, but in a different way …You'll see."

Weeks went by, and nothing happened. Then one late September evening, Grandmama was preparing supper when she looked out our kitchen window and saw a cat—a long, lean white cat—jump into our garbage pail and knock it over. She ran out to chase it away, shouting curses at it. She did not have her thick sweater on and when she came back into the house, a chill gripped her. She leaned against the door: "That was not a cat," she said, and the odd tone of her voice caused Father to look with alarm at her. "I cannot take back my curses. It is too late." She took hold of Father's arm. "It was all white and had pink eyes like sacred fire."

Father started at this, and they both looked pale. My brothers and sister, clearing the table, froze in their gestures.

"The fog has confused you," Stepmother said. "It was just a cat."

But Grandmama shook her head, for she knew it was a sign. "I will not live forever," she said. "I am prepared."

The next morning she was confined to her bed with a severe cold. Sitting by her, playing with some of my toys, I asked her about the cat: "Why did Father jump when you said the cat was white with pink eyes? He didn't see it, you did."

"But he and Stepmother know what it means."

"What?"

"My friend, the juggler, the magician, was as pale as white jade, and he had pink eyes." I thought she would begin to tell me one of her stories, a tale of enchantment or wondrous adventure, but she only paused to swallow; her eyes glittered, lost in memory. She took my hand, gently opening and closing her fingers over it. "Sek-Lung," she sighed, "*he* has come back to me."

Then Grandmama sank back into her pillow and the embroidered flowers lifted to frame her wrinkled face. She placed her hand over mine, and my own began to tremble. I fell fitfully asleep by her side. When I woke up it was dark and her bed was empty. She had been taken to the basement of St. Paul's Hospital, where the sick Chinese were allowed to stay. I was not permitted to visit her.

A few days after that, Grandmama died of the complications of pneumonia. Immediately after her death, Father came home. He said nothing to us but walked up the stairs to her room, pulled aside the drawn lace curtains of her window, and lifted the wind-chimes to the sky.

I began to cry and quickly put my hand in my pocket for a handkerchief. Instead, caught between my fingers, was the small, round firmness of the jade peony. In my mind's eye I saw Grandmama smile, and heard, softly, the pink centre beat like a beautiful, cramped heart.

TEN

IN September, a month before Grandmama's death, everyone was worried about me. I was desperate to start school again, anxious to prove that I was now grown up like my older brothers, Kiam and Jung. But the school doctor rejected my attempt to get back into the classroom.

"Sek-Lung still has breathing problems," he told Kiam to explain to Father. "I recommend he stay with his home studies and try again next year."

Father gently nodded his head, and First Brother shrugged his shoulders. There was no argument against the science of medicine. My two older brothers and my older sister Liang were instructed to tutor me at home for another year. The school sent Kiam home with a pile of books and mimeographed worksheets to keep me busy.

Grandmama could tell I was deeply disappointed.

"No cry," she said, opening a series of jars filled with sharp-smelling powders and stems. "I make you better. Make your lungs stronger."

"No more herbs!" I protested.

•

Being sent home from school the first time, in Grade One, had been all my fault. Jung had warned me to keep to myself, to mind my own business; and for the most part, Jung's tough-guy reputation protected me from the school bullies. But after the second week of classes, I forgot Jung's warning and cheerfully waved my hand in the air to earn a Good Deed Star from Miss MacKinney for cleaning some blackboard brushes during recess.

On the school steps, I stood proudly in my new short pants and clapped the brushes together in the chopping-board rhythm Stepmother used with her cleavers. There was no wind that day. Chalkdust clouds rose in the air and hung thickly about me. Chalk particles rasped my nose and throat, sent me gasping in wild alarm. Two older girls ran to help me. I began to sneeze. Blood poured out of my left nostril. Worried about staining my new short pants, I bent forward and pinched my nose to stop the bleeding, then very quickly doubled up for lack of oxygen.

"Cripes!" one of the big girls said, looking incredulous. "Breathe through your mouth!"

I did.

The two panicked girls pushed me up the wooden stairs and into the school hallway towards the Main Office. When I tripped, both of them grabbed me by my suspenders and dragged my blood-streaked body into the nurse's office.

Finally, propped against a leather chair, I calmed down enough to gulp down air reeking of iodine. The school nurse put a cold compress on my nose and efficiently wiped the blood off my bare legs. My grey flannel short pants were ruined. She knelt down and made me gargle some blue-tinged, mint-tasting water, but nothing stopped my lung-rattling wheeze. My sister, Liang, was called out of Miss Dafoe's manual training class to take me home to recover. I knew Liang wouldn't mind that much; she hated Miss Dafoe, who taught everyone how to read a ruler by whacking their knuckles if they couldn't point out the quarter-inch mark.

"You're a damn mess," Liang said, pulling me along the street. "I'd better not have to wash you up, too."

Grandmama began boiling up some bitter herbs for me to drink; she held my head back, rubbed my chest with Tiger Balm and made me breathe in a haze of eucalyptus vapours.

Three days later, the Vancouver City Medical Officer visited our home. He undid my shirt and sniffed the air. The Tiger Balm made his nose curl up. He poked about our rooms.

"Is it always this damp?" he asked.

"Only rich not damp," Father said, in the broken English that he used with white authorities.

The doctor checked all of us for TB.

Everyone passed the tests. I didn't have TB but my lungs were tight. I had night fevers.

"Sek-Lung must stay home until he can breathe clearly," the doctor said.

When Grandmama was alive, I told her how desperately I wanted to go to school and be grown up like First and Second Brothers. Kiam and Jung came home and opened impressive books, made handwritten notes using long wooden nibholders to scratch out inky words and formulae. Then they dipped the nibs in a screwtop bottle of Bluebird ink. Sometimes Kiam let me press a sheet of blotting paper over his writing, and hold it in front of the hall mirror to see if I could read the words reflected back.

Liang impressed me with her ability to read rapidly, turning the pages of *Beautiful Joe* and *Little Women* with sudden smiles or tears. Sometimes she read aloud to me, simplifying passages for my benefit. I liked the dog story the best.

Watching them all go to school in the morning, I wanted to be taught my lessons by a real teacher like Miss MacKinney, with her shadow of a moustache and her steel-rimmed glasses, whose class I'd been in for those first two weeks. I liked the way she broke into a smile and her blue eyes lit with laughter when she discovered I could read English words (though I could not pronounce the words exactly right). To her I wasn't any different from the Japanese, Ukrainian, Russian, Jewish and Italian boys and girls in her class.

"Nivver mind, Sek-Lung," Miss MacKinney said. "Ah've an accent as weel."

A year of tutoring me had made my sister and two brothers impatient and touchy. Second Brother Jung pounded the table to get me to spell properly; Sister Liang slammed the Third Reader shut if I asked her to slow down, and First Brother Kiam groaned each time he had to repeat, and repeat, the seven-, eight- and nine-times tables with me. Liang complained that it was unfair that she had all her Chinese School homework, too, because I had only to do English homework. Sometimes Kiam or Jung were cheered by my progress, but I always felt cheated, locked out from the mysteries of Strathcona's monumental red-brick edifice. On warm days, strolling past the long rows of opened windows, I would turn to Grandmama with earnest longing.

"Listen," I told her, "they're singing."

A piano would pick out a lively tune and a chorus of voices followed like a happy army. The broadleaf maples would rustle in the wind. Grandmama and I would sit down on some steps for a few minutes and look at the North Shore mountains, listening to the trees and the music.

Going to school meant a lot to me.

"You go next year," Grandmama promised, even as she was weakening under her eighty-third year. "You get stronger."

"How?"

"We find way."

After Grandmama's funeral at Ocean View Cemetery, I began to look to the ghost of my ancient guardian for help. I knew that Grandmama, though dead and buried in her pine coffin, would never desert me. She would see that I started school next September. I only needed to *see* her, in spirit, to know everything would go well next time. I did not doubt that the Old One had died. I saw Grandmama laid out against the white sheets lining the pine casket, her eyebrows pencilled in, her face waxed. But I did not cry because I knew the Old One would never leave me.

I wandered about the house, absent-mindedly; opened Grandmama's bedroom door and stared hopefully into the silent cluttered room. Her last windchime caught the morning light and barely moved. Stepmother promised to clean out Grandmama's room after the Chinese New Year in February. Sister Liang was to have the room for herself. I resented Stepmother's promise and began a campaign of sulking: how could she give Grandmama's room away? I refused offers to go to the picture show with Third Uncle and ate barely half my bowl of rice at meals. I grew thin and sulked. I had to be pushed to do anything beyond my solitary make-believe war games. Any time I was taken out of the house, I put on a strange, open-mouthed look and whispered openly to Grandmama.

Chinatown people turned away, muttering behind my back. *Poor Sek-Lung...Spent all his seven years with Poh-Poh... He can't get over it.*

Stepmother's *mahjong*-playing lady friends gave her sensible advice, urged her to be patient, and fed me sweetmeats and rare oranges. Father received sympathy from both his political friends and foes. No one wanted to debate China's future with him; no one wanted to deal with a man who had a haunted son. Kiam and Jung periodically rolled their eyes. Sister Liang refused to take me out anywhere her jitterbugging girlfriends might see or hear me.

The truth was, the Old One's ghost was tugging at me and would not let me go.

When she was alive, Grandmama had taught me that spirits and ghosts were everywhere because the Chinese were such an ancient people; so many Chinese people had died that their ten-thousand million ghosts in Old China inhabited "the ways of the Han people." Whether one was a peasant or royalty, Grandmama said, Old China people took it for granted that these ghosts lived constantly alongside them.

They were mischievous spirits and frightening demons, these good and bad ghosts. They could upset, or bring into harmony, the *yin* and *yang* forces—the *fung-suih*, the *wind-water* elements that helped to balance our "hot" and "cold" natures. *Wind-water* shaped our destiny, cured our illnesses, brought good or bad fortune. How else to ensure good fortune? How else to ensure good health and keep away from bad? Wasn't the Old One slowly bringing back my laboured breathing to normal with her mix of ancient herbs and balms? Didn't each mix require an external balance, like wind and water, her fingers massaging the *che* "energy" points located on the bottom of my feet?

"Bad and good ghosts," Grandmama had told me, "know those points, too."

Grandmama also had told me that in Vancouver only a small population of Chinatown ghosts could bother with us, really no more than a hundred or so, and most of these were somewhat confused by not being able to go with their bones back to Old China.

Inevitably, as a reward for my faith, the Old One came back, as she had promised, to help me in my resolve to start school when next September came.

In late January, three months after her burial, things began to happen to me which the family preferred to call "incidents."

The back door would suddenly swing shut by itself, in exactly the way Grandmama (when she was alive) had shut it to prevent chills from creeping up her back.

"It's Grandmama," I insisted.

"The humidity," First Brother Kiam cut in, matter of factly. "Damp weather swells the wood."

"The house is very drafty," Father said. "It's an old house."

"The wind again," Stepmother said, pulling her sweater to her.

"It's both," Second Brother Jung nodded, looking at everyone else but me.

Sister Liang said nothing but stared at me, unsettled and unsure. I sidled up to her and whispered, "Did the door ever shut on its own when Grandmama was living with us?" Liang's eyes widened.

Once, before lunch, I saw the Old One on the staircase, as if waiting for me. She was wearing her favourite blue quilted jacket, one hand on the worn oak bannister. I called out to Second Brother Jung. He ran to my side, stopped, and stared up at the staircase. It was empty, though he was not sure of an indistinct shadow like a veil, flitting away.

ghost

One cloudy afternoon, at precisely 3 P.M. (I can still hear the hall clock chiming), the Old One came back to visit me again. This time when I called out, Stepmother rushed out of the kitchen and stood by my side; she looked up and down the hallway, at nothing.

My actually seeing Grandmama on our staircase and in the hallway became the subject of debate in the family. No one wanted to believe me, though, no one really wanted to doubt me either, for the world of Chinatown was the world of *what if...*

That is, *what if* Mrs. Jong hadn't sensed there was something wrong one day and so decided not to sit in that seat by the exit on the Hastings streetcar, the very seat that a truck minutes later slammed into? *What if* Mr. Chan hadn't dreamt twice of the numbers 2-4-6-9, the very ones that won the numbers lottery? *What if* the Soon family hadn't, each of them, dreamed of their village home burning down; how would they have known to warn the family by cable to get away, three weeks before Japanese bombers actually devastated the empty house?

If visions and good sense didn't combine to make us pay attention, what then was the meaning of anything? Grandmama would have understood perfectly: signs and portents were her lifeblood. She had always said to her friend Mrs. Lim, "You only need to pay attention."

I overheard big Mrs. Lim across the road ask First Brother Kiam, "Have there been any more *incidents*?"

I couldn't hear First Brother's answer, but Mrs. Lim's strong voice shouted back, "Usually these things last for a year or two."

Kiam groaned.

Then one spring day, on a hot dry afternoon, the three front parlour windows mysteriously slammed shut: *Bang! Bang! Bang!*

"It's Grandmama," I announced, and everyone glared at me.

Father quickly "fixed" the front windows: he put a building brick on each of the three narrow window ledges to hold them open when we needed fresh air. Each ungainly brick stood precariously on a thin ledge, waiting to fall.

"Father," Kiam politely warned, "shouldn't you use smaller bricks?"

"Why?" Father shot back. "And have Poh-Poh push them over like feathers?"

mock

Everyone laughed but me. I didn't care.

Father also "fixed" the mysteriously closing back door. Now there was a simple hook and chain to hold it shut, though the chain sometimes rattled as if someone were pushing against the door.

"The wind," Stepmother said softly.

"Definitely," Father said, daring any of us to suggest otherwise.

There was little sympathy for my clinging to the Old One's presence. Father even took me to the herbalist to be examined. The old man found nothing wrong with me, except for my throat, which was a little swollen.

"Why is he wheezing so much?" Father asked.

"Too much damp these days," the herbalist said, as if it were obvious. "Some children breathe like this until they grow up."

I was given an extract of powdered lotus leaf and eucalyptus oil, mixed with a honey base, to coat my throat. When Father asked about my seeing the Old One, the herbalist shrugged.

"Is the boy hurting anyone?"

ELEVEN

WEEKS went by. The family became used to my unabated
faith in the Old One's return.

Stepmother went back to her mending and knitting; Father, to
reading his three Chinese newspapers; Kiam, to turning the pages
of his thick science and math books, and keeping account books
for Third Uncle; Jung, to checking out the *News-Herald* and
Vancouver Sun sports pages to see how the Brown Bomber was
doing. Sister Liang, however, lingered beside me to hear more.
Sometimes she liked to hold the inch-wide jade carving that Poh-
Poh (as Liang called her) had left to me before she was taken to
the hospital. Liang liked to look at its pink centre, run a finger
over the minature carved petals, and remember how Grandmama
had spoken of her friend the travelling juggler and magician.
Liang begged me to tell her everything I knew about Poh-Poh's
first boyfriend. But I decided it was useless to tell her much; she
always wanted to hear the boring parts. For example, she asked if
the magician and Poh-Poh ever really kissed. Because I would
never tell her, we always ended up arguing about where Poh-Poh
had gone after she died. Liang knew how to annoy me.

"Poh-Poh's a-moldering in the grave," Liang taunted, "just like
John Brown's body!" Then she broke into song: *"Poh-Poh's body*

lies a-moldering in the grave—the truth is marching on—"

"Ghosts don't *need* bodies!"

"You don't know anything about the Old One," she said. "Poh-Poh's *dead*! Ask *Dai Goh*!"

Dai Goh—First Brother Kiam—had won a prize in science at King Edward High School. Even Father referred to him for information about the new fire bombs the Japanese were dropping over China's cities, about how they worked, like demon dragons spewing flames for hundreds of feet in every direction. Kiam knew about facts; he would, of course, verify that the Old One was dead. I knew Grandmama was not there in the way you would assume she was there if you were like, say, First Brother Kiam, coming to *scientific* conclusions. Dragon fires were real, measurable, scientific; my seeing and talking to Grandmama were not.

Kiam had never been close to the Old One. He also prided himself on being modern, beyond what he called "all that illogical stuff"; he was learning physics and something called the Atomic Structure. He was first in his math and science classes at King Edward High. But whenever I mentioned seeing Grandmama, as I did at least twice standing by the kitchen stove, twice on the staircase, countless times by doorways, Kiam quickly reiterated the "facts": *She's dead. Buried. Gone.* She was, he patiently explained, disintegrating into basic atoms and molecules. Bits of matter.

"She is so there," I shouted. "I saw her by the back door this morning before breakfast."

"And what were you doing downstairs so early?" Stepmother asked, as she threw some vegetables into the wok. The leaves and stalks sizzled and danced. The kitchen smelled of fresh peanut oil, root ginger, coriander and crushed garlic.

"I heard Grandmama calling me," I said, matter-of-factly. "She wanted me to say—"

I stopped; my heart started to pound.

"Wanted you to say *what*?" Jung said, slamming a bucket of sawdust into the hopper. The kitchen stove sighed as the sawdust slid down the tin sides of the chute.

"Nothing," I said.

Stepmother looked at me with apprehension, but I could say no more.

I knew if I had said, "Grandmama told me, *Old way, best way,*" the family would laugh at me. Father and Kiam had been saying how we must all change, be modern, move forward, throw away the old.

"After all these dirty wars are finished," Father lectured to Third Uncle, "those who understand the new ways will survive."

Third Uncle dragged on his waterpipe as if he could not hear.

Another time, even more mysteriously, the Old One appeared on the staircase landing above me. There, in her favourite blue jacket, she stood and pointed her finger past me, and when I refocussed my eyes, she disappeared. I looked to where she had pointed. There was nothing there but our front door window looking out across the street at Mrs. Lim's tree-shrouded shack.

Mrs. Lim, I knew, liked the old ways, as if she had never left Sun Wui. Mrs. Lim told Mrs. Chang she thought she saw the Old One in the upstairs window looking across at her. When Mrs. Chang, shaking an armful of gold and jade braclets, reported this to Stepmother over the *mahjong* table, Stepmother slammed her cards down.

"Just old-fashioned talk."

None of the ladies around the table said another word. When we got home that evening, Stepmother threw her coat down.

"Don't you dare repeat Mrs. Lim's crazy words about seeing the Old One." Her voice rang with frustration. "Don't you dare mention any of this to your father when he gets home. He has the war in China to worry about."

What no one could accept was this: *Grandmama had never left me.*

By the end of March, Father and Stepmother were pleading with my Chinatown uncles to intervene, to join forces against my madness.

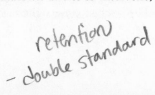

retention
— double standard

"She's shipped out, Sekky," Third Uncle said, bluntly. "Your Poh-Poh's shipped out."

I went on playing with my tin soldiers.

"Gone," said Uncle Dai Kew. "You'll see your Grandmother in Heaven when you get there one day. Just like the Bible tell you so."

I wished I had never gone to church with Uncle Dai Kew. The Bible explained everything to him, even his gambling losses.

I turned away.

One night, when we were in bed, Second Brother Jung was talking to me about the new job Stepmother had managed to get in the woollen factory, about how he himself was trying to get odd jobs at the wharf, how everyone would be working soon because we were poor, how Father and First Brother Kiam worried about the rent.

"Sekky, you have to understand," he warned me, "everyone in the family is caught up with work and school."

Jung went on; he really only wanted to talk to himself. I fell into a trance; my breathing seemed easier, grew stronger. I looked past Jung and suddenly saw the Old One standing at the end of Second Brother's bed.

"Sekky," Jung said, "what the hell are you staring at?"

"Nothing," I said, startled, and caught Grandmama's smile before she vanished. I felt good about seeing Grandmama, felt the oxygen fill my lungs, and went to sleep, smiling. But Jung, I know, sat up in his bed for a long, long time, staring at nothing but moonlight. He was desperate for his own room, never mind the irritation of having to share it with a kid brother who was always seeing a ghost. I could not help it: my heart, my *eyes*, had not lied to me.

After another one of my "incidents," I heard Father swear to Third Uncle that if he could ever raise enough money, the Old One's bones would be dug up and taken to the Bone House in Victoria.

Liang told me about her friend Monkey Man sailing home to

China with a shipment from the Bone House—two thousand pounds of old China men bones from the lumber, fishing and railroad camps. But the war changed a lot of things. Now such back-to-China bone shipments were discouraged. Overseas shipping space was restricted to war munitions and emergency supplies, and to the transport of living men for the purpose of killing other men.

No one in the family really wanted to talk about ghosts, not when they were speaking around me. On the contrary, they insisted only on the facts of life and death.

First Brother Kiam insisted on the Big Fact: Death meant the end of someone's activity on earth. There were no such things as ghosts or demons or spirits. In response, I quoted from Mrs. Williams, who taught at the Methodist Sunday School, about the Holy G-h-o-s-t and how it was everywhere. Everywhere. Like Grandmama. Though naturally Mrs. Williams only understood about Christian ghosts with their pink faces and huge white wings and never mentioned Grandmama in her blue jacket.

"The fact is," Third Uncle said to Father, "you haven't paid your respects properly to your dead mother. You must *bai sen*, you must *bow*. Pay your respects! All this political talk you talk, one world, one citizenship! You forget you Chinese!?!"

Father jumped out of his easy chair and stormed out of the house. When he slammed the door behind him, one of the building bricks on the front window ledge tipped over and fell onto the porch. The window slammed shut, cracking the glass.

Everyone turned to look at me.

Soon after that, Grandmama's room was cleared out and Father asked the family, including Third Uncle and Uncle Dai Kew, to prepare for a final ceremony. Everyone seemed to know what was going on, except me.

Kiam went across the street and came back with Mrs. Lim. The big woman was dressed in a blue silk jacket, the same colour as Grandmama's. Two men came with her. Father said the one with the bald head and long black jacket was a Buddhist monk, an old friend of his who worked on the CPR steamships long before the war in China started. The other man was taller and wore an ill-fitting western suit; he had long oily hair that dangled over his collar. We all walked upstairs into Grandmama's old room.

I stood in the doorway and looked inside, feeling the Old One's presence. The place was empty, except for two large clay bowls. Outside the freshly clean, curtainless windows, I could see the distant line of North Shore mountains like resting lions.

Mrs. Lim took me aside.

"It's time," Mrs. Lim whispered in my ear, "for the family to let the Old One go."

But they had already let her go, I thought.

The tall, long-haired man, Mrs. Lim told me, was a *fung-suih* expert, a geomancer who understood the harmonious flow of wind-water forces.

"If only your Father had asked him for advice about your Grandmother's burial," Mrs. Lim shook her head, "Poh-Poh wouldn't be bothering you now."

The long-haired geomancer looked older than Father. He had narrow eyes and waved his hand in the air and sniffed for emphasis, like the doctor at school who had tapped my chest and told me to take a deep breath. The bald-headed monk bowed to Father; he had a long face and spoke in a clipped dialect unfamiliar to me. The services of the monk and the geomancer were called upon (I was told years later) because of my stubbornness.

The two men put on white gowns over their own clothes; they planted burning incense sticks in the red clay bowls placed at the east and west corners of Grandmama's room. Smoke trailed upward; rhyming whispers rose into the solemn air. The family was now being prepared to surrender Grandmama, as Mrs. Lim told me, to let the Old One go.

The long-haired geomancer and the bald-headed monk, Third Uncle, Mrs. Lim, and even Uncle Dai Kew, encouraged our household to *bai sen* for future prosperity, for good health and long life. To think of the Grand Old One. To pay our respects to

Grandmother. Having done all this, Father felt satisfied and assumed my silliness would stop.

But it didn't.

I saw Grandmama three more times. So did Mrs. Lim, who swore it was no mere shadow drifting between our house and the O'Connors' next door. Liang went pale, said she felt a chill that day, even though it was sunny and hot. Kiam looked sympathetic. Jung said he thought the back door just now shut by itself.

"You forgot to chain it," Father said, looking to Stepmother for support.

Stepmother said nothing. It was no use arguing with the Old One, dead or alive.

I took a deep breath.

"Grandmama wants us to *bai sen* once more," I blurted.

Kiam groaned. Father turned away. But that April afternoon in our parlour Uncle Dai Kew raised his voice.

"What harm could it do?" he argued, putting down his Bible. "You can respect your mother and still be modern."

Uncle Dai Kew turned his Bible to a page showing some women bowing at the feet of Jesus.

"Look here, look at the white people here. Look at them in the church, bowing all the time, and they run electric motors."

Father relented.

"I bring you incense tomorrow," Third Uncle said. "I bring you special wine and paper money to burn. The Old One will never fear poverty in the other place."

"I'll make steamed chicken with black mushrooms," Stepmother said. "That was the Old One's favourite dish."

"I'll ask Mrs. Lim to bring red sauce for good luck," Father said. "Everything should go well."

The next afternoon, Stepmother set up one of the small end tables in the parlour, put down a white cloth, and on it placed dishes of food, a red clay bowl and Grandmama's picture. On each side of the picture, Father hung small banners with black and gold-edged Chinese characters on them. The Buddhist monk came again and bowed before the picture. He lit sticks of incense.

We each took a turn and bowed three times, paying our respects to Grandmama's formal portrait; then, and hereafter, the monk assured Father, it would be all right for everyone to talk directly and loudly to the Old One.

Using a formal dialect, Father greeted her, and burned a sheaf of gold and silver paper money. Flames curled into the air.

Father talked to Grandmama about keeping the family in good fortune and good health. Stepmother bowed and, looking at me, said, "Good health for Sek-Lung…" twice.

"Poh-Poh," said First Brother Kiam, "please see me through my scholarship exams."

Second Brother Jung whispered something, but no one could make out what he said.

"Please let Sekky start school in September," Sister Liang said, and she crisscrossed her fingers for double luck.

It was my turn.

"I'm getting stronger, aren't I, Grandmama?"

I could feel the oxygen in my lungs, the tightness gone; even the burning incense didn't bother me. Grandmama looked sternly back at me.

Stepmother set a plate of fruit before the Old One's picture, bowed three times and said nothing.

To *bai sen* meant atoms and molecules did not count.

"You're looking stronger," Father said.

I knew my improving health had to do with the family talking to Grandmama. Jung said I wasn't snoring or wheezing any more in my sleep. I felt I would never have to gasp for breath again, never feel my chest tighten with fire, nor my head burn with fever.

"See," I said at dinnertime one night, eating an unheard of third bowl of rice, "Grandmama said I would get better."

"Jesus!" Kiam moaned, but nothing could remove the smile on my face. Liang gave me a wild-eyed, monkey-faced look, and slurped up a spoonful of bitter melon soup. Jung shook his head like a boxer waiting for the bell. Father and Stepmother glanced quickly at each other, said nothing, and pushed more steaming rice into their mouths. Grandmama, in her favourite blue-quilted jacket, leaned on her elbow against the kitchen doorway and smiled back at me.

I did not mention this last fact to anyone. There was no need to cause any more incidents.

TWELVE

AFTER the family had decided to respect Grandmama's spirit, to bow three times, burn joss sticks, and pray before the Old One's gilt-framed photograph—that is, to *bai sen*—the Old One no longer haunted us. Now, when I picked up the coin-sized jade peony, remembering how Grandmama used to hold it up to the light and tell me stories, the carved semitranslucent stone was a reminder that she was gone.

A few days later, Father had Kiam hammer in three nails on the parlour wall facing the front windows. In between two elegant scrolls of memorial calligraphy, Father hung up Grandmama's portrait. The front room, however, and her upstairs room, which was now more or less Liang's bedroom, never quite lost the smell of myrrh. Mrs. Lim said the lingering fragrance was a good sign, and Jung said he liked the smell, because the scent reminded him of the Tong Association assembly hall where on special days, rows of incense and thick red candles burned before warrior gods.

A kind of peace settled over our household.

That summer, seven months after Grandmama's death, a long time for a young boy, I flung myself into life without her.

I wanted to grow up fast, to have my chance to fly a teeth-baring Fighting Tiger over the skies of China, to storm over Europe and bomb and strafe as many of the enemy as possible, to mow down as many Nazis and Japanese as my older brothers and their grown-up pals vowed to kill.

I imagined Stepmother and Father, even Liang, and brothers Kiam and Jung, standing at the Vancouver docks to wave me off while a military band with trumpets and drums and bagpipes played on and on. And I, handsome in my military uniform, would promise to stay healthy and never wheeze again.

That year, 1941, I had my first outdoor summer, with my two older brothers packing me off to soccer games and football practice, encouraging me to be as physical and as robust as they were.

All that summer, whenever he had time off from his work at Third Uncle's warehouse, Kiam had me chasing and kicking soccer balls on the school grounds, sometimes goodnaturedly laughing at my awkwardness. Jung took me to the Hastings Gym, where he and his pals taught me how to put up my fists to defend myself.

All the foot-stomping, jumping, pushing and shoving I had been forbidden to do because I would choke and wheeze, all the pent-up physical energies inside my bony frame, suddenly exploded. I was a new boy.

When my two brothers were working, or when they were too busy to bother with me, I hitched up with a half-dozen or so bloodthirsty boys—boastful eight-, nine- and know-it-all ten-year-old comrades. We were constantly bending down our shorn heads in a football huddle to plot out endless movie-inspired war games.

We were, of course, all "good guys" fighting the dirty Nazis and Japanese. We broke into threes and fours and soared into snarling, arm-stretching, attack-and-dive flight patterns, loudly dropping brick and concrete bombs down the grassy slopes of MacLean Park. We roared through clouds of playground dust in oversized shipping cartons devised by Joe Eng to look like Sherman tanks, setting cardboard towns and cities on fire with stolen matches. We slammed together ear-crunching, dented garbage-can lids, and cheerfully yelped ourselves dry with the cheap thrill of murderous victories as we sent smaller children scrambling and screaming out of the range of our howling gunsights. And one late afternoon Alfred Stevorsky, the oldest of all of us, jumped over a garbage pile and plucked out a discarded bakelite doll the size of a real baby. He sat it up against a pile of bricks.

"Watch this," he snarled.

He poured out some liquid from a small paint can, took out a match from his shirt pocket, and set the half-dressed doll on fire.

We all watched with fascinated horror as the baby-sized head began to melt. Its rose-coloured cupid mouth twisted into a wide gaping grimace. Its two large glassy eyes burst from their wired sockets and, slowly, one after another, drooled down the distorting flaming cheeks.

"That's what real bombs do," one of the Han boys said. "That's what my Uncle Bing told me."

Alfred Stevorsky unbuttoned his fly and pulled out his show-off cock. A long stream of urine splashed over the mess.

The enemy was everywhere. The *Vancouver Sun* newspaper said so. Newsreels said so. Hollywood and British movies said so. All of Chinatown said so, out loud.

On June 20, 1941, at 10:15 P.M., shelling from a Japanese submarine hit Estevan Point on Vancouver Island; then, a day later, shells hit the Oregon coast. An unidentified submarine was spotted in the Strait. It's true, I thought. The enemy is everywhere.

Every household along the West Coast was ordered by the government to hang thick blackout cloth over each window. Air raid sirens screamed practice warnings and frightened birds flew into the air. On certain clear days at noon, foghorns and sirens tested Warning and All-Clear patterns. Kiam and Father agreed with the series of editorials in the *Sun*: the Japanese along the coast were potential spies and traitors. Letters in the newspapers demanded that something be done with the "infiltrating treacherous" Japanese in B.C. Gangs of older, jobless boys roamed back streets hunting for Japanese. Fights broke out. There were knifings on some streets, and on Fourth Avenue and Alberta, a Japanese boy, trying to protect his mother, was shot dead. Stepmother told Father to write something about that, to protest the killing.

"They're killing Chinese boys in China," Father said, in Stepmother's dialect. "I lost three cousins, the youngest seven years old. You lost your Mission Church friend when they bombed Canton. What the hell am I supposed to write about?"

Our war games went on unabated, fed by movies, spy comics, drum-beating parades, trading cards, fund-raising drives, recruiting posters and war toys of every kind. I had a dozen tin American pursuit bombers and British fighter planes. I remember how pleased I was to trade away an early Curtiss B-24 and a chipped-wing Hurricane (it had a broken tail as well) for three chunky Sherman tanks for much-needed ground support.

The gang treasured bits and pieces of army and navy surplus military clothing salvaged from the First War. Alfred Stevorsky had the best outfit. His older brother gave him a patched-up U.S. Army coat, with what the brother swore was a real bullet hole in the left arm, and Alfred's mother opened up a trunk and gave him an RAF captain's hat with a stiff brim. Some of us, like the Han boys, got our stuff from second-hand clothing stores along Hastings Street. I had Father buy me from the Army and Navy Store's clear-out sale a British-made leather aviator's cap, with its genuine cracked flight goggles and authentic earflaps and a mysterious number inked inside the right flap. The world was full of secrets.

When September came, the school doctor put his cold stethoscope on my chest and pronounced the slight wheezing to be some kind of allergy. I nervously passed the rest of the medical exam;

[margin handwriting: "violent war games? again a violent our conversation?"]

then I confidently completed a six-page English reading test, matching cartoon pictures with English words, wrote a paragraph of my choice, passed everything—and was allowed to start at Strathcona in Advanced Grade Three. I was joyful: it would be as if I had not missed a single day of school.

Grandmama had kept her promise. No longer would those towering red-bricked Strathcona School buildings along Pender and Keefer Streets be a mystery to me: I was starting school in five days. Kiam and Jung gave me some new pencils and three blank exercise books. Even Liang gave me things: a stick-pen holder with an unlicked nib and a large ink eraser she hardly ever used. Stepmother stitched a brown corduroy carrying case for me. Father showed me a new Waterman fountain pen he said would be mine as soon as I learned to write properly.

I might even start Chinese School.

Advanced Grade Three at Strathcona was a class for immigrant kids who knew too little English, or who could understand English but not read or speak it well, or who for whatever reason were starting late and needed extra attention, like me.

Jung had taught me to use my fists, so I even-stevened in two recess fights and lost one. It was worth it; I learned to spit blood, just like the elders spit out tobacco. I didn't really enjoy the fights, but I enjoyed the attention. Except for a few scrapes, plus a few name-calling sessions during the first two weeks of recesses—*Sick-kee Sekkk-kee!*—everything was going A-okay.

In Miss E. Doyle's classroom, at least, there was no name-calling; in class, no pushing, no kicking. Not even whispering. Her commands were simple, and simply barked: "Sit." "Eyes front." "Feet flat on the floor." And all the boys and girls obeyed.

"I am the General of this class," she said, looking particularly at a front row of tall boys whom she had placed there on purpose, including my friends Alfred Stevorsky and Joe Eng.

Big Miss Doyle waved a steel-edged ruler just like the one my

Grade One teacher, Miss MacKinney, had waved. With her large palms, Miss Doyle brushed the stiff lapels of her brass-buttoned tartan jacket.

"All of you are my soldiers, and some of you, like Joseph Piscatella here, need more English before you are finally marched out of my care. Some of you need pro-nun-ci-a-tion lessons."

She looked at the tall boy in the front row.

"I can tell your *spoken* English is much improved this year, Joseph."

Miss Doyle looked around and nodded at one or two familiar faces. She noticed my aviator's cap folded neatly on my lap.

"Next time, Sek-Lung," she said, "that stays in the cloakroom."

"The boys at recess called him Sekky, Miss Doyle." A red-haired girl with braces on her legs smiled at the teacher.

"Thank you, Darlene," Miss Doyle smiled back, "but you remember from last year how you should raise your hand and wait for permission before speaking out in class."

"Yes, Miss Doyle."

After the daily roll call, rain or shine, warm or cold, Miss Doyle assigned one of the bigger boys, like Joseph, to pry open a window. She asked for other volunteers to water the row of flower pots she carefully seeded at the beginning of every school term. The seeding was part of her nature lesson. At the end of June, the best students were awarded plants bursting with blooms.

"Perhaps, Sek-Lung," Miss Doyle said, looking directly at me, "you might like to help Darlene with the watering jug on Mondays."

"Yes, Miss Doyle."

Joe Eng snickered.

"—and Joe Eng will help on Thursdays and dust the windows as well...yes, Joe?"

"Yes, Miss Doyle."

No one snickered.

In Miss Doyle's class, we sat with our backs straight "like soldiers," with our hands folded in front of us. Our hands sat pressed against a book opened to the correct page, its number chalked on the blackboard; and our feet, for Miss Doyle's inspection, were to be flat as an iron against the floor.

Miss Doyle, with her loud gravel voice, was the guardian of our education. With hawk-eyed precision, she reined in her Third Graders with a kind of compassionate terror, blasting out a delinquent's full name as if she were God's avenging horn: each vowel of any name, however multisyllabled, whether it was Japanese, East Asian or Eastern European, Italian or Chinese, was enunciated; each vowel cracked with the clarity of thunder. She walked so heavily that the floor boards squeaked with stress. And if you pleased her, she would seem to be amused, and sharply pulled her opened red jacket tightly about her thick body so that her large breasts poked up. Alfred Stevorsky always liked that. *Alfred = S's*

Frank

Most of us, like Darlene or Joseph, liked to please Miss Doyle, but she was, like a mother, easier to annoy than please and, like a father, careful to display authority, in her case, the strap hanging next to the large Neilson Chocolate Map of the World at the front of the classroom. She used the leather strap to point out the latest battles in the British Empire—which was all the red colour on the map—or the battle in England itself.

Each afternoon, we waited with excitement for Miss Doyle's descriptions of the day's battles and victories. No matter how small the conflicts or how great the number of casualties, Miss Doyle rarely talked of people killing each other, but always mentioned "rescue" and "courage" and "kindness."

She also regularly read aloud letters from her brother, whose name she enuciated clearly for us: "John Wil-lard Hen-ry Doyle." He was a fire marshal for his district of St. Martin's, London.

"A fire marshal," the General said, "is someone assigned to take charge of putting out fires caused by the bombing. But his main job, boys and girls, is to save lives, not buildings."

She repeated her only and older brother's full name so that we would not think, she said, that our own variety of names was any more unusual.

G
bravery

"A name is a name," Miss Doyle emphasized. "Always be brave enough to be proud of yours."

Bravery was a central theme in her class. I saw her brother in a fireman's outfit climbing ladders and walking through flames.

In his world, bombs fell night and day, injured people were pulled out from under collapsed buildings, children were hurt but brave. Miss Doyle kept her brother's picture in a small silver frame on her desk. He looked very young in the picture, very tall, and the small girl beside him, looking up at John Willard Henry's big smile, was Miss Doyle herself.

Miss Doyle read us sections of her brother's vivid letters, which thrilled us all.

I remember listening to how the smoke rose in furious clouds over a place called *Pick-a-dill-lee* Square; how in a place called Kensington Gardens, a statue of a boy named Peter Pan was not disturbed even an inch by the concussion bombs. There were ghastly smells coming from burning factories and houses, the awful weight of collapsed walls and twisted steel girders, the cries and screams from the mysterious dust-choking darkness beneath trembling beams. There was rescue and valour, and unending hope for the nightmare to end. "We will never surrender," John Willard Henry wrote, quoting a man named Churchill, who, Miss Doyle emphasized, was a loyal friend of the King and Queen.

"When I was a little girl," Miss Doyle said to the class, "my brother John used to read the story of Peter Pan to me. It is a book written by whom, Darlene?"

"Mr. J. M. Barrie."

The letters inspired everyone in the class to believe in "the just cause" and bravery. We saved our pennies to help our families buy more war bonds. One day, when John Doyle noted that the bombs were coming closer and closer to St. Martin's, I noticed the red-haired Darlene dropping her head to her desk, as if she were afraid. And Joe Piscatella tensely bit his bottom lip, following every word of the brave John Doyle.

"Adventurous times, my dear Tinker," he wrote in one letter,

using a pet name for Miss Doyle, *"but we'll pull through."*

At night, in bed, I prayed to Grandmama to keep John Willard Henry safe from the bombs. Some nights I dreamed of a tall man wearing a fireman's hat, standing with the Old One, safely. I would learn to be as brave as Miss Doyle's wonderful brother. Sometimes the gang would play rescue war games, but it never seemed as much fun as sky diving, blowing apart cities and torpedoing ships.

We pleased Miss Doyle when we were brave; that is, when we raised our hands to answer her questions, or ventured to speak aloud. Most of us knew the humiliation and the mockery—"Me wan'nee fly lice! Lot-see lice!"—the tittering, brought on by our immigrant accents. On streetcars and in shops where only English was spoken, people ignored you or pretended they didn't hear you or, worse, shouted back, "WHAT? WHAT'S THAT YOU SAY? CAN'T YOU SPEAK ENGLISH!?!"

Miss Doyle never ignored us, never tittered; she stood strictly at attention as if to compliment our valiant efforts when we spoke or read out loud, daring anyone to mock us.

We were brave, she said, just as the King and Queen, their framed portraits hanging separately above us, encouraged us to be. Miss Doyle pinned up on the cork board by the back cloakroom a newspaper picture of King George and his Queen talking to a group of British people; they were all standing in front of a bombed-out building as if it were an ordinary day for a chat.

"Their Majesties always enunciate perfectly," Miss Doyle informed us, loudly.

Day after day, we absorbed her enunciated syllables, the syllables of a King and Queen. Without our fully realizing what was happening, our English vocabulary multiplied and blossomed. When I prayed to Grandmama, asking her again and again to help Miss Doyle's brother, the fire marshal, I prayed more and more with English words, pronounced perfectly. Grandmama, in the other world, somehow could understand all languages.

Though every girl and boy found out quickly enough what

irritated the General, no one was ever certain what, besides bravery, would really specifically please her.

There weren't that many chances for anyone living in Canada to be truly brave. Murderous bombs were not falling down on Vancouver as they were in London, though they fell down every day in Miss Doyle's brother's succinct, suspense-filled stories about rescue and valour.

Reading aloud from those three-folded onionskin pages, Miss Doyle told us about the darkest days of the Battle of Britain in the gentle light of her brother's rescue stories. As she carefully folded each letter and returned it to its heavily stamped envelope, we could feel our backs stiffen with courage.

One of her brother's rescue stories was so exciting that I told it to Jung. There were struggling baby noises coming from a dark bombed-out section of a hospital building, and John Willard Henry's team of five men and a woman named Grace risked everything to reach the trapped child. When Grace poked her hand through a small cleared-out space to reach for the whimpering infant, the woman screamed, jumped back. The child was covered with hair. Finally, John Willard Henry reached in and pulled out a small frightened terrier.

"*I have the nipped finger to prove it,*" he wrote. "*Damn odd business, this risking your life for a puppy!*"

Miss Doyle even said the word *damn,* just like her brother wrote it.

Jung laughed, then waited until I finished laughing, too.

"Want to know something?" he asked me, carefully.

I nodded *yes,* thinking that he was going to tell me that story was probably made up, but I was ready to let him know that it was all in a real handwritten letter sent from England.

"You don't know, do you, Sekky?"

"Know what?"

"Last Christmas—Miss Doyle's brother—blown to bits."

My mouth dropped open. I refused to believe Jung, who years ago had been in Miss Doyle's class and hated her because she strapped him for pulling the fire alarm.

"Everyone knows he's dead, Sekky," Jung persisted. "His picture was in the *Sun*. Ask Kiam."

I dared not ask Kiam, nor did I ask anybody in the class, not even Alfred Stevorsky or Joe Eng. After all, if John Willard Henry was really dead, why didn't someone in the class say so? Why didn't Miss Doyle say so?

bravery?

Tormented all week, I did not even say a prayer to the Old One. No one knew I still talked to her. Grandmama should have warned me. *this picture of bravery is dead*

I waited after school to ask Miss Doyle about her brother. She had just put another of his airmail letters away and dismissed the class. We could hear Mr. Barclay's class next door stampeding out like cattle, but everyone in Miss Doyle's class left in the usual orderly fashion. Miss Doyle was busy cleaning off the blackboard.

I could hear Darlene's braces clunking away.

"Sekky," Miss Doyle said, turning around. "You're still here."

"Miss Doyle," I began, "was Mr. Doyle blown to bits?"

She looked puzzled, then her eyes glazed over. Her face registered shock, betrayal.

I wanted to get out of the room. I abruptly turned and rushed to the cloakroom to get my jacket and hat.

"Sek-Lung," Miss Doyle thundered my name, "come here."

With my coat and hat in my hand, I walked slowly back to her. She had used me, tricked me, made me care for someone, made me pray for the safety of someone who was already dead.

Miss Doyle gave me a wide-eyed YOU'D BETTER PAY ATTENTION look.

"That first day," Miss Doyle began, speaking to me as if I had forgotten to help Darlene with the water jug, "that day when I started to read my brother's letters, you must *remember* that I... *oh, my God*..." she took my hand. "You were away that day."

It was true. I had been away from her class one afternoon.

"Oh, Sekky, you went to the nurse's office!" Miss Doyle's voice suddenly went soft, as if she were once again the little girl in the picture, "I did. I told the class of John's death. Yes… he is… dead …" And then Miss Doyle used Jung's words, my words, a child's words, in a whisper I could barely make out, "…*blown to bits.*"

In uneasy silence, I let Miss Doyle lift my arms and push them through my jacket; I let her half guide me to the front of the room. Passing her desk, however, I pushed against her and stopped to study the picture in the small silver frame.

In the picture, I could see how brightly the little girl's blonde hair shone; her smiling face said, *Nothing in the world can ever go wrong.*

I took my pilot's cap from her hand and walked out the door. I knew I still liked Miss E. Doyle.

Miss E. Doyle made it a rule never to tolerate interruptions or careless behaviour in her class.

Not only did she prefer to stand at attention for most of the time she spent with us, she expected every boy and girl in her class to adopt her military bearing, her exact sense of decorum.

We were an unruly, untidy mixed bunch of immigrants and displaced persons, legal or otherwise, and it was her duty to take our varying fears and insecurities and mold us into some ideal collective functioning together as a a military unit with one purpose: to conquer the King's English, to belong at last to a country that she envisioned including all of us.

After morning prayer, in a carefully modulated stage whisper, Miss Doyle told us to open our eyes and keep our bowed heads before her, then "carefully and quietly" to put our fingers under our desktop ledges and lift. A single whoosh sound filled the room as the tops of desks moved upward, like so many wings. Books and pencil boxes came clattering out, and desktops fell back down. We were now to remember to keep our feet flat on the floor.

When we were all ready, she would say, "Excellent." That was the signal to be "at ease."

In training us, she never hesitated to use her desk ruler repeatedly on our burning backsides, nor was she slow to engage the leather strap on our stinging bare hands. And few of our poverty-raised, war-weary parents or guardians expected a teacher, male or female, to do any less.

Once, from the back of the room in the unnatural silence that was the miracle of her careful training of her troops, we heard a delinquent pencil box crash to the hardwood floor like a bomb.

We all turned to look: on the floor, in the middle of the back aisle, sat an absurdly large *Grand Dutch Coronas* cigar box the size of Miss Doyle's Holy Bible. The lid was held tightly shut by thick-knotted yellow twine.

Some of us stared straight at the leather strap hanging on the wall, afraid even to blink. Some of us turned to see Tammy Okada in a grubby flowery dress, pale with fear, her dirty knees shaking.

Tammy Okada, of mixed parentage, had tightly braided brownish pigtails and wore obvious hand-me-downs; her English was terrible. None of the girls wanted to play with her, not even those who were more or less her own kind, the Japanese girls. Tammy Okada was a stupid girl, thick-waisted from a poor diet, not much blessed with looks. She always had to borrow someone else's pencils because she could never untie her own twine-knotted box. Yet she was too proud to let anyone help her undo the twine.

For some reason, Miss Doyle had never forced Tammy to open her pencil box; instead she always commanded one of the other students to lend Tammy a ruler or an eraser or whatever. And now the cigar box had slipped off her desktop and banged onto the floor.

The eagle-eyed General could see right away whose stupid makeshift pencil box it was.

Miss Doyle walked straight up the aisle, bent down and snatched up the cigar box. The box immediately broadcast a rolling noise, as if it held no more than a tiny solitary item: a single steel marble, perhaps, or maybe a small round ball of foil, rolling inside...round, round, round. We could all hear the loud rolling hiss coming from the box as it was held in mid-air, frozen in Miss Doyle's surprised grip. Now everyone knew: a box almost ten inches square and three inches high, and it was practically empty!

Empty! This absurd discovery caused three or four of the girls in the class to trade smirks across the aisles. Florence Chan giggled. Elizabeth Brown threw her head back. Alfred Stevorsky snorted. Joe Eng started to guffaw, but thought better of it when the General's blonde head did not move. The classroom grew still, waiting, watching. Tammy Okada instinctively held her hands over her scalp as if she expected Miss Doyle, her grey eyes glistening, to take the box and break it over her head.

For a long, long moment, the big woman did nothing. Miss Doyle's stillness also warned the rest of us that her uncanny radar was *O-N.* The slightest hint of another giggle or snort, or even a misplaced sigh, would mean the strap. We held our breath.

The General loudly cleared her throat: *Ahem!*

In three seconds, like disciplined soldiers, we sat up, hands folded, feet flat on the floor, eyes front, staring at the Map of the World. Still, I couldn't resist turning my head a little, straining the corner of my eyes to sneak a look: General Doyle, unsmiling, still held the knotted box in her enormous grip. She focussed her steel-cold eyes on Tammy Okada.

"Take out your books and put them in a pile," she said to Tammy, each word clear and sharp as a warning bell. She stood silently watching, as the brownish-haired girl, eyes edged with tears, dropped her shaking hands and nervously emptied her desk.

Miss Doyle put her hand out, gripped Tammy's shoulder, walked up the aisle and stopped before the one remaining empty front seat.

"*Here*, Tammy Okada," Miss Doyle carefully enunciated each syllable, "you will be able to pay much better attention, *yes?*"

From my seat in the middle of the room, I could see Tammy Okada's braided pigtails visibly trembling.

"You will become my best student, *yes?*"

Tammy Okada's back, in spite of herself, seemed to straighten a little.

"Sit."

Miss Doyle walked away with Tammy's cigar box still clutched in her hand. We figured this was the last anyone would ever see of that pathetic dirty box. We all waited to see if Miss Doyle would throw it into her desk drawer of confiscated stuff, or if she would toss it into the wastepaper basket; after which, she would slowly dust off her big hands and walk over to the hanging strap.

I thought Tammy Okada must feel like a leaky submarine. I was feeling a little sorry for her when Miss Doyle walked past the wastepaper basket and strode directly to the front of her own cabinet-style desk. She reached down into a bottom drawer out of everyone's sight. There were snipping noises. Miss Doyle threw away cut pieces of knotted twine and rummaged noisily, but we could not see what she was doing. Then we heard the smart *Snap! Snap!* of elastic bands.

Still unsmiling, Miss Doyle walked back to Tammy Okada's front row seat and placed the big cigar box on the desktop. The whole class could hear a weighty load of contents shifting and rattling with what every boy and girl suddenly knew to be the best possible pencil-box paraphernalia anyone could ever dream of owning: stuff from the General's own hidden cave of seized treasures.

I imagined the years and years of confiscated collectibles— coloured pencils of every hue and length, mechanical pencils, pen nibs, holders, crayons, jacks, pencil sharpeners, paper cutouts, elastics, marbles, stencils, erasers, fold-away rulers, Crackerjack miniatures, maybe even a *compass*—all poured into that single box. Tammy Okada, unbelieving, ran a shy finger over the crisscrossed rubber bands.

"Tammy Okada," Miss Doyle's crisp enunciation did not falter, "your pencil box, *yes?*"

"Yes," Tammy said, in a voice so soft we barely heard it.

"*Jeez,*" Elizabeth Brown breathed.

The rest of us sighed.

Miss Doyle picked up a chalk, tapped the blackboard for attention and began to teach us how to use the letter *S* to show possession. The General printed in big letters: *Alfred's book...Sekky's cap ...Tammy's pencil box...*

"You're all paying attention, *yes?*"

"*Yes*, Miss Doyle," we sang in unison, like soldiers.

We had learned to answer the General's tone-dipping *Yes?* or deeper *No?* with "*Yes*, Miss Doyle" or "*No*, Miss Doyle."

Jung, who had been in Miss Doyle's class many years ago, advised me not to raise my hand to answer a single question, not even if I knew the answer.

"It'll work in your favour if the General hollers your name and you surprise her with the answer."

Then up would go her ample breasts.

The girls in the class grew to admire Miss Doyle and would hold themselves high like her, chin back, sweater buttoned to the absolute top. The oldest boy, aged twelve, just arrived from Poland, would widen his eyes at Miss Doyle. "Denny"—his real name was too easy to make fun of and too hard to pronounce—liked to please Miss Doyle, too, though he, like Tammy Okada, only fitfully spoke half a dozen English phrases. Miss Doyle strapped him once, and at recess he muttered, "I kill that bitch... I kill!" But by the next day, Denny only wanted to copy a straight line of words, neatly spaced and correctly spelled, line after tidy line. Like the rest of us, he wanted to earn the General's gold star stuck on the top of the page.

At recess, our dialects and accents conflicted, our clothes, heights and handicaps betrayed us, our skin colours and backgrounds clashed, but inside Miss E. Doyle's tightly disciplined kingdom we were all—lions or lambs—equals.

We had glimpsed Paradise.

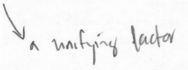

THIRTEEN

AFTER surviving those first few weeks into September, I was like the other Advanced Grade Three kids, wanting to please Miss Doyle. And yet, when her staunch authority focussed on me, I suddenly wanted to be forgotten, left alone, ignored.

"Sekky, you are playing with—*what?*"

Against her thundering authority there was no appeal. For example, if an innocent boy went home and complained Miss Doyle had unfairly seized his favourite tin fighter plane, which happened to slip out of his pocket during Silent Reading, that boy would get a worse strapping at home. It was a hard life. I missed my freedom.

After school, every day, I tried my best to maintain my membership in Alfred Stevorsky's defiance-loving, war-battling gang. I rushed through my homework in front of Father or Stepmother when either was around, and escaped outside as soon as I finished.

Father, Stepmother, brothers Kiam and Jung, and even sister Liang, were all working wherever and whenever they could. Our household was constantly short of money. My older siblings also went to Chinese School.

I played.

I was, after all, supposed to be too weak for doing any kind of real work and, of course, too young to do anything that others would take seriously. I wasn't allowed to go to Chinese School either—"Too much stress for the boy," the Strathcona School doctor had told Father.

"Let the boy play," Dr. Palmer said to Father, who heard the word "play" and thought how foolish to waste away those hours.

Though he knew better, Father saw each of his three sons as Confucian scholars, as if his B.C.-Chinatown boys could reflect the Old China he himself remembered as a child. There, in Sun Wu village in the county of the Four Districts, if a boy was not too poor, after his labours in the family shop or after his toils on some ancestral field, he looked forward to an encounter with reading and writing. Settling into a creaking chair with brush in hand, he sensibly studied the *Sam zi jing*, the *Three Character Classic*. At least that was what the elders told the Chinatown sons. In Old China, no scholarly child actually played after age six. He put away childish things, found in learning his recreation and inspiration.

"In China," Third Uncle told me, "there was a poor boy who caught a hundred fireflies and kept them in a jar. Know why?"

I waited for a story as wonderful as Grandmama used to tell me.

"So he could have enough light to study at night."

I thought it would be fun to catch the flies, but too much of a strain to read at night.

"Nighttime is for dreaming," I remembered the Old One used to say, "for signs to appear."

Besides, such a boy I was not. Here I was, almost eight years old, playing. Playing until I was too tired even to dream. The gang and I became neighbourhood terrors.

I not only shouted words I learned from play-boxing with Jung's friends at the gym, but words like *chink, nigger, bohunk, wop, jap* and *hymie* quickly infiltrated my playground vocabulary. I knew enough not to say those special words in front of bigger boys, and never in front of an adult, but they somehow were overheard by neighbours and reported to Father and Kiam. Though Jung said "I don't give a shit," Liang pretended to be constantly outraged about my reckless phrases, especially about the expressions that described girl-parts and dog-parts. She always looked like she was going to faint but still managed to tell Father what I said.

One day, I got bored.

Alfred Stevorsky and the other boys had gone to sneak into a three-ring Barnum circus at Exhibition Park, but First Brother Kiam wouldn't give me the few pennies for the Hastings streetcar to get there and back. Kiam was not as much fun as he had been in the summer; nowadays, he worried about the war, his school projects, his work at the warehouse, or his girlfriend, Jenny Chong. He told me not to wander too far away.

I took my cardboard carton of war toys and stepped outside the house.

From our porch, I noticed a jumbled row of bundled *Sun* and *Province* newspapers on our sidewalk, stacked along with other stuff to be recycled for the war effort, all waiting for the pickup truck. I could see the two- and three-foot-high paper stacks standing in for the haphazard mountains surrounding the Burma Road. The Japanese were attacking. I took out my favourite Curtiss P-40 Warhawk with the Flying Tiger teeth painted on both sides of its nose. First Pilot Sek-Lung was going to drop some bombs over the Burma Road. I snapped on my leather pilot's cap.

The "bombing" was a neat game Alfred Stevorsky had invented with matches he borrowed from his house. First, you slightly dampened two matchheads with your tongue, just *barely* damp. Then you struck the thick, sulphurous head of one matchstick with the head of the other; and as one dampened match started to sizzle and smoke, you snapped it into the air with your middle finger. The "bomb" would quickly shoot skyward and then spiral downward, trailing circles of white smoke, before it burst into flame. If you timed things right, the "bomb" burst white-hot exactly as it "hit," like the kind of smoke-and-fire incendiary bombs all of us saw in the newsreels. One afternoon, the gang pooled our pennies together and brought seven large boxes of matches to practise on in the alleyway. I got pretty good at it.

With the matches I "borrowed" from a distracted Kiam, buried in his schoolbooks and Canadian army recruiting pamphlets, I strolled off our porch and stood over the curbside piles of newspapers and snapped away. I meant only to create smoke and sizzle, not flames.

I got each match to spiral down in a trail of smoke and sizzle out perfectly, just singeing the tops of the bundled newspapers. I flew over the whole mountain range, striking pairs of damp matchheads together, one expertly after another. With each one, I caught my breath, pursed my lips, and made the roaring sound of a diving fighter plane. Then, while I was busy bombing to death thousands of Japanese troops, out of nowhere descended Mr. O'Connor, swearing a blue streak, with a full bucket of water to douse the pile of papers burning wildly five stacks behind me.

It was the best bombing run I had ever seen, just as I had day-dreamed. I wished all the boys could see this: hot white smoke and fire like molten gold swirled upward; waltzing grey ashes, like flak, suddenly enveloped my Warhawk. The sooty air burned my nostrils.

Even Mr. O'Connor's endless choice of colourful phrases added immeasurably to the effect.

But after no more than three or four minutes, there was only the choking smoke and the sound of dripping water, and through the afternoon haze, Mr. O'Connor looking dampish in his wet trousers, his grey eyes like Miss Doyle's looking piercingly at my bomber.

When Father and Liang came home, Father was not happy at all with the blackened sodden mess in front of our house. If you ask me, Mr. O'Connor did not have to use so much water, as I quietly explained to Father.

An hour later, Stepmother came home and Father gave her that look that said *something happened*. Father had Kiam take me upstairs to await my fate. Then Kiam left for his date with Jenny Chong.

"Tough luck, kiddo," he said, and shut the door tightly behind him. I could hear him dancing down the stairs, exchanging some words with Father, then leaving the house.

Upstairs in the bedroom I shared with Second Brother Jung, I could hear my parents' voices against the clatter of dishes and the sound of my sister's sudden laughter. Then I heard Jung come home, and minutes later, I heard him say, "Holy shit!" And there was more yelling. I spilled out my box of military toys and set up a war game with some soldiers and tanks. Jung knocked on the half-open door and came in.

"You're grounded," he said. "Father says you're going to have to stay at Mrs. Lim's house any time no one is home with you, if she'll have you."

Mrs. Lim, who lived across the street, used to speak three or four shared dialects with Grandmama when the Old One was alive. Together, they always talked about Old China and Old China ways and traded Chinatown secrets. They also exchanged herbal remedies: Grandmama knew all about the *che* power, the *essence*, of roots and herbs, of crawling and swimming things; and Mrs. Lim knew all about the leaves and the healing parts of large animal organs.

Mrs. Lim habitually wore black, as if she still lived in the peasant world of Old China. Every time she came over to visit us, Mrs. Lim and Grandmama talked about how I should be raised in the old ways, the best ways, how I needed to address my elders properly and remember how to speak their names in the right way. She compared me to her daughter, Meiying, when the girl had been given to her years ago at the age of eight.

"Nearly same age as you now, Sek-Lung" Mrs. Lim would say.

"Meiying learn everything very fast."

Some days, from our porch, we could hear Mrs. Lim yell at her adopted daughter, yell at the neighbours, yell at us boys if we played too loudly, yell at anyone who crossed her path. But mainly she yelled at her daughter.

Meiying never protested. Perhaps she knew that her own mother had not wanted her. Meiying's mother, an actress once, and a gambler, so the talk went, did not know who of the many bachelor-men whose bed and food she shared was the father. Coming home with the day's groceries one afternoon, Mrs. Lim met up with Meiying's mother in front of the Fast Service Laundry.

"Take this bitch-girl from me," she said drunkenly to Mrs. Lim, pushing her thin eight-year-old away.

Mrs. Lim took Meiying home, and people said Meiying's mother disappeared with a man who took her to Toronto. She left her daughter some clothes, a couple of silk shawls and pieces of Chinese Opera costumes, and a small Chinese Opera doll with an exquisite white-painted head. The doll was styled and dressed as a princely scholar. Mrs. Chang said it was a doll given to Meiying's mother by the Canton Opera Company when she left China. A fortune-teller told her the doll was her future husband, who would be a handsome man living in a royal household and who would always be studying a foreign language. "Wouldn't you know it," Mrs. Chang laughed, as she told the story to the *mahjong* ladies, "Mabel finds a man who studies the racing form every day and lives in Toronto on King Street! Oh, so royal! Such a scholar! Well, Tommy Fong's certainly handsome, even when he gets as drunk as Mabel."

Meiying turned out to be a blessing for Mrs. Lim; she had a quick mind, shed few tears, and went gratefully from her own mother's drunken chaos into the widow's firm Old China ways. Grandmama repeated Meiying's mother's story many times to my sister, Liang. Liang always said, "We're in Canada, not Old China."

"We in Chinatown," Grandmama said. "Things different here."

Mrs. Lim and Grandmama would both shake their heads with frustration at my sister's stone ear: *"Aiyahh, ho git-sum!" Aiyahh*, they exclaimed, *how life cramped one's heart!*

Liang wondered how the beautiful Meiying, with her long hair and perfect set of grades in Chinese and English school, could tolerate living even one minute in Mrs. Lim's shack. Liang, many years her junior, admired Meiying from a distance.

"If only May," Liang said to me one day, calling Meiying by her English name, "had a different mother than Mrs. Lim…"

The only good things we could say about Mrs. Lim were that she had the grandest climbing yellow roses in the neighbourhood and that she made the best noodles whenever we shared our flour and eggs with her.

"Stepmother is across the street talking with Mrs. Lim," Jung said to me. "If old Mrs. Lim agrees to take care of you, you'd better wear your pilot's cap. Flaps down."

I pushed my largest tank over a row of soldiers.

I had always been glad I was not a girl-child. When Jung told me that I was to be put under the thumb of Mrs. Lim because Stepmother and Father had had enough of my war games and of the neighbours' complaints, I envied my sister Liang for the first time. Liang was lucky. She could work sometimes and also go with Father anywhere she wanted. Mainly, Liang dried and stacked dishes at Hon Lee's Cafe (and would get ten cents for that, too) or stuck on address labels at the *Chinese Times*. She liked being with Father, and sometimes she even got to stay at the newspaper office as he struggled to finish a piece of writing to meet the deadline.

Father worried about China, about the civil war there between the Communists and the Nationalists; he worried about our schooling and worried about the Japanese; he worried about Kiam wanting to fight for Canada when Canada did not want the Chinese. He worried about Stepmother, always angry. And then, of course, he worried about Jung working instead of going to school, and about Liang wanting to wear oversized sweaters like a clown, and he worried about me. There was nothing, it seemed, that Father did not worry about. And things he worried about, he wrote about in the newspaper, and then worried about what others would think.

I liked going to the newspaper office with Father, but on the third visit I accidentally knocked over a small tray of English type while reaching for the capital letter "S." The tray of letters was used to print up English names and Vancouver streets. Not all the metal pieces spilled onto the floor and disappeared under the printing machines, the editing desk and the front counter, but the owner said I was not to be found there again. I think he meant that I could not go near the trays of type again, but Father would not listen to my argument.

Any place Father took me, shortly after the second or third visit, someone didn't want me around again. Once I sat on a glass-topped counter at Ming Wo's, and it broke. I wasn't hurt, but half a sack of rare dried shrimp was wasted. The owner himself had sat me up on the counter so I could see how he worked an abacus; it wasn't my fault. But Father said that was that.

Mrs. Chang said that Liang should be old enough to handle me, but Liang refused to think about it. Besides, Father and Stepmother didn't trust Liang to be home by herself with me. My sister and I didn't exactly getting along.

Eleven months after the Old One's death, my sister insisted that I still had not returned to the world shared by everyone else in the family—"the real world," as she pointed out, with twelve-year-old wisdom. To frighten her, I pretended I saw the ghost of Grandmama.

"Poh-Poh's dead," she said, indifferently turning over a *Movie Story* page with a big picture of Sonja Henie on skates. "It's time you grew up, Sekky."

I made a crash landing with my Spitfire.

"And stop playing all those stupid war games. You don't know anything about war."

I was in Liang's room, which had been Grandmama's room before she died.

I sniffed the air and said, "I can still smell the Old One." Liang shut her eyes in disbelief.

"Will you get out of here?" she said. "It's *my* room now."

I looked around. The room was freshly wallpapered, in a design of white and pink roses. There was a small dresser, the trunk she had been given by her friend, monkey-faced Wong Suk, who had returned to Old China years ago, and a desk rescued from the dump and painted sky white. The desk was missing a bottom drawer. A wooden chair, also painted white, sat on a little rug.

"It's a boring room now," I said, more to myself than to anyone else.

"Get out," Liang said and started to write secrets into her diary, making sure that I could see the letters of my name being capitalized across the page, waiting for a wicked entry. I didn't care. With Grandmama gone, everyone was my enemy. I went downstairs to lock myself in the pantry's cool semidarkness.

Only a week before, I had accidentally had thrown one of my fighter airplanes into the pantry. When I climbed up to retrieve it, I found a whole shelf of Grandmama's herbal remedies. Familiar fragrances, sharp and bitter flavours, made my tongue and nose go moist with anticipation. Stepmother had put all these "dangerous medicines" on the highest shelf she could find. Mrs. Lim had helped her put aside the valuable dried sea horses, the rare hard black nugget of bear spleen, the squat bottle of ground deer antler; she named the powdered herbs and brown ointments no one else could guess. On the shelf were these: the still mysterious seeds like peppercorns with tiny spikes, the packets of bitter thick-veined leaves and mandrake roots, the tubes of BB-like pills, the tiny cosmetic pots of sweet-smelling ointments, a tin or two with half-torn labels. And a small tin of Bayer Aspirins. Nothing was to be thrown away; nothing to be wasted. Roots and leaves. Dried things that once had crawled and hopped in the moonlight.

"With the old one gone," Mrs. Lim told Stepmother, "I only can know half as much."

The pantry now held all of Grandmama's herbal knowledge. My sister's secrets, even if she was scrawling my name into her private diary, could not compare with the Old One's secrets. Revitalized by the medicinal scents, I returned upstairs. Liang was still scribbling away in her diary.

"Boring," I commented.

"You're boring, Sekky," she said. "Why can't you just go to your room and think of—*Mrs. Lim?*"

Father and Stepmother told me that Mrs. Lim would probably strangle me after my first day over there.

"This is going to be fun," Liang said. "I can hardly wait for next week."

On the Monday before I went to Mrs. Lim, Miss Doyle noted that my voice was snappy. At recess, I foolishly picked a fight with Jack McNaughton and lost. I couldn't even concentrate on my war games.

Mrs. Lim had been invited over for tea so that I could get used to her. Stepmother and Mrs. Lim chatted. I pretended I had polio and couldn't move. They paid no attention.

By Wednesday, I had grown stubborn and hostile, angry that I was not yet as strong and independent as Jung nor as smart and grown-up as Kiam. At least I wasn't as ugly as Sister Liang. I did everything to ruin their time with me, if they stayed around at all. I was a brat. I whined and sulked and fought, except of course, with Father. To cross him would be dangerous. Father became louder and angrier with each report from China. Territories, counties and provinces fell to the Japanese. The BBC announced the

father's
stress &
anger

arrival of Commonwealth soldiers in Hong Kong. Soon Canadian troops would be there, too. Father was sure Hong Kong would be the next to fall. How could the British, two oceans away, direct the defence of Hong Kong? The Burma Road, China's lifeline, had been lost. The Flying Tigers had failed to halt the enemy. Japanese troops drove deeper and deeper into southern China.

By Thursday, Stepmother was trying her best to prevent Father from ruining our dinner with his spluttering rage against "the dog-shit Japs!" She stopped him from detailing the horror stories about the Japanese atrocities against the Chinese population.

"But the children should know what kind of dog-screwing bas-tards those Japs are!"

"They know too much already," Stepmother said. "You think they don't know? Ask them if they know nothing!"

"They bayonet pregnant women!" Liang volunteered, her eyes wide with terror.

"They bury alive villagers and nuns," Jung joined in.

"They cook up Chinese babies," I said, with dark authority, for all of us at recess had traded stories and begun to turn away from the Japanese boys and girls in the schoolyard. In the older grades, there were already fights between gangs of "good guys" and "Japs."

Around all the tables and cafe counters of Chinatown, people wailed or whispered the news of family losses, an aunt here, a friend there, a father, a mother, a sister. There were tales of incred-ible enemy cruelty. A cousin wrote from Shanghai how the Japanese army were burying people alive, women and children. Another wrote how she witnessed living people, tied to posts, being used for bayonet practice. There were even darker rumours: the Japanese had camps for medical experiments, there were spe-cial camps for women hostages. A dozen incidents of mass slaugh-ter were exposed in the newsreels: machine guns ripped across a line of defenceless citizens; bombs fell on civilian targets; starving refugees poured into the ravaged countryside; the sanctuary of churches and temples and hospitals were all violated; in one news-reel of captured enemy film, a Japanese bayonet lifted up what seemed to be a woman's head, her long dark hair matted with blood.

"I want to join the Canadian military," Kiam said.

We all turned to see what Father would say.

"You're not a citizen of Canada," Father said, calmly. "You were registered in Victoria as a *resident alien*. We've had this talk before. When the Dominion says we are Canadian, then we will all join up!"

Kiam closed his chemistry book. I knew he had been talking to his friends again, and to Jenny Chong. Father would not say another word. Father and Jenny Chong's father did not agree on many things.

On Friday, three days before I was to go to Mrs. Lim's, Third Uncle came to visit with us. Whenever he came, Stepmother said very little so that Father would not lose face. If things became too heated because Third Uncle and Father could never agree on the politics of the Old China and the New China, she interrupted sweetly with an offering of more rice or soup or another cup of tea. About one thing, however, the two men were in absolute agreement: the Japanese demons must be driven out of the Middle Kingdom. Third Uncle and Father were working on the script of a Chinese Opera to raise Save China War Bonds.

Behind all the grown-up war talk, my tanks and planes roared, killing every Japanese in sight. I absorbed Chinatown's hatred of the Japanese, the monsters with bloodied buck teeth, no necks, and thick Tojo glasses; I wanted to kill every one of them.

During school recess, the gang and I gave surly looks to the Japanese boys and girls we didn't know. When the recess monitor wasn't watching, we shoved "the slant-eyes" in the back or punched them in the arm. Of course, sometimes a guy from another class mistook me for a Jap. Alfred Stevorsky and Joe Eng straightened them out. But we had to be careful: the older Japanese boys hit back. A boy with a German-type name gave Joe a black eye. Alfred got his best jacket torn. And I got my face pushed into the mud once. But we gave as good as we got. Our

[handwritten margin note: violent war game]

teacher, Miss Doyle, started to stand at her window and watch us at recess. If she caught any of us starting a fight or anything, she used the strap.

The Japanese kids started to keep to themselves; even the ones in Miss Doyle's class we used to be friendly with stayed more and more away from the rest of us. Some of the much older boys, white and Asian, began to protect the smaller Japanese kids from those who wanted to bully them. Some of us stood around, confused. But this was all kid stuff. Hearing about the war happening overseas was okay, but I wanted the actual fighting to start happening in Canada. The Chinatown talk was that it would, that there would soon be casualties.

Each day I looked into the sky and waited for the fall of bombs. I thought of Singapore and London and wished I was there.

The Japanese attacked Thailand, Borneo and the Philippines. There was more talk about enemy submarines—more Japanese ones—lurking beneath the B.C. coastal waters; there was growing anger and fear and hatred for anyone Japanese.

After school, I had to watch other boys go off to MacLean Park with their war toys while I went straight home and chafed over the crisis that mattered most to me: my own war games, and if I would be allowed to play them in the dungeon of Mrs. Lim's rundown shack. There would be no gang of boys there, only myself, hidden behind a hedge of roses. Myself and my arch enemy: fat old Mrs. Lim and her bossy yelling.

Something dark seemed to possess me. Why should I not get my own way? Why should anyone think I could not be trusted? There was a war on, and boys needed to practise the arts of war. No one was on my side. I was surrounded by traitors and enemies. Before I was sentenced to Mrs. Lim's, I had tasted freedom, and now it was gone. That first summer after Grandmama's death, I'd kicked soccer balls and exhausted my older brothers; I'd worn boxing gloves and lost fights; I'd spat blood; I'd threatened and sworn at my sister; I'd set the mountains of Burma alight with flames and fought a hundred battles against the Japanese and won each one.

Mrs. Lim didn't have a chance.

FOURTEEN

IT was settled. By the first week of October, I was forbidden to meet my friends after school, warned not even to speak to any of them, especially not with any boy kicked out of Chinese School. Instead, right after English school, I was to go directly to Mrs. Lim's.

Father swore that if he heard I was even one second late presenting myself at Mrs. Lim's, he would take the kitchen cleaver and decapitate all my toy soldiers, and with his foot crush my five tin tanks into pie plates. He swore that he would then stand at MacLean Park and give away my precious fighter planes to the very first boy who walked by, white, black, brown or yellow, "even if it a Jap boy."

Then he would demand that the Reverend Father Chan put me into the Bad Boys' Orphanage, where Christian Brothers who wore hoods like Death confined trashy boys, whipped them, and threw away the key. I would be the only Chinatown boy at that orphanage; I would shame all the Chinese people on earth.

To tell the truth, I did not once take the threat of the Bad Boys' Orphanage seriously. After all, we weren't Catholic. In class, Miss Doyle had already explained that Catholic families go to Catholic places, and Protestant families go to Protestant places. Same for

Jewish people. Same for Hindus and Buddhists. All the people in the world belonged to families and had to stay with their families.

But when Father raised his booted foot over my box of war toys, as if to flatten everything right there and then into pie plates, it sent a shudder through me. Father's eyes were wild with anger; his voice, choking. So I hurried after school to meet the fifteen-minute deadline agreed upon by both him and Mrs. Lim, each sealing the bargain with a handshake, Father's hands clasping Mrs. Lim's pudgy fingers. The two followed that up with a deadly round of Chinese sayings, in a classical drumbeat rhythm too ancient for my *mo no* ears. I heard hissing snakes and growling lions.

Breathless because of my five-block sprint from Strathcona, I stood on the street and glanced up at Mrs. Lim's shack, perched on wooden stilts, high atop an escarpment of rock. Two rickety staircases, separated midway by an even more precarious-looking platform landing, pitched skyward towards a jutting wooden porch.

Our neighbour Mr. O'Connor told First Brother Kiam that the peculiar shack had once belonged to a millworker named Jamieson, who bought the undesirable property for twenty-five dollars in 1895. People laughed at him, but he swore a man could make his home anywhere he liked. With salvaged lumber from the mill, and an ingenious pulley system, Jamieson built the two angled, chain-anchored maple staircases first, hammering metal spikes every three feet into the rockface. The finished stairs shook at every footfall but were, Mr. O'Connor said, "built sturdy enough to last to the end of the century." Then, with a younger brother, Jamieson carried each board and beam up the two flights of stairs and drilled a foundation of pilings and stilts, levelling the craggy surface with Portland cement and sacks of thick black earth. One lumber season after another, the two brothers steadily brought home the timber and, after long labour, finished the shack.

Almost immediately, an argument broke out between the

Jamiesons. It could have been over gambling debts or a woman. Or too much drinking. Neighbours heard shouting that night. Then nothing. One shoved the other over the porch railing of the house. They found the older brother with his neck broken at the bottom of the stairs. The surviving brother disappeared. Years later, the city offered the house for sale at a public auction. Only a crazy one-eyed China man raised his hand and shelled out the minimum two hundred dollars to buy the worthless property. That was Mr. Lim, of course. He borrowed half the money from his Tong Association and was still in debt for his Head Tax. An elder warned Mr. Lim that the house might not be lucky.

"Can a poor man afford a lucky house?" Mr. Lim said.

In 1933, Mr. Lim was killed working at the same mill where the Jamiesons once worked. A pile of lumber tipped over on his blind side, crushing him. The widow put her X on a piece of paper, witnessed before a lawyer, and thereafter, every month, money was put into her bank account in Chinatown.

Mrs. Lim told Stepmother that before Mr. Lim went to work that fateful day, "With his one eye, my husband saw the white man's ghost lying at the bottom of those steps. But I never saw anything. I sent him back down. If you don't work, I said to him, how can we eat?"

Mrs. Lim put her pudgy hands to her eyes, rubbing them in disbelief.

"Why did I let him go?" she cried. "Signs—I know signs—why didn't I listen to him?"

Mrs. Lim broke down and cried.

Mr. Lim died before I was born. Kiam remembered him as a gruff man who had poor hearing and spoke too loudly, like many labourers from Old China who worked beside pitiless machinery. On steep mountain slopes and by rushing waters, their voices had to drown out the chopping of the mechanical Iron Chinks in the fish canneries, defy screeching eight-foot crosscut mill saws. In their hearts, Father said, the China men sang ancient songs and thought of other mountains, other seas. Such men built the Great

Wall and pulled ships through the cloud-piercing gorges of the Yangtze and never surrendered.

"You remember: we Chinese," all of the Old China men drilled into my brothers and me, between their sips of tea and hacking up the bad waters, "Never forget, *we together Chinese.*"

I was Chinese and would never surrender. I carried my three-inch Red Ryder pocketknife with me, ready to do in Mrs. Lim if she was too mean.

Now, my fate decreed, I had to climb those two rickety flight of stairs and be babysat by the fat old widow. There was no choice. But I hesitated on that first step: the planks looked unstable, ready to collapse. I wondered how my older brothers had ever carried up Mrs. Lim's groceries, the boxes of firewood, the gunny sacks of sawdust; how they negotiated those steps, as steep as the cliff edges of the Yangtze. *Never surrender!* I could look between the thick planks and see, at eye level, the first two sets of chains bolted to the staircase frame, anchoring it to the rock face, taut and moist, smelling of iron. I took a deep breath.

"Mrs. Lim! I'm coming!"

At the very top, I could see the grey shack and the wall of imperial yellow roses Mrs. Lim had planted the spring of Mr. Lim's death. A curtain of brilliant end-of-summer blooms nodded in the early October breeze; a few petals drifted down. The roses were Mrs. Lim's pride, bright as beacons, hiding the pilings on one side and from spring to fall scenting the tiny porch landing. The porch was just large enough to hold a dark old sofa. I suppose it seemed like Paradise to her, a fat woman, sitting on that lone chair above the street, peering through her shelter of roses and leaves and thorns to look down at the rest of the world. From the bottom of the street, however, it just looked like a dump with sharply angled walls of grey and a smaller wall of yellow pushing against the sky. Riding a cool breeze, a scattering of yellow petals floated down. One landed on my head.

I started climbing, carefully, one step after another. I tried not to look down. Tried not to shake the staircase. It trembled and quaked under my feet. The chains clanked. I thought about how it must have felt to be pushed over the porch railing, like the Jamieson brother, and hear your neck snap. I pushed on.

At the platform landing, I decided to pause a bit. I sat on a bench seat built for that purpose. Hang on a bit. Just to look around. I have to do this every school day, I thought, bitterly. I looked out at the houses across the street, the free houses: one of them was ours, then Mr. O'Connor's, then the Chens and...

A raspy voice called out my name: *"Sek-Lung!"*

I glanced up just in time to see Mrs. Lim on the porch, turning around and ambling back into the shack. The front screen door slammed. I knew what torture she had in store for me: ten thousand Chinese sayings to memorize.

I remembered how an RCAF pilot would not be afraid of any kind of challenge—not of anything—like James Cagney in *Captains of the Clouds*, like Deuce Granville and his Jumping Jeep Men, like Terry and the Pirates. I closed my eyes and scaled the last flight, pulling myself, hand over hand, like a blind mountain climber. The staircase bounced against the escarpment. When I landed on the porch, the thing seemed to sway; it creaked loudly, then stopped. All these years, I realized, these steps and this porch had held Mrs. Lim's weight.

A breeze brushed against the porch, stirring the leaves and flowers. Leaf shadows danced everywhere. The air was sweet with scent. Enemy cunning. Inside the house, Mrs. Lim had a secret button that her pudgy thumb would press; underneath the porch, instantly, a spring would trip and send me soaring. I saw my body pitching skyward, flying, planeless, to the bottom of the escarpment. Father and Stepmother would discover my broken body, neck neatly snapped. I moved a few cautious steps forward. Was Mrs. Lim ever breathless when she reached the top?

"...in..." a voice said, from somewhere in the shadowy hallway, "...come in."

It was a soft voice, breathless. Maybe Mrs. Lim had used up all her volume calling down my name.

I peered into the semigloom of the house. A pot-bellied stove with a sawdust hopper stood in the middle of a square hallway. A neat stack of firewood sat in a galvanized bin between two partly curtained doorways. Sacks of sawdust leaned against one wall. I pulled open the screen door and walked in. The floor creaked.

There was an open doorway to my left. Over the damp wood, I could smell sweet herbs mixed with a strong salty aroma of pickled cabbage. There was the sound of water angrily boiling, and from an angle I could see a black iron stove and clouds of steam rising from a pot and kettle. Overhead dangled a straw-hooded lightbulb, throwing strange shadows against the ceiling and a warm light on the walls.

"Here," a voice said.

Mrs. Lim sat at a large kitchen table, dressed in a dark blue smock, her broad face lit impassively by the overhanging light-bulb. Her wide arms rested on a basket of peas and behind her, a triple line of glass jars sat along the sink. My heart sank. I hated washing anything, even myself. At her black-stocking, slippered feet were more baskets of peas waiting to be shelled, assorted bunches of unwashed leafy vegetables, pyramids of dusty red and green peppers. A quick glance and I could see on a wall of newspapered shelves above the table piles of sun-dried bok choi to be bundled with raffia; small crates of twisted roots, deep dishes of pungent herbs and spices, dried mushrooms, piles of velvet-coloured bark, thorny twigs, all waiting to be cleaned, cooked, ground up or chopped. All the womanly tasks she and Grandmama, Stepmother and Liang used to do together in our kitchen: now I had inherited the labour. I was to spend eternity shelling, washing, sorting, chopping...never to see daylight again. Never to eat anything but bitter peas, drink herb-infused teas, chew salted cabbage. My mouth went dry; my teeth tasted of chalk.

To the left of Mrs. Lim's elbow, a neat row of rippling silver caught my eye. I gulped. An array of honed knives and hefty cleavers of varying sizes and shapes gleamed on the gingham oilcloth that covered the table. I quickly counted seven readied weapons, each blade longer and sharper than the last.

Mrs. Lim scowled at the useless sight of me standing dumb-struck before the baskets and crates and the sink of woman's work. She went on shelling peas with lightning speed. She was truly mean: she didn't even offer me something to eat.

"Here," a voice repeated.

It was amazing. Mrs. Lim's lips had not moved. I looked again. The scowl remained frozen in disapproval of the spoiled *mo no* boy standing before her.

"Behind you, Sekky."

I turned around. It was Meiying, Mrs. Lim's daughter. Her long hair flowed over her shoulders, and she held a large silk shawl shimmering with autumn colours.

"Let's go," she said and pushed open the torn screen door.

It slammed shut. She was gone.

I looked at Mrs. Lim. Behind me, I heard Meiying's quick steps disappearing down the staircase. The stairs rattled. Reaching for a handful of peas, Mrs. Lim waved me away.

I could not believe I was to leave. After a moment's pause to see if Mrs. Lim would pick up a cleaver, I turned around, pushed open the screen door. I imagined a cleaver just missing the back of my head. I hit the first stair even before I heard the screen door slam. But the trembling, banging staircase stopped me. I grabbed for the rail and hung on. The stairs banged and banged against the escarpment wall. Meiying was rushing down the last flight of steps in double-time, unafraid of the chain-pulling, shuddering stairs.

I held my breath—*if a girl isn't afraid!*—and plunged down the precarious steps as fast as Meiying had. I leapt off the last shaking step and stood gasping before her. Street dust bellowed around my patched Buster Brown boots. I felt like Robert Preston, leather-neck, landing on Wake Island, machine gun blasting away.

The staircase banged one last time. I stared at the thin girl before me. Meiying tossed the large silk shawl about her shoul-ders.

"We're going to the playground, Sekky," she said, turning. "Keep up."

She raced ahead of me; she was so much taller, her legs so much longer, faster.

"Wait," I said, but thinking of the baskets of peas, the salt cabbage and the scowl-frozen Mrs. Lim in the tiny dark kitchen, I ran to catch up.

Between breaths and the pounding of my boots hitting the pavement, I felt my lungs expand, contract, expand, and without any warning, heard myself yelling *FU-UCKkkk!* exactly as if I were Alfie Stevorsky or Joe Eng. It was the one word Father once slapped Jung across the face for saying; it was the very word that First Brother Kiam warned me Father would cut out my tongue for uttering, if I even *pretended* to say it. I could see Mrs. Lim's cleaver suddenly strike the wall, quivering.

Meiying ran on.

When I was almost eight, girls were not exactly my favourite people. But Meiying was not like most girls.

Meiying called me Sekky, instead of Sek-Lung, as if I was her friend. When she visited Stepmother, she always brought Liang and me some jaw breakers or gum or Five Flavour Lifesavers and never, never, asked us about school. I liked that about her. She didn't even mind if I slipped and called her May, her English name, even though Father scolded me.

I knew Stepmother liked her; sometimes, they spent time chatting together while trying out hairstyles or make-up. Mrs. Lim would sometimes linger over her cup of tea, taking quiet pride in her adopted daughter's popularity with the married women in the community.

Everyone liked Meiying. Father even pointed her out as someone my sister Liang should emulate. Liang, at twelve, her teeth slightly bucked, wished she could be as tall and as elegant and as smart as Meiying. But Meiying was seventeen, far beyond the reach of my sister's giggling group of girlfriends. With her tightly curled hair, Liang moped about, sunk deep in her Sloppy Joe sweaters. Meiying walked briskly and wore deep-coloured cardigans, and her long black hair shone, spilling over her shoulders.

First Brother Kiam liked her looks, too, I could tell, but he wasn't attracted to the fact that she did so many things so well. Meiying knew enough Mandarin, for example, to explain a phrase or two to Kiam, who was studying the dialect because Father felt it would be the official language of any New China "when the people win." Meiying knew some Mandarin because her mother for years had sung in concerts in the local Chinese Opera, in the classical dialect, before she gambled and drank too much and gave Meiying away to Mrs. Lim, leaving her with some clothes and a foot-high Chinese Opera doll with the painted white face of a scholar.

And now Meiying was to be my babysitter. If I had to have a babysitter, Meiying was better than Mrs. Lim. She runs like Second Brother Jung, I thought, and liked her for that. I wished she were a boy. I could really like her then. Still, I hoped Alfred and Joe and the rest of the boys were not around to see her tagging around with me.

When Meiying slowed down, I made a dash to be a step or two in front of her. She took a moment to catch her breath, which made me feel better.

"We're going to the park, Sekky," she said in English, putting a slim hand on her chest. "You'll like it there because they're having a baseball practice."

She tried to fasten my shirt collar; I pushed her hand away.

"At least button your jacket."

I let my jacket hang open. I only wished I had my leather pilot's cap with me. What I said next would have had more authority.

"There's no baseball at MacLean Park now."

I thought of MacLean Park, where my friends might be gouging out minature trenches with sticks, shooting away whole battalions. Older boys played soccer there, but rarely baseball.

"There is," she said, "where we're going. You'll see."

Instead of turning south on Jackson, over the cobblestone roadway towards MacLean Park, Meiying turned north and walked even faster. The mountains in the far distance were already topped with snow, but flowers were still blooming in Vancouver yards. We were walking away from familiar territory, away from the boundaries of Chinatown. I tried to catch her attention. What was she doing?

Meiying's hand reached back for mine; I avoided it and gave her my special blood-chilling heartless look, something I copied from the movies. One eyebrow twisted up like a crazed Charlie Chan; the other eyebrow narrowed into a fiendish slant. She ignored me.

"Walk faster," she commanded. "What have you got in your pocket?"

"Nothing," I said. "Just one of my planes. A Spitfire."

"They have an excellent attack range," she said.

Good faking, I thought.

"Deadly interceptors," she went on, hardly pausing to witness my surprise.

"The Luftwaffe's long-range Messerschmitts haven't got a chance," she said.

Shit, I thought, *she can even pronounce the names correctly.*

She pretended to dive-bomb, then flew ahead.

From the cockpit of my Spitfire, I machine-gunned her.

"Keep up," she said. Her shawl lifted from her shoulders and gave her outstretched arms wings against the wind. I made machine-gun noises, but she refused to fall down.

We kept running north (now she was a Stuka), flew towards Hastings Street. At last she slowed down to a brisk walk. Making the machine-gun noises had completely used up my wind. Then it dawned on me: this was the *bad* end of Hastings Street. The streetcar tracks gleamed like pewter.

I had been warned to stay away from this "hoodlum end" of Hastings Street. I let Meiying walk ahead a few steps to see if she would stop, if she would realize she was going the wrong way. Instead, her pace increased. She double-timed over the tracks, unfazed by the bell-ringing streetcar headed towards her.

"Watch out!" I yelled, but she ran on.

The Hastings streetcar rumbled by, the driver shook his fist; I had to run faster.

I swore to myself that if we ran into the Han twins in this neighbourhood, I would murder her.

The two Han boys lived in No Man's Land, where the few no-class *Haka* ("guests of Old China") lived, where hoods and drunks and, Jung said, "wicked ladies with no place to sleep" stood about. I fell back a few more steps. Hotels and bars and little shops with handwritten English signs stood on each side of Hastings Street; Meiying turned down a side street. I felt for the rusty jackknife in my jacket. Meiying stopped, took a small compact mirror from her cardigan pocket. She wet her lips and peered at herself, smoothed her long hair and arranged the shawl around her shoulders.

"Do I look okay, Sekky?" she asked.

"Where are we?"

M crosses all borders

"We're almost there."

She pointed towards the end of the block, where a small crowd had gathered. Then, it came to me: Powell Ground. It was officially called Oppenheimer Park, but Chinese and Japanese found the name difficult to pronounce. And Oppenheimer Park, Powell Ground, was Little Tokyo—Japtown—enemy territory!

Meiying pushed ahead, barely noticing my blatant loathing. I thought of air battles over Burma, imagined Jap Zero fighters going down in flames. *Banzai!*

Powell Ground had a dingy, dusty baseball diamond surrounded by a green border of grass and weeds and three trees in one corner. Across from the playground, dozens of Japanese stores, with large lanterns, neon signs and names painted in gold on the windows, fronted Powell Street. Even from where we stood, I could see how uncluttered and clean the store window displays appeared, compared to the casual disarray of Chinatown stores. A large two-storey churchlike building stood on one corner, and wood-framed houses, like our own, bordered the side streets, planted with neighbourhood victory gardens.

Like the soldier I was, I knew Meiying had made a bad mistake: only a girl would think that every playground was the same. I walked quickly and stood with her at the edge of the small crowd. Someone broke into a laugh. Among a few words of English, I could hear rising clipped-toned voices, foreign tongue babble.

I tried my best to whisper discreetly to Meiying. "This is Japtown—we shouldn't be here."

"Why not?"

"We're not Japs," I said. Girls were so thick.

"You're not *afraid*, are you, Sekky?"   challenges him

She lifted a corner of her shawl, as if to indicate the crowd of striped-shirted ballplayers a hundred feet beyond us, some of them with bats in their hands, swinging them in wide arcs. A few men tossed baseballs into the air and began throwing them hard-smack into their teammates' thick leather gloves. They were all *Japs*. The enemy.

"No," I said loudly, a soldier standing guard, fists ready. "I'm not afraid of some dumb Ja—"

She put her hand over my mouth. Then she reached down and took my fist and gripped it. Tightly. My other hand, deep in my jacket pocket, palmed the cool handle of my Red Ryder knife. I thought of Mrs. Lim's collection of knives and cleavers.

The crowd was mostly Japanese. Older women sat on picnic blankets, reaching into baskets, unwrapping small trays of food; children ran around them, laughing. Three Japanese men moved closer towards us. Meiying pretended not to notice them. My three-inch knife wasn't too sharp and had a chipped rusty blade, but if we were surrounded…attacked…it would still make a nasty hole in some.…The three men walked right by us. Everyone ignored us; we must have blended in. Some of the

younger women had shawls on like Meiying's. Others pulled
sweaters tightly around themselves. The men looked ordinary,
some in fedoras and wide pants, some in tweed jackets like
Father's. I had to remind myself that they were the enemy.

Then a guy's voice behind us said "May!"

We turned around. It was a young Japanese man, wearing a
baseball uniform that had letters in English on it: ASAHI. He was
as tall as Meiying and maybe a bit older. I was wondering who he
was when she smiled back at him. That shocked me. She released
my clenched fist and looked down at the ground. The three
Japanese men standing close to us turned to stare, then slowly
moved away. They didn't seem happy.

"Is this the boy, May?" he asked, when he reached us.

"Yes, this is Sekky," she said. "He's okay."

What did she mean, *okay*?

Meiying put her hands on my shoulders. For protection, I
thought. She seemed half glad to see him, half confused.

He turned his head, slightly embarrassed that he had attracted
attention. He had a high forehead, deep black eyes like coal, thin
lips; his hair was shiny with hair cream. He looked like a Chinese
movie soldier, a Good Guy, in one of those films we saw at the
China War Effort Fund Drive. But he was *Japanese.*

His fingers reached for hers, the tips brushed against hers; hers
moved slowly between his.

"The news is much worse today, May," he said.

I could see his fingers tighten over hers; she didn't pull away
but went on listening to him.

"There's more talk about us being the enemy. Being traitors.
The *Sun* printed letters about putting us away, there's talk about
us registering—"

"It's only stupid talk!" There was a sudden urgency in her
voice. "We can still see each other after school, Kaz. We can still
meet after choir."

But he turned away from her and I only caught his last word:
dangerous.

He brushed his other hand against her arm. Meiying suddenly remembered me.

"Go over there, Sekky, by that first tree, by that bench." She let go his hand; he stepped back. "You'll be fine. Kaz and I will be watching out for you."

I refused to move.

"Play with the Spitfire you brought with you. Go on."

"Spitfire?" The slim Japanese gave a funny laugh. "Everyone's at war! Even—"

Stupid Jap, I thought.

"Go on, Sekky," Meiying pleaded.

The desperate tone in her voice caused me to move; my head was filled with mixed thoughts. The spot was far enough away for me not to be able to hear them talking. I was trying to figure things out when the ballplayers on the field started shouting a chant in Japanese. One player pitched a ball directly to home, then another player threw a ball to the same catcher. In a split second, the catcher caught the ball, snapped it whizzing to first, caught the next one, hurled it away even faster to third...suddenly five, six, seven, eight balls were in play, and the diamond was exploding with baseballs smacking into leather gloves and instantly being whipped away. All the players became incredible jugglers, chanting in rhythm and catching, throwing, catching. When I thought they could not catch or throw a ball one split second faster, they gave a shout in unison and abruptly stopped. They were as good as the star players on the Chinese Students Soccer Team, passing the ball with their heads and feet, faster and faster and faster. For a moment I forgot I was watching the enemy. And that one of them was standing too close to Meiying.

The first baseman looked around, adjusting his glasses with his glove. He called out "Kazuo! Kazuo!" whistling and yelling the name out comically. When he spotted Kaz standing so close to Meiying, his smile turned angry. No one on the diamond moved.

Kazuo broke away from Meiying and ran out onto the field, ignoring the cold stares. He swiftly swooped down to collect all the baseballs, scooping them up as he ran by, tossing them neatly one after another to a bat boy standing on the pitcher's mound, who unerringly caught them and put them into a canvas bag. Then both of them ran to home plate; the smaller boy, about my size but heavier, began to organize the equipment behind the catcher's cage. Kazuo bent over and took out a stiff thick brush and cleaned home plate. A large menacing man in a black jacket walked over to Kaz and began to shout at him. He pointed angrily at Meiying, shaking his fist and spitting in the sand. Some of the Asahi men began to stare at Kaz, then at Meiying standing alone. I ran back to her and stood guard.

The stout catcher came towards us and shouted in English, as if we might be deaf: "Leave Kazuo alone, little girl! He's already in enough trouble with his family over you!"

The man in the black jacket was still shouting at Kazuo, arms gesturing wildly, threateningly. But Kaz continued brushing off home plate, as if nothing were bothering him. Nothing. His hair shone in the afternoon light.

Meiying turned to me and took my free hand. It was sweaty. Some of the women on blankets pointed at us, chattering. We had crossed a line. No one would have minded if Kazuo had kept his distance and we, ours; if this girl and this boy had remained onlookers and not trespassers.

They stared at us, waiting.

"Let's go, Sekky," Meiying said.

She bent down.

"Walk slowly," she whispered. "Don't let anybody think we're being chased away. Don't look back."

A half block away, I turned around and could see the row of store display lights clicking off early to meet the blackout rules. These were the same Japanese stores selling Japan-made goods that everyone in Vancouver was boycotting. Buy their toys and food-stuffs, and you buy a bullet aimed at the Chinese. Father had joined a rally in Chinatown that piled up all our Japan-made goods—clothing, toys, bamboo racks, games, junk dishes of all kinds—and smashed them or set them ablaze.

I was thrilled to have met the enemy, yet still so reluctantly dazzled by their baseball skills that I found myself tongue-tied and mostly silent. I would begin to speak, stop, then begin again.

dash

The whole adventure was inexplicable and deeply exciting. I wanted to shout, to give my Tarzan yell. I had expected to be tortured by Mrs. Lim today; instead, I had become a soldier and confronted the enemy.

I knew, of course, Meiying was involved in something shameful, something treasonable.

Everyone knew the unspoken law: *Never betray your own kind.* Meiying was Chinese, like me; we were our own kind.

"Keep your business in your pants," Third Uncle had warned Kiam when he got interested in a white waitress at the Blue Eagle who liked to dance with him.

I could see Father's outrage if he ever found out, and I shuddered to imagine how horrified Stepmother would be: *No, no, not Meiying, not the perfect one!*

There was no getting around it. She must have known Kazuo for a long time. She was a *traitor.* Her boyfriend was a Jap, a monster, one of the enemy waiting in the dark to destroy all of us.

Yet I felt oddly relieved. Uplifted even. Powerful. We had just been in the heart of Little Tokyo, a place where even Alfred Stevorsky or Joe Eng would never go, at least not without a gang of much older boys. How I wanted to run into them, even if it were the Han boys, and tell all my pals everything. But there was no one around.

The faster Meiying walked, the more boldly my mind embraced my new knowledge: *I, Sek-Lung, could turn her in.*

I glanced up at Meiying. Her eyes seemed to glitter; perhaps the wind was too strong.

"Don't cry, May," I said. "I won't tell on you."

"Promise me," she said, between holding back her tears, "promise me you'll go back to Powell Ground with me again."

I was taken aback, but heard myself say, "I promise."

I thought of secretly borrowing Jung's large scout knife. After all, going back to Japtown could be dangerous, just like in a real war zone. A few years ago, one Halloween night, mobs of white men in masks and armed with clubs had rioted in Japtown, smashing plate glass windows, kicking down doors, looting whatever they could carry away.

Everyone in Chinatown talked about that night.

Some recalled another night, years before I was born, when a similar mob had hit Chinatown. "Years and years ago," Third Uncle told us. "You bet they yank us Chinkee pigtails. Cut off, like this!" Years before that, there had been white mobs in San Francisco that left, some said, three China men, limbs and necks broken, hanging dead from lampposts.

But I wondered why we, the Chinese, had not joined the Halloween mob that attacked Japtown.

Perhaps I could do some damage in my own way, weaken the enemy. Trap her. Trap them both. Meanwhile, I could pretend to be Meiying's friend: I could be a spy. Turn her in later to the Tong or the RCMP. Would they tie her hands behind her back, blindfold her, and *bayonet* her? I saw the Japanese soldiers do that in the war photos Father brought home from one of the Chinese newspapers. Kiam and Jung saw the same thing in the newsreels. The Japanese tied up people with barbed wire and hung them up for live bayonet practice. But Chinese soldiers gave away spearmint gum and cans of food to refugees and were cheered wherever they went.

Meiying tightened her grip on my hand. We stopped at the corner store and she bought me a double-scoop chocolate ice-cream cone, a Sergeant Canuck comic and a Captain Marvel one. We walked over to the Good Shepherd Mission and found a clean step to sit on. A laden chestnut tree spread its arms above us. I started on Sergeant Canuck first. He was a Sergeant of the B.C. Police, fighting spies and traitors. Meiying sat quietly beside me, looking at nothing except the large-leaf shadows on the sidewalk.

It was almost too windy for me to hold down the pages of the comic book and still lick my cone, but I managed to finish both. Then I opened my second comic. The first story was about how Billy Batson could shout "Shazam!" and turn into Captain Marvel.

I looked away from my comic and saw how pale Meiying looked, how hopefully she watched me. I thought about our time together. We had both walked into Japtown. In fact, I knew we were headed to Little Tokyo by that last block. Yet I hadn't stopped her. If I were being honest, I would have to admit that I pretended I didn't know what was happening until the last possible moment. If she was a traitor, what was I?

I remembered how Kazuo had kept brushing home plate, how he ignored that big man crowding over him. Meiying caught me lost in thought.

"What are you thinking?"

"He's a sporty guy," I said, meaning to say that I liked his nerve. But I guess she thought that I liked *him*. She broke into a smile, as if a wonderful thing had just happened between us.

"Oh, Sekky! If only you were the whole world!"

She threw her arms around me, totally catching me off guard, then quickly let me go.

"Read this Marvel comic three times, Sekky," she said. "Then tell me all the stories about Captain Marvel."

I did. Meiying listened and never once corrected me or called me stupid. I even invented spy bits as I went along, just to improve things, to make one story out of the many. She taught me how to decode SHAZAM. Each letter stood for something like Strength and Hero and Amazing…I soon forgot she was really just a girl who was babysitting me. I even forgot about fat Mrs. Lim. The October wind blew sharply, and some chestnut clusters fell onto the sidewalk.

"It's getting late," she finally said. "I promised to get you home by now."

We stood up. Pushing myself off the step, I brushed beside her and could smell a drift of Three Flowers perfume, mingling with the fresh wind and the dried grass along the sidewalk. It was the same scent Stepmother used, and I liked it. I kicked at some fallen chestnuts. She laughed and kicked them back at me.

"We'll go again tomorrow," she said. "I'm to take care of you every day after school. Ma is too busy with her canning and herbs to look after you."

"Sure," I said, casually.

The next day, Kazuo was not there.

Nor was he there for the rest of the week. Mrs. Lim began wondering why we liked the outdoors so much.

"Sek-Lung needs exercise," Meiying would say. "The school doctor said so."

"Too much fresh air no good," Mrs. Lim shook her head at the madness of white doctors. "Burn out his lungs."

On rainy days, there was no practice, and Meiying knew he would not be there. Then we stayed in and, together, helped Mrs. Lim in the kitchen with her chores. She said we were useless and in the way, but, generally, Mrs. Lim ignored the two of us, and let Meiying make a game of our washing and sorting and chopping. At those times, Mrs. Lim sometimes sat back and watched Meiying confidently hand me vegetables to wash before drying or pass me seeds to be put into small paper packets. These were sold by Mrs. Lim to Chinatown merchants: the dried vegetables to the local cornerstore grocers, the herbs to the herbalists in the dark corners of stores. "Don't spill the profits," Mrs. Lim nagged.

We snacked between washings and drank small cups of tea. Mrs. Lim would open a steaming hot fold of lotus leaf, filled with savoury sticky rice. With a string between her pudgy fingers, she divided the mold of rice into three portions, one for each person. The lucky person got the portion with a bit of red Chinese sausage. Everything seemed at peace, and I was surprised at Mrs. Lim's long silences. On such afternoons, she chose to sit on the porch sofa and watch the October winds strip her rose bushes of petals and leaves, and listen to our voices singing from the kitchen. One day, I noticed the rose bushes were completely bare. What was left looked like a treacherous tangle of barb wire, which made me think of battlefields and trenches and added to our pretend games in the kitchen.

On sunny days, we ran anxiously to Powell Ground to see if Kazuo would be able to meet Meiying by the bench under the trees. There, Meiying would tell me what Kazuo had said to her at school that day, how he had almost failed his history exam, how he had a fight with some boys who were calling him "a dirty Jap." I said nothing, but imagined my solders firing away.

All the Japanese kids at Strathcona were sticking together now; they made up almost half of all the classes. They kept to themselves, said little, only waited to see who else would be mean to them. Miss Doyle and other teachers stood at the school exits to make sure no one attacked them. Some of the teachers and the older boys took to walking some of the younger kids home. More and more Japanese parents brought their kids to school in the morning and, after school, waited anxiously for them.

One day Jung met me and Liang after school and said, "No one better think you're a Jap." He pounded his fist in front of Alfred Stevorsky and his boyfriends, then kick-boxed into the air. "I'll beat the fuckin' shit out of them."

Jung took Liang to Chinese School and watched me as I ran to Mrs. Lim's. Kiam was busy guarding Third Uncle's warehouse, as robberies were more and more common. The Depression squatters at False Creek, right in Chinatown, were being cleared out by the police. "Join the Army!" the younger men were told.

At the high school Meiying and Kazuo attended, Meiying told me, the Japanese boys fought back, defended their own kind, dared anyone to call them names. Meiying said, "Kaz and me, we still talk."

"Why?" I asked.

"We're friends, Sekky," she said. "Friends have alliances. You know what allies are?"

"Yes," I said, but knew that she meant they were sneaking around.

After waiting half an hour, if he didn't appear, Meiying would pretend to finish reading her book.

"I guess Kaz had to help his brothers with the store," she would say sadly. "They must be very busy today."

We would then leave Powell Ground and decide either to go window shopping all the way downtown to Woodward's store or even Eaton's, or stop midway at the Carnegie Library at Hastings and Main, just off Chinatown. Meiying left me in the Boys and Girls section with a pile of books for me to read at a table by myself. She went to another section upstairs, where I found her flipping through large picture books about Japan. Then we would walk about Chinatown, looking in the windows at tin toys, and remember to ask for Mrs. Lim if any new shipments of rare food-stuffs had arrived from China. Everything was getting scarce. Even soy sauce and cooking wine were being watered down. On the last day of October, the newspapers said that Halloween was can-celled.

Now that it was November, the streets darkened very early. We walked past houses with their blackout curtains pressed against windows and door frames, past volunteer men and women who carefully checked each window and door to see that the law was being strictly obeyed.

"You Japs?" a man in a brown jacket said to us.

Meiying showed him the tin buttons pinned on our lapels that had the Chinese flag proudly stamped on them. Kiam had got them for us from Chinese School. I also had one that said: I AM CHINESE.

"Get home," said the man. "It looks like snow."

We didn't rush. Meiying walked as if we had every right to be walking as we did, slowly. Our breath clouded before us. We laughed. Part of the sky was clear. Stars shone through, and we glimpsed an early moon. Then the clouds thickened and snow fell. I studied the sidewalk for boy's treasures, for lucky pennies or lost toys or an unbroken conker.

The chestnut trees had dropped their hard dark-brown seeds long ago. The Han boys had gone around claiming they had the champion conkers. Boys were everywhere boring holes in the horse chestnuts, stringing them, and challenging each other to bashes. Meiying taught me to swing my chestnut at a sharp angle, like a Spitfire soaring skyward for a kill. I beat both the Han twins' conkers, one smash after another.

By the time Meiying took me home to my house, I was happy and exhausted. Usually, everyone was home by then. Father would be unfolding his bundle of Chinese newspapers, worried about the China Front, shifting in his big sofa chair, growing angrier and noisier about the invading *dog-dung Japs*. Stepmother and Liang would be setting the table for our late supper. Jung would be dialing the RCA radio from one end to the other to catch the latest sports news. First Brother Kiam would be upstairs listening to Artie Shaw or Benny Goodman on his own Philco radio. Kiam's part-time work at Third Uncle's warehouse had almost come to a halt: no import shipping was reaching Vancouver harbour.

Nothing at home was out of the ordinary, except that I knew Meiying had entrusted me with a highly treacherous secret. If her widowed mother, with her deep village loyalties and Old China superstitions, found out about Kazuo, she would spit at Meiying, tear out her own hair, and be the second mother to disown her.

If Chinatown found out, Meiying would be cursed and shamed publicly as a traitor; she would surely be beaten up, perhaps branded with a red-hot iron until her flesh smoked and flamed. In the Chinese propaganda movies that Stepmother sometimes took me to see, there were violent demonstrations of what happened to traitors.

One November afternoon we waited much longer for Kaz than our usual half hour. Snow had come and gone, though the mountain tops were white and glistening. It became too dark to be sitting on that park bench, too dark for me to see my soldiers in the dirt trenches I had dug, too dark for Meiying to pretend she was reading her book.

"Let's go," I said, impatiently.

When we got to my house, Meiying paused, knocked on the door and delicately gathered one end of her shawl and pressed it gently against her eyes.

"Just some dust," she said. "Do I look all right now, Sekky?"

I nodded my head.

Stepmother opened the door, let us both in and said nothing to Meiying. As I removed my jacket, it seemed to me they stared at each other for a long time. Then Stepmother silently embraced her. I peeked out from the parlour window after the door closed. I watched Meiying walk across the street and swiftly climb the steps up to her own house. I could see Mrs. Lim, wide as the door-way, waiting for her daughter. She had her arms folded impatient-ly across her apron; her large body seemed to cause the old wood-en porch to sag. I could hear her shouting at Meiying. Her stupid daughter of a worthless person had left her bedroom window open again. And hadn't she paid good money, prayed ten thousand prayers, to have the Buddhist monk seal up the windows against the broken-neck white demon? The harsh voice seemed physical-ly to hammer away at the thin figure crossing the porch. A flash of red and gold caught my eyes, and Meiying disappeared into the darkness.

I stepped back from the narrow side window and was surprised to see Stepmother still standing stock-still before the closed door. She saw me staring at her.

"Hang up your jacket," she said, and turned quickly away from me.

FIFTEEN

As November turned into December, Stepmother made arrangements with Meiying to take care of me after school. And since Mrs. Lim did not like Meiying working part time any more at the Blue Bird Cafe, where her beauty attracted the same kind of men her mother once knew—only these men were in military uniforms—everyone was satisfied.

Some days Meiying seemed very happy. I watched her in her bedroom as she tied her hair with long, trailing scarves—many-coloured pieces left behind by her runaway mother that made me think of battle flags and warrior banners. The scarves were hung beside a foot-high, red-cloaked Chinese Opera doll sitting on her dresser and leaning against the mirror. Some days she sang and let me play with the doll.

Carefully, I put my finger up inside its small jewelled head and moved its puppet-jointed arms so that the slippered feet danced. The delicately drawn face and the rich red cloak reminded me of an enchanted prince. And in the late afternoon light, her black hair falling over her shoulders as she opened another book to read, Meiying looked like a princess. I could see why Kazuo would like her, but I still couldn't see why she liked him.

Those pleasant first December days, in spite of the frosty air, she smiled so effortlessly and laughed so freely that I sensed she had somehow spent some time with Kazuo at her English school. On certain days they continued to meet at Powell Ground, too. Swathed in thick sweaters, and the gloves and wool scarf Meiying knitted for me, I would play cut-the-pie with my pocketknife while they held hands and walked away from me for a little while. They always disappeared inside the empty doorway of the Methodist Church building. Some days she came out rebuttoning her coat. Of course, it was very warm inside the church. I didn't mind. I always got new comics after that and a treat of candy or cherry coke. Kazuo once gave me some Japanese candy that tasted of seaweed. I thought it had poison in it, but they both ate it to show me it was safe.

Another time, Kaz gave me a baseball, and we threw the ball around. He showed me how to spit on it and rub the stitching part before winging it. The best time happened when Kaz, because he was as tall as Kiam, bent down to box with me. I threw Kaz a fake left and got to hit him hard on the jaw. Of course, we were just supposed to be shadow boxing, like Jung had taught me in the summer. "Goddamn!" he said and rubbed his jaw. I kept punching at him. Meiying pulled me back, but he laughed and lifted me up into the air and threw me up, up, up; he caught me by my feet and began to swing me around and around and around, higher and higher. It was dizzying and thrilling, and when he stopped, catching me mid-air, the world kept spinning. I almost threw up.

"Now we're even," he said, and Meiying pushed him, knocking him over and falling on top of him; I quickly recovered and jumped him. We ended up laughing and rolling around on the ground.

It was fun that day.

All this time, Meiying and I never once openly discussed with each other the understood and forbidden topic of her sneaking around to visit her boyfriend. Sometimes he pinned on the I AM CHINESE button that Meiying got for him, and we met at the Carnegie Library on Hastings and Main, between the boundaries of Chinatown and Little Tokyo. Not that I minded the sneaking around part. It was fun.

But he was, after all, still a Jap.

And though no strangers could tell that Kazuo was Japanese when he held hands with Meiying and walked us part way home, one day I thought for sure that Stepmother, who'd left work early to pick up some pills at the Main Drug Store for Third Uncle, saw the three of us stepping out of the library together. It was directly across the street from the drug store.

As soon as Meiying spotted the familiar face, she pushed Kazuo away. He quickly dropped Meiying's hand and ran down the steps in the other direction. Meiying waved to Stepmother and brushed her hand against her skirt. She pulled her coat collar up against the wind and began walking down the library steps, as casually as possible. I followed. But before Stepmother could even ask anything, Meiying said, "Everything's fine...can I carry this?" which I thought was curious. Stepmother nodded her head and handed over a cloth bag of groceries.

"Did you have fun at the library, Sekky?" Meiying asked, as if she hadn't been with me earlier to meet Kazuo at Powell Ground.

For some reason, I suddenly felt I had to lie, too.

"It was okay," I said, and we walked home, barely able to make out the North Shore mountains in the winter afternoon light.

At home one evening, my curiosity got the better of me. I asked Father, "Are all Japs our enemy, even the ones in Canada?"

Stepmother sat stiffly; her set of four knitting needles stopped clicking. Father shuffled his newspapers with authority.

"Yes," he said, with great finality. He looked sternly across at Stepmother. "All Japs are potential enemies...even if Stepmother doesn't realize that."

"Well, Sek-Lung," Stepmother began, "some Japanese persons were born here and—"

Father sharply snapped his papers. Kiam looked warningly at

me, trying to signal me to shut up. Then, in an effort to lessen the tension, he said, "The ones who are born here are only *half* enemies."

Liang laughed, tossing her head back. "That's stupid," she said, daring to defy First Brother.

"It's *not!*" I exclaimed.

Stepmother looked at me, startled, then smiled broadly, as if she understood something beyond me. She picked up her knitting. In the stillness, the long metal needles clicked and stabbed into the air.

"Are you enjoying your after-school hours with Meiying?" Stepmother asked.

Her tone confused me, but I thought she just wanted to change the subject, to avoid the storm of Father's dark looks directed at her.

"Yes," I answered. "Lots."

It was true. Meiying entertained me well. Last week we'd run into the Han boys, and she took us all to the soda counter at the corner store across from MacLean Park. We ordered cherry cokes. Sitting in the only booth, Meiying's eyes lit with fire as she told us stories, scary ones, about the ghosts in Chinatown. There was the opera ghost whose shape could suddenly be seen pushed against the front curtains; the Shanghai Alley ghosts of the laundrymen who died from despair of ever seeing their families again, their footsteps treading the narrow steps; ghosts of those who died from hunger, from love; water ghosts from False Creek who moaned and gave warnings. They were just like the spirits and demons Grandmama used to tell about.

"The smell of a ghost," Meiying warned us, "is like the smell of burning incense, just as the ember touches the wood."

We boys were entranced.

When Meiying tired of telling tales, she let us play war games on the mostly deserted grounds of MacLean Park; she settled disputes about the efficiency of weapons or the firepower of planes, urged us to draw the enemy in and then strike. A tactic, she said

with authority, as old as Robin Hood's forest ways. Larry Han
asked her why she knew so much.

"Aren't we all at war?" she answered.

When the two Jenson boys, Ronny and Rick, deigned to play
with us, and we had arguments, she taught us how to form
alliances. "Fight against a common enemy," she said. "That's what
friends do."

While we played, Meiying often sat by herself on the bench,
huddled against the chill, looking at the library books on her lap,
the pages glowing under the street lamp. The pages would sometimes turn in the wind, but she did not notice.

Whenever it rained, Meiying and I stayed in her tiny room to
the left of the pot-bellied stove.

Sitting on her bed, she read stories to me, or made up war stories from dramatic pictures I cut out from *Life*. "Tell me about this
picture, May," I said. She helped me to set up my soldiers on her
desk and positioned my tanks behind "hills" and on "bridges"
made of books, and watched my favourite planes battle oncoming
bombers.

"Now," she commanded, if I paused and might interrupt her
reading, "protect that bridge."

"Do you think we will win the war, May?"

A tank rumbled over an open geography book.

"I mean, will we win against the Tojos?"

She looked at me sourly.

"Will we win against the *Japs*?" I repeated.

"Monday the fifteenth is your birthday," she said, changing the
subject. "You'll be eight years old in a few days. I'm making something special for you."

It would be a sweater, of course, because she had already commented on how tightly the ones I had fitted me. That was boring.

"You didn't answer me, May," I persisted. "The Japs are fighting in Hong Kong now. Mr. O'Connor's son is there with the
Commonwealth troops. Miss Doyle says we're all allies."

"Yes," she said. "Everyone in Chinatown is talking about the

Canadians fighting there."

I thought of Mr. O'Connor's son on his last visit home in October. A bunch of us boys stood around admiring him. He looked good in his uniform and thick woollen army coat. He walked over to our yard from his father's house and showed Kiam some pictures of his buddies. Kiam used to be in the same class with him, but Jack O'Connor had quit school to enlist. I admired his heavy army boots, with the khaki puttees anchoring his pants. Later, Mr. O'Connor and Mrs. O'Connor got into a taxi with their son to take him back to the docks.

I thought of Jack O'Connor charging into Hong Kong with his army buddies, guns blazing.

"Will us good guys win the war, May?"

"Of course we will! Why, Sekky, we have good alliances!"

"Then all the Japs will be killed?"

Her eyes widened in shock. I had breached our code. I was sorry to have asked that question, even more sorry when I heard her answer, at last, "Yes, yes...I...suppose so."

That Sunday morning, Jung and I were awakened by hard pounding on our front door. Jung swore and got up from his bed. I peeked out from my blankets. Voices were raised; there was shouting. Someone came running up the stairs,

"Stepmother, Stepmother!" I heard Father yell, "The Americans are going to have to fight the Japs!"

Footsteps ran back down the stairs.

Jung and I pulled on our kimonos and ran downstairs. Third Uncle, still in his winter coat, was standing impatiently at the parlour doorway, telling Kiam to "open" the radio: "Open it up! Open it!"

The front tube warmed; I could see its pinpoint glow behind the edge of the large dial. There came the familiar sharp buzzing sound; we smelled electricity, then heard static...a voice said, "... Pearl Harbor has been bombed..."

Liang said, "What's that?"

"The tide has turned," Father said. "America is going to be China's ally!"

"Dirty Japs!" Jung said.

"Father," Kiam said, "I want to join the Canadian Army!"

"Yes, yes," Father said, forgetting the countless times he had told Kiam not to think of such a foolish thing.

Third Uncle and Father were charged with excitement. Jung took a boxer's stance and started shadow boxing. Kiam bent down closer to the radio. Stepmother pulled her dressing gown tightly around herself, looking worried. She was standing behind me and I could see her face in the wall mirror. She put her hands on my shoulders and gently squeezed them.

I thought of Powell Ground and the slim boy holding Meiying's hand, laughing at my Spitfire.

The second week of December, we began a new routine. Meiying told me we were going to meet at my house. "That way you won't have to rush home, Sekky," she said. "I'm still not feeling well enough to be good company."

When I got home from school, Meiying would be upstairs in Stepmother's bedroom. Both women would talk quietly while Stepmother prepared herself to go to work at the woollen factory.

Sometimes their conversation, in a formal dialect, was agitated, and I was told not to come upstairs but to get something to eat. I realize now that the kitchen was the farthest place away from the bedroom.

Then Meiying would take me to play with my boyfriends at MacLean Park. She sat on a bench, wrapped in her dark coat, book unopened.

Once Meiying came to Strathcona School to pick me up. Her face looked bruised, and there was a small cut over her left eye. She told me it was nothing. There had been a fight at school; she'd defended herself. Everything would be okay. She turned pale, uneasy, and told us she had a queasy stomach. I drank my cherry coke in silence and watched her grip her glass of water and stare at the empty soda counter.

On the Monday of the second week of December, Meiying did not arrive on time for Stepmother to leave for her shift.

I remember that day because it was December 15, my official birth date. Meiying had promised me a special treat. The day before, the first Sunday after Pearl Harbor, I had a big dinner with the family, and a fake-chocolate birthday cake from Woodward's with my name spelled Sekee. Father bought a freshly killed chicken from Keefer Poultry and Stepmother made my favourite dish: braised white-meat chicken smothered with salted black beans and special black Chinese mushrooms.

I waited for my special surprise from Meiying, but she did not appear. When I asked about her, Stepmother said she'd forgotten to tell me that Meiying had some kind of flu.

I got a pair of socks, a rare package of All-Sorts all the way from England, some lucky money from relatives, and a new pair of suspenders with sheriff badges on each strap. Kiam gave me two new Dinky Toy jeeps. Jung made me a set of Sherman tanks out of empty Spam tins and large rubber bands. Each tank emitted a clacking noise when you pushed it along the ground. Liang clipped off the blonde hair of one of her smallest dolls, painted the hair with Chinese black ink, and dressed it up in a Flying Tiger pilot's outfit Stepmother helped her to sew—except the doll had blue eyes and didn't have a pilot's leather cap.

"I'm working on that," Liang said.

I missed Meiying; I asked if I could take a piece of birthday cake across the street, but Stepmother said it was best to let her rest.

"Mrs. Lim says May's throwing up a lot," said Liang. "Save her a piece of cake for tomorrow."

Now it was Monday, our regular after-school time together, and Meiying was late. Stepmother was to be at work in ten minutes, but she refused to leave the house and let me wait alone.

Instead, she stood by the front window, looking at the street.

"Have you been going to MacLean Park with Meiying?"

"Yes."

"Always?"

"Sometimes we go to Chinatown or Woodward's or the library," I answered. "But usually we go to MacLean Park. For cherry sodas or ice cream or a new comic."

"No other parks?"

Stepmother seemed too curious.

I did not hesitate.

"Nope."

Stepmother sighed. When she turned back to the window, there was a knock on the door; it was Meiying. She had on my favourite scarf, a trailing red and black one floating with amber butterflies over her dark navy winter coat. But it was not tied around her hair neatly. The long silk material fell loosely around her shoulders, as did her hair. She said to Stepmother, "I'm fine," and then they both quickly walked upstairs. They closed the bedroom door, but I could hear their whispering. When they finally came down, Meiying's hair was combed and the scarf neatly tied in place. They both walked stiffly. I thought their odd behaviour was because of my birthday, my special treat, which they both were conspiring to hide from me. I guessed we were going to the John Wayne movie, or to inspect the new war toys at Eaton's Toyland. Maybe I was going to get my pick of a new fighter plane and not just some dumb sweater. Meiying brushed by me, empty-handed. I could smell Three Flowers perfume.

"We going to the Odeon?" I asked, but neither of them paid me any attention. Stepmother pushed my arms into my coat, buttoned me up tightly. She handed me my leather pilot's cap without even looking at me. Instead, Stepmother frowned sternly at Meiying and said, "Make this the last time."

They were talking in code to each other, like secret friends, allies, just as I did with the Han boys when the white boys that sometimes played with us could be tricked, defeated, by the conspiracy of our speaking Chinese. Stepmother watched Meiying and me leave the house. As we rounded the corner, going north, I knew where we were headed. I pulled the flaps of my cap down and buckled up, ready for battle.

Meiying walked quickly, and I kept pace. She seemed too wan to walk so quickly.

"Hurry, Sekky, they're breaking up the Asahi team."

The words "breaking up" made me think of war, of fighting and winning. We passed some soldiers and sailors walking on Hastings Street and then Powell Ground was before us. Meiying stopped, took out her compact and fixed her hair. Each word she spoke sounded as if it were wrenched from her. She pulled at my arm.

"Kaz left school so I haven't seen him. Hurry, Sekky!"

We ran the last block.

As my boots pounded on the pavement to keep up with Meiying, I could hear Third Uncle's raspy voice shouting, over the loud words of the parlour RCA, "The filthy bastards! The back-stabbing, whoring Japs!" Then we were standing on Powell Ground.

Meiying and I were back on enemy territory.

There were a few men in the park. Each time someone appeared, another man ran up to him, and soon one or both of them departed. I recognized the catcher from the Asahi team. It was the first real cold day in December; the skies threatened snow. The trees were skeletons. A voice suddenly shouted to us in Japanese, then in English.

"No come here today! Everything over! Go home!"

But Meiying took my hand and we did not move. We must have stood there for twenty minutes, watching men come and go, watching fragments of a crowd begin to gather and quickly disappear. The wind felt damp. A Japanese woman started to cry, then quickly returned to her car with two children. Behind her, I could see the storefronts decorated for Christmas. A giant red paper crane floated in the middle of one window display, draped with tinsel. Twinkling lights surrounded it. A man waved at a group and they ran into a building, shouting in Japanese. Lights began to go off all along Powell and Jackson Streets, until the windows reflected only the grey sky. People in the street suddenly appeared like ghosts, disappeared, then noisily reappeared.

Then, at the other end of the park, Kazuo came running towards us, with a boy almost exactly my height at least ten feet behind him. The boy with Kaz seemed taken aback to be hurried along to our part of the field.

"May, you shouldn't have come," Kazuo said, catching his breath. "Didn't Mr. Barclay give you my letter? He told me he only meant well when he first got us together. He's sorry—"

"Sorry?" Meiying gasped, as if she were choking.

Meiying reached out and pulled Kazuo to her. They held each other closer than I had ever seen. I looked at the chunky boy behind Kazuo and dared him to say anything.

"Where will you go, Kaz?" Meiying's voice sounded sad. They held each other very close.

She buried her head on his shoulder and began to cry. It made me think how weak girls were, just like everyone said. I started to concentrate on the enemy boy across from me. He was bunching up his fists; maybe he couldn't stand a girl crying either. I wished for the nerve to say aloud, "Jap!" the way Father would say it. I stared at the boy until he stared right back. I mouthed it:

Jap!

Chunky didn't flinch.

He pursed his lips and mouthed back,

Chink!

I began to tighten up my fists, getting ready to bloody his stupid eyes.

Suddenly Meiying stepped back from Kaz.

"Kazuo, take this with you."

She raised her arms and a silk scarf flashed against the open sky and her long hair suddenly flew out in the wind. She folded the material with its dancing butterflies and pressed it against him.

"Keep this scarf to remember us."

"Don't, May," he said, "don't make things so hard for me."

She turned away, started running, and shouted, "Sekky, we must go home!"

I shot one last hard look at the boy, giving him my best tough guy glare. I meant to give the same ugly look to Kazuo, but he seemed to be crying. I was shocked: how could a grown man *cry* over a girl?

When I turned to follow Meiying, she was already a great distance away, her hair streaming behind her. I shouted, "Wait! Wait!"

Meiying stopped to wait for me. We paused for a last glimpse of her friend, the tall shadow with the small ghost beside him.

We walked home, past the Good Shepherd Mission, the crunch of dead leaves marking our every step; each of us wordless and deep in thought. The cobblestone road felt slippery, treacherous, as we crossed alleyways and sidewalks. Finally, we were at the bottom of our steps. Meiying reached into her coat pocket and took out a small gift-wrapped parcel, pressing it into my hand. Barely whispering "*Happy Birthday, Sekky,*" and only with the faintest smile, she left me.

I looked at the small parcel in my hand and tore it open. The red paper separated and a hand-sized blue notebook emerged, the kind you can still buy in the Five and Dime. I opened the book. Inscribed on the first page, both in her Chinese calligraphy and in English, were my name and the title, neatly printed: A PILOT'S ADVENTURES—A STORY FOR MY FRIEND SEK-LUNG.

From between the pages, a red packet fell out. That was my lucky money. I lifted the flap. It was five dollars, more money than even Third Uncle had given me.

For the rest of the week I did not see Meiying. Stepmother stayed home from work and said Meiying was really sick with flu. She explained that the extra shift at the factory was temporarily shut down. Supplies for the factory were scarce or had not yet arrived.

Whenever we were alone together, Stepmother pestered me with questions about Meiying,

"Where did you go to play?"

"The playground."

"Was it always MacLean Park?"

"Sometimes we read comics in the soda shop."

"No, I mean the playground."

"MacLean Park," I lied, "always the same." A soldier would never break a promise not to tell.

Somehow Stepmother was satisfied with my answers. She could always tell when I was lying, but this time I fooled her.

"Sometimes we stayed at Mrs. Lim's," I added, to be sure, "in May's bedroom, reading and stuff."

"Yes," Stepmother said. "Remember to tell Father that if he happens to ask."

Christmas came, but we hardly noticed, because on Christmas Day, Hong Kong fell to the Japanese. The Canadian soldiers there were reported killed or captured. Father knocked on the O'Connors' door with a small box of English Toffee and said how sorry our whole family was and how it was just a matter of time before their Jack would be home again. Frank O'Connor agreed and thanked Father. Mrs. O'Connor did not even smile, Father said, but took the small box of candies from him and gently closed the door. From then on, whether day or night, the blackout curtains were never raised again at the O'Connors.

The New Year came. Chinatown burned a few firecrackers, and lucky packets with coins were given to children, but no one knew if the coming year would grow darker.

That first week of January 1942, Father came home to say the Japanese were being taken away. Camps were being built for them. Chinatown heard that Japtown was to be seized and auctioned to the highest bidders. Even Chinese businessmen would be allowed to bid on the real estate and the stock; there were stores and houses, fishing boats and cars, radios and pianos, everything you could imagine Third Uncle ran to the Tong Association to raise money so he could bid. Father said there was justice in this. "Look at all the real estate they're taking in China..."

"We don't want any of it," Stepmother said, putting down her knitting on the table in front of Grandmama's framed portrait. "We want none of it."

"You should hope!" Father's tone was contemptuous. "As if you should have the money to buy anything!"

"And if I did—!"

"You should have chosen a damn rich man!"

"I *chose*? I was *bought*!" Stepmother said, for all at once she could not stop herself. She stood up, as if pulled against her will. "Even Jook-Liang and Sek-Lung—my *own* two children—call me Stepmother!"

"That was the Old One's decision," Father said. "*She* decided, *you* accepted!"

My heart beat against its cage; they rarely argued like this.

"If you hated it, why didn't you say something?" Father said, his voice rising, unspoken pain in his eyes. "You two women agreed."

Slowly, deliberately, Stepmother sat down.

"My love," she said, so softly I could hardly hear, "and all these years, *where was the tongue of my husband?*"

When I stopped playing with my Sherman tanks to listen for more, they fell silent.

Kiam held his brush suspended in air. Jung was coming down the stairs but had stopped. Liang bent her head down over her book. Stepmother picked up her knitting. The click of the needles began measuring the seconds. Father looked at the picture of Grandmama.

"One of you go make some tea," Father said, absently.

Kiam hesitated, then got off his chair and went into the kitchen.

"Liang, come here," Stepmother said. "It's time I show you a new stitch."

Father watched me as I raised my Spitfire over the Sherman tanks. I pretended to crash-land and made spectacular noises. Jung shouted from the hall that the Han boys were at the front door for me. We were joining other boys to form alliances and play war. Fresh snow had fallen. We could make mountains and bomb them, make caves and hide snipers in them.

"Sek-Lung," Stepmother said, encouragingly, "Go out and play."

"Just a minute," Father said. "Where do you go with the Hans?"

"MacLean Park," I said. "Just down the street."

"I know where it is," Father said. "That's the only park you ever go to?"

"Always."

I selected some planes, dashed past Jung who was holding up my coat, grabbed my cap and ran out the house. As I started down the stairs to join the Han twins, buttoning up my coat and pulling on my pilot's cap, Mrs. Lim came rushing on her fat legs across the street. Her eyes were wide with shock; her body shook. She was frantically waving me to go back inside. I jumped back up the porch stairs and banged on the door, calling for Stepmother. Something ominous in the way Mrs. Lim raised her arms made me cry out for Father, too.

Jung was still at the door when Father and Stepmother ran past me and down the stairs. Mrs. Lim was almost collapsing. She gasped, *"In her room! Meiying!"*

A kind of dreadful excitement gripped me. I rushed across the street, following Stepmother, who hurried up the shaking and rattling staircase into the house. I watched from the front doorway. There was a stillness, an immense silence when I thought the world had been stopped forever. I heard Stepmother wail, *"Aiiihyaah! Aiiihyaah! Lim Meiying! Lim Meiying!"*

I slowly walked into the hallway, past the pot-bellied stove, turned left, and stopped before Meiying's bedroom. I pushed between the doorway and Stepmother. She was too stunned to stop me. I looked down, half directed by Stepmother's eyes, and saw Meiying.

She lay curled up, head to knee, beside her cot, her hair dishevelled like unravelled silk threads, her eyes shut tight against some paralyzing pain, her thin body angled across the peeling linoleum floor. One arm, caught between her legs, seemed to float on a spreading pool of blood.

Recovering, Stepmother started to yank me back out of the room.

"An ambulance! Tell Mr. O'Connor to phone for an ambulance! Hurry!"

I stumbled, fell, slipping on a thin line of blood. Stepmother took hold of me, her grip as tight as steel, furiously turning me away. In that push and shove, something else caught my eye: two long knitting needles glinting between Meiying's legs.

"Run, Sekky!" Stepmother shouted. "Run!"

I ran down the stairs, half jumping each plank as Meiying had taught me how, unafraid. Mr. O'Connor told the metallic voice on his phone to send an ambulance to our street. He gave Mrs. Lim's address and Mrs. Lim's name. Then he shut the door behind him. Mrs. O'Connor peeked through a crack in the window.

We waited and waited. Perhaps the ambulance was slow because it was wartime, but I still recall Mrs. Lim saying, between bitter tears, "We are Chinese; they take their time."

And then they finally arrived.

One of the ambulance men seemed gruff, as if we were unclean, as if the task was crazy, climbing up those two rickety flights of stairs. The other man was polite and had a kind voice. But it did not matter. When they reached Meiying's room, there was no movement, except Stepmother's nodding head.

Later, Stepmother said they put a blanket over Meiying; the one with the kind voice said he would have to get more straps and a

where was your tongue

different dolly from the ambulance. There was no hurry, the other said. First the police would have to come, then a doctor. And after all, they didn't want to break their necks over these dangerous stairs.

Stepmother came down and took my hand and walked with me back into our house. Mrs. Lim, sobbing, came with us. Father held her hand. Kiam had taken Liang and Jung to Third Uncle's place in Chinatown.

Stepmother went upstairs to her bedroom.

I thought of Meiying and her whispering together in that room, sitting before the dresser mirror, sharing Three Flowers perfume, easily chatting away, fluttering voices, like butterflies of palest amber, gossiping.

I followed her upstairs.

She was looking in the dresser mirror, with an old silk shawl around her shoulders. It was the one with gold flowers that her girlhood friend in Old China had given her when she herself was just a girl, a shawl Meiying had once admired, as girls will. I thought, as Meiying must have often thought, how lovely she looked. Her eyes were wet.

"Mother," I said. "I'm here."

She reached out to me. I took her hand and pressed into her palm the carved pendant Grandmama had left to me.

[handwritten marginalia: not Stepmother | not Poh-Poh]

[handwritten note: he retains the most old Chin + then he has (auth)? to change things ⟶ gender embrace, ranks + names]

ACKNOWLEDGEMENTS

For early encouragement and support, heartfelt acknowledgement to Earle Birney, Jan de Bruyn, William and Alice McConnell, Cherie Smith, and Jacob Zilber.

For her identification of the dozen dialects extant during Vancouver's early Chinatown history, I wish to acknowledge Amy Tang of the Language Institute (Canton). For their generous advice, colloquial translations, evocative late-night discussions of the past, and for information on Old China and North American Chinese phrases and sayings, I thank Kathleen Chim, Richard Fung, Paul Andrew Kay, Toy Lowe, Paul Yee, and my colleague Alfred Shin. Thanks also to Marsha Ablowitz, Lena Chow, Randy Enomoto, Angela Fina, King Lee, Ann McNeil, Patricia Reid, Almeta Speaks, Earle Toppings, and Larry Wong.

Appreciation to Patsy Aldana, Ray Jones, Judith Knelman, Saeko Usukawa, Jim Wong-Chu, and not least, Denise Bukowski. And for her unstinting, frank advice throughout my struggles with this first book, I especially thank Mary Jo Morris.

Appreciation to friends and relatives of my Vancouver Chinatown years; and to my former associates at Cahoots Theatre Projects, and to the many supportive colleagues and friends at Humber College, Toronto.

Grateful acknowledgement to the Toronto Arts Council for their award of a writer's grant in support of the early stages of this work.

And, not least, appreciation to the members of my extended families, the Noseworthys, Schweishelms and Zilbers, and to certain loyal companions throughout the decades—you have kept me going, always.